# Army of the Lost Rivers

# ARMY OF THE LOST RIVERS

Carlo Sgorlon

Translated by Jessie Bright

ITALICA PRESS
NEW YORK
1998

ITALIAN ORIGINAL
© 1985 ARNOLDO MONDADORI EDITORE, S.P.A., MILANO

TRANSLATION COPYRIGHT © 1998 BY JESSIE BRIGHT

ITALICA PRESS, INC.
595 MAIN STREET
NEW YORK, NEW YORK 10044
WWW.ITALICAPRESS.COM

All rights reserved. No part of this publication may be reproduced, stored in a retrieval system, or transmitted, in any form or by any means, electronic, mechanical, photocopying, recording, or otherwise, without the prior permission of Italica Press.

LIBRARY OF CONGRESS CATALOGING-IN-PUBLICATION DATA
Sgorlon, Carlo, 1930-
[Armata dei fiumi perduti. English]
Army of the lost rivers / Carlo Sgorlon ; translated by Jessie Bright.
p. cm.
ISBN 0-934977-62-3 (alk. paper)
ISBN 978-1-59910-143-9 (e-book)
I. Bright, Jessie, 1930– . II. Title.
PQ4879.G6A8913 1998
853'.914– –dc21 98-43358
CIP

Cover Illustration: Cossack army, New York Public Library Picture Collection.

VISIT OUR WEBSITE AT:
WWW.ITALICAPRESS.COM

# Introduction

As we grow older we become in a sense, anachronisms. Our responses, at least our automatic or unconscious responses, and maybe many of the conscious ones also, are conditioned by experiences that may now be hopelessly out of date. In a whimsical mode it could be said we are immigrants in time who haven't quite adapted to our new country. Of course immigrants have to make certain efforts to deal with external factors in the world around them, but people in their late sixties may sometimes feel equally awkward when confronted with hip twenty year olds or when faced with the necessity of coping with rapidly changing technology. An American who goes to live in Britain has to learn to drive on the left side of the road, and a person born in 1930 may be stressed by the necessity of "walking through" seven recorded voice mail messages saying: "Press one now if you...," when all the caller wants is to know whether his or her last ATM transaction really was recorded accurately or when the flight comes in.

What if a whole population becomes an anachronism? What if they find themselves trapped in opposition to overwhelming historical events to which they can only react in terms of obsolete values and habits? And then what if this whole population is transplanted geographically to a distant place where language, culture, and much of the terrain are radically different from what they remember both consciously and unconsciously? That's what happened to the people in this book.

When the Bolshevik revolution swept over Russia one of the last pockets of resistance was among the ethnic group known as Cossacks, a people descended from nomadic Tartar tribes who roamed the steppes of Central Asia and by the fifteenth century had mingled with Russian elements living in certain river valleys between the Caspian and the Black Sea north of the Caucasus Mountains. They managed to maintain a significant degree of autonomy within the Russian Empire until the eighteenth century when they were forced to submit completely to the authority of the czar. Carlo Sgorlon uses the names of those rivers to create the ambiance of his novel: the Don, the Terek, the Kuban, the Donets, etc. And when he mentions those names he is reinforcing his major theme.... But more about that later. At any rate perhaps the word "Cossack" most readily brings to mind an image of the elite corps who protected the czar and enforced his policies... including, alas, carrying out pogroms against Jews in the shtetls. And certainly the Cossack is pictured on horseback because the horse was an essential feature of Cossack culture and identity. Sgorlon refers frequently to the conflict between the "White" forces led by Kerensky against the "Reds" or Bolsheviks, during which the Whites were supported by these Cossack cavalry units. But, as everyone knows, the Whites lost, and the Cossacks became a sort of ultimate anachronism, unable to stop living their lives in terms of a dream, a desperate hope that they might take up the battle once more and defeat the huge Communist apparatus. To put it differently, their greatest desire was to return in time to the era before the Revolution. Then came World War II and Hitler's disastrous invasion of the Soviet Union. Many Cossacks refused to defend a regime they detested and eventually, along with other elements who had been political prisoners, they made a deal with the Nazis to fight with them against the Red Army in the hope they would be able to regain their lost land, or in Sgorlon's picturesque phrase, their lost rivers, and live again as they once had. It didn't work of course and even the German high command had a backup plan. They actually promised the Cossacks that if they couldn't go back to their native region they could have Friuli — Sgorlon's and other Friulans' native region in the northeast corner of Italy — as their new homeland, to be called *Kosakenland in Nord Italien*. It might seem quite unfair and even a bit ironic for one totalitarian government to give someone else's land away to the opponents of yet another totalitarian government without consulting the people living there. But anyone who knows a little history — the U.S. government's track record in dealing with native Americans might come to mind — will not really be surprised that governments and military high commands aren't always fair to indigenous populations.

Thus Sgorlon's story begins in the fall of 1944 with the massive influx of thousands of Cossacks into the small towns and villages of a rural mountainous area, which had known some of the bloodiest battles of World War I — Caporetto for example — and which was also a center of partisan guerrilla activity after the armistice of September 1943 between the Badoglio government and the Allies. Along with them arrived smaller numbers of other minority groups from the same general geographical area, for example Circassians and Kalmucks. Yet another factor was soon to come into play, an event which, until recently anyhow, wasn't terribly well known. In January of 1945 at the Yalta Conference, Roosevelt and Churchill agreed to Stalin's demand that after the war ended all opponents of the Communist regime, all "counter-revolutionaries," should be turned over to Soviet authorities.

Thus, in general, the protagonist of this novel is an ethnic group, a transplanted population who were driven out of their homeland in those lost river valleys, then were moved in long marches to what is now Belarus, then to Poland, and finally down through the Balkans to Friuli. The frequent references to Carnia refer to a mainly northwestern zone of Friuli, a mountainous area adjoining the Alps that border Austria. In such a situation there are indeed many opportunities for reflection upon the effects of incongruities in both space and time. Flying Fortresses themselves may seem anachronistic in the 1990s, but even in the 1940s the idea of Flying Fortresses destroying an army that traveled entirely on horseback, or fighter planes strafing and dropping cluster bombs on people riding in covered wagons must have seemed not only anachronistic but acutely painful to contemplate.

Among the most frequently recurrent expressions in the Italian text is *"la patria,"* a substantive that presents certain problems to an English-language translator. The bilingual dictionaries suggest "country, home(land), fatherland, motherland," but none of these terms have quite the same overtones in English as *la patria* has in Italian. But then the word "home" as we say it doesn't have an indisputable equivalent in Italian. In fact the Italians often borrow it directly. No translation can be a perfect equivalent — this one certainly doesn't pretend to anything more than a relatively honest approximation — but finding an equivalent for that particular expression is an interesting task when the theme of the novel is the loss of *"la patria."* For contemporary men and women, who have lost so many of the traditional elements that once gave them a sense of worth and clear identity, loss of home or homeland is particularly sad. It implies the loss of the cues and clues to answer those universal human questions in collective terms: Who am I? Where do I belong? To whom or what am I finally accountable? In many of Sgorlon's novels we find him expressing a regret that modern rootless, consumer-oriented, materialistic societies no longer value such things as a stable relationship to the earth in general as well as to a particular place in some river valley or a particular island or a mountain chain that has shaped the culture of which the individual is a part. The tragic adventure of the Cossacks in the novel is particularly appropriate for developing these ideas. But this does not mean there are no significant individual characters. There certainly are and one of them is not a Cossack but a young Friulan woman, named Marta, who resembles in many ways the women in some of Sgorlon's other novels. Her interaction with other individuals brings out Sgorlon's ideas about the similarities of all people when it comes to a need for a homeland, about the terrible pain and difficulty of the *"senzapatria,"* who have lost their homeland. Marta's sympathy extends to the invaders as well as to those whom the invasion has harmed or displaced and above all to the victims of the recurrent insanity known as war. But these things don't need to be explained to the reader of *L'armata dei fiumi perduti*. The novel reflects on such things, but it is a narrative, which like all narratives should not be given away in an introduction.

A word about the author himself, a modest man who would probably think such a word wasn't necessary. Carlo Sgorlon was born in 1930 in Cassacco, a small village outside of Udine in Friuli. He was educated at the prestigious Scuola Normale di Pisa, and he also studied in Munich. He has published some twenty volumes, a few collections of short stories as well as a long list of novels. He has lived all his life in his native region and the people of that area regard him with great pride and affection. But he also enjoys a national reputation as a writer and has won many distinctive literary prizes and honors. For instance, this novel, first published in 1985, won Italy's most coveted literary prize, the Premio

Strega. His earlier volume, *Il trono di legno* (*The Wooden Throne*, published by Italica Press) won the Premio Campiello.

Perhaps it would be useful to conclude this introduction with a translation of the author's own brief preface to the story:

"This novel is a 'mixture of history and invention.' The characters are the products of imagination but the double tragedy of the Friulan and Cossack people is among the little-known events of the Second World War. I relied upon a number of different kinds of information: ideas, suggestions, motifs, songs and refrains taken from books published in Friuli about this subject. Among these works were *La terra impossibile,* by Bruna Sibilla Scizia, and *L'armata in fiamme,* by Pier Arrigo Carnier. But my major inspiration came from Leo Tolstoy's *The Cossacks.* However, in a general sense I based the novel on my own sympathetic memories of those strange, primitive, sometimes almost barbaric, invaders, whom the ruthless indifferent cruelty of history had robbed forever of the possibility of having a homeland, a *patria.*" He concludes by thanking Signora Luciana Franz Barbieri, who helped him with the transliteration of Russian, Ukrainian and Tartar words.

Professor Adrian Wanner of Penn State University helped with the English transliteration of those same words. His patience and expertise were invaluable, and if the translator missed certain nuances those imperfections should not be attributed to him. A more recent work by Pier Arrigo Carnier, *L'armata cosacca in Italia,* published in 1990 by Mursia was an extremely useful reference in preparing this translation.

— Jessie Bright

# Army of the Lost Rivers

# The Kidnapping

After the regime collapsed in July Marta thought things were going to change and the end of the war was surely at hand. With each passing day she wondered why the new government didn't sign the armistice since there was nothing else they could do now anyway. Hadn't this exact same situation brought down the previous government? But actual events were one thing and logic was quite another: they rarely coincided. Thus she couldn't even manage to reassure her landlady, Signora Esther, with whom she had lived for many long years. The Signora, a Russian Jew, was the widow of Aaron Heshel, a famous orchestra conductor. They had fled to Italy during the revolution. Whenever Marta set about convincing Esther she needn't be afraid anymore because the war would be over in two or three weeks, the words mysteriously disintegrated and speech died in her throat.

By now Signora Esther was so obsessed that agents in some shadowy police barracks or hideout were spying on her and plotting to come after her that nothing could calm her. She was suspicious of anyone who set foot in her house, an old country villa just outside a tiny mountain hamlet, which she had acquired and moved into after the persecution of Jews had become overt. In fact her son Caleb had died when his bicycle went over a steep embankment as he was trying to escape from a gang of hoodlums pursuing him.

She often stood at one of the attic windows, scrutinizing every movement on the path to her house. Fear left her no peace, even waking her up at night so abruptly she could hardly breathe. Nor did the assortment of bottles and jars of every dimension, spread out like a complete set of chess pieces on her dresser and bedside table, do any good. The slightest noise or discernible change in her surroundings left her breathless with alarm. It was as if the terror that had tormented Aaron in his last days had now entered her. In fact Marta wondered if maybe these weren't symptoms of an early decline.

Marta recalled stories told by Haha, an old gypsy who often camped with his tribe in caravans by the river not far from the house. Horrified, he had talked of rumored deportations of Jews and gypsies to Germany. Considering the pogroms and persecutions Esther had already seen and experienced in Russia before she left that country, Marta understood the weight of her current anxiety, a weight too heavy for a woman of her advanced years. Every now and then, when they encountered one another, Esther would throw her arms around Marta and hold her tight, as if hoping to draw some kind of security from that contact.

"What is it, Signora? What's the matter?"

"I don't have the strength to go on. I'm tired. Tired, you understand? I just don't want to be myself anymore. I wish I were somebody else, or even something else: a crow, a frog, a grasshopper...a creature nobody would notice and I'd be left alone to live in peace...."

Then she'd begin to cry. Big tears would roll down her dry and wrinkled cheeks, ruined by too much powder and makeup. Marta didn't know what to do or say. She too felt alone and powerless. Nor could she expect any help from Anita, who was totally absorbed in trivialities. Anita had lived with them ever since the army sent her brother Arturo off to Russia. He was a shoemaker who had left his home town in the south with his sister to escape an ugly sequence of murderous feuds between rival families. But unfortunately the war caught up with him and he was drafted. Marta and Arturo were engaged but she didn't want to get married before he went away. There were too many uncertainties hanging over them. Church weddings and celebrations and confetti just didn't seem right in times like these. She had fallen for Arturo because he was lively and cheerful, as well as clever, possessed of a shrewd peasant wisdom. But she also loved him because he personified a figure she had imagined in childhood and then gone on elaborating: the "poor soldier," the perennial victim of all wars. At that time in her village in the upper Natisone Valley she had watched two armies pass like floods, first the Italian and then the Austrian. It was then she first heard the song:

*Alas he was just a poor soldier who knew he had to die*
*Far from his wife and home and under the colonel's eye....*

For her, all soldiers, herded here and there, forced to fight on first one front then other, resembled the "poor soldier" of those melancholy lines.

Meanwhile the war wasn't ending — it was starting all over again. Like the circular story of Signor Intento, the tale that never ends, just keeps repeating itself. The September armistice, so long awaited and finally realized, hadn't ended the war at all. Instead it brought masses of German troops into Italy through the Alpine passes and down the mountain roads. It reminded Marta of that other invasion after Caporetto. She was only a little girl at the time but she remembered it vividly. This German invasion, which could sometimes be detected even from the villa, in the sound of distant trucks on the state roads or the buzzing of motorcycles or barking of police dogs, was only one more episode in a long long series of foreign occupations that had plagued Friuli from the very beginning of its history.

By now the war had arrived at her door and it was only a matter of time before it would begin to bark and bite. She felt its presence as something akin to the most frightening and unreal fairy tales she'd heard as a child, but she also knew war was relentless and unstoppable. It would always be there in the world, ready to destroy everything from top to bottom, like a plague or some kind of lethal fungus. Nonetheless people had to toughen themselves and not give in. The indestructible tenacity of her peasant ancestors was part of her own nature and she knew it. They had always set about rebuilding the moment the hordes of invaders disappeared over the horizon.

Every now and then she took a walk in the woods to a spring half hidden by beech trees and moss, or to a prehistoric cave carved out of a mountain. She felt the war would never find its way there, not in any form. Listening to the bells of the local church, or those of neighboring villages reminded her of the bygone holidays and country festivals of her childhood, long lost memories of the tiny town where she'd grown up hearing a half-Friulan, half-Slavic dialect. The bells merged with the evening in a momentary intensity that distilled her inner longing for peace, the same longing inherent in the heart of nature, in reality itself.

Sometimes after Signora Esther and Anita were already fast asleep in their beds Marta went on with her housework, listening to the night sounds of crickets singing in their holes among the grasses of the garden and the courtyard, or the hooting of horned owls or cries of barn owls or screech owls that might be nesting on the roof or in the loft. She was sure the nucleus of nature would remain intact — a fresh inviolable center the war could never touch or harm. The wind rustling the cornstalks mattered more than any invader. Then she'd get hold of herself, realizing she'd let her mind wander far beyond some invisible boundary. With a certain effort she'd return to the present, where she felt surrounded by multiple dangers advancing with the stealth of so many cats.

At a certain point Marta noticed a change in Anita's behavior. She was becoming evasive, seemed to avoid working in the same room with Marta, refusing even to meet her eyes. Some of the village women came to report that Anita had been seen with transients. Knowing how naive the girl was, grown up in body, yes, but with no common sense or prudence, Marta panicked. Anita had no one. She had been confided to her care, but how could Marta follow her every move?

She decided to try to keep a closer watch and took Anita with her on her woodland walks or excursions into the village. The mountains, covered with beeches and firs, were changing color with the autumn chill, and the first snows had already dusted some of the higher slopes.

One evening, as they returned to the villa after an absence of several hours, Marta caught a glimpse of the gypsy caravans in the distance, camped in their usual place among the bushes by the river. On a closer look the caravans seemed to be empty. The gypsies had apparently gone off in search of food, a search grown obsessive as the war grew more vicious. The horses, tethered to stakes driven into the ground, moved restlessly in the evening solitude.

"Let's go take a look. Maybe we'll find old Haha," said Marta to the girl.

"And his grandson Elias," added Anita, who loved children as much as children love toys.

With a certain effort they made their way down through the underbrush to the caravans. A dying campfire was still smoldering under an overturned kettle. Unfinished rush chairs were scattered about along with other signs of a struggle. The horses sensed the two women's approach, maybe even recognized them and began to whinny in distress. Marta peered inside the caravans, noting an unusual and puzzling disorder. She couldn't figure out what had happened to drive the gypsies away so precipitously, as if in terror, but of what? She couldn't imagine. Whatever it was, it was certainly serious. She considered going down to the village to see if anyone there knew what happened, but then, stricken by sudden doubt, she decided to return to the villa, in case something had gone wrong there too. They rushed home and as Marta looked around her heart sank. Bit by bit the evidence confirmed her fears. Doors stood wide open and Esther's clothes lay tossed about on the floor.

"Signora Esther! Signora Esther!" she called but the only answer was the wind blowing in through the open windows. It looked as if Esther had fled in terrible and mysterious haste, after throwing together a few paltry possessions. Had she been taken suddenly ill? Or was she too overwhelmed by the pervasive dread that they all felt. But where would she have gone? Perhaps some latent terror had exploded in her mind like a summer storm and driven her instantly mad. But no, that couldn't be so because it would mean the same madness had fallen upon the people in the caravans.

They searched at length for the signora, calling her along the paths, in the woods, in the village. Then they went back to the villa and there in a corner of the courtyard, where the ground was soft and swampy from a recent rain, they found tracks of truck tires. Marta's intuition stirred but her thoughts remained vague and confused as if fear kept her mind from forming clear, precise images. The specter of war had passed there, through the villa and among the caravans, provoking a frightful sequence of events.

Arturo's dog Baldo whined desperately in a corner as if he were to blame for what had happened. Marta decided to consult the family of tenant farmers who lived closest to the villa, to find out if her suspicions were correct. But as they approached the farmhouse they could see all its doors and windows closed and bolted. They heard dogs barking, but no one answered their shouted appeals. The tenants were barricaded inside, as if in a fortress.

"We'll come back tomorrow," said Marta.

"Yes, tomorrow," agreed Anita.

They went to bed in the same room, as they had for some time now. But Marta couldn't sleep. At midnight she was still tossing and turning, her mind on Esther's empty bed in the next room. Anita, however, despite the major scare she'd experienced, fell into a deep sleep almost at once. At a certain point Marta heard a tentative knock on the door. She got up, opened the window and sensed more than saw Haha standing in the middle of the courtyard. She put on a bathrobe and a coat and hurried downstairs to let the old man in. He was so frightened he could barely put words together.

"The Germans," he stammered. "The Germans.... They came...!"

"I thought so. I saw tire tracks in the courtyard...."

"They had a truck and two motorcycles. They surrounded the caravans and took everybody...."

"What about you?"

"I was in the woods, looking for kindling. Only a miracle saved me. They got Signora Esther too...."

How on earth they had found out Esther was Jewish remained a mystery, because, as the saying goes, only the wind and the river knew that. For this very reason Marta thought there was something magnetic and supernatural about the Germans, an ability to read people's minds, find out their deepest secrets. Nothing could escape them. Armed to the teeth, they had arrived in great numbers from distant places and carried off those poor souls so scared of their own shadows that catching a stray chicken took the maximum of courage. Haha couldn't get hold of himself. In fact on his face one could read more clearly than ever his old terrors from those earlier times when other German brutalities had stood revealed. Although it was nothing new, it was still an enigma why they had to take away women and children. And why people like these who not only weren't involved in the war, but were so suffocated by fear they didn't even dare raise their eyes to look at the new invaders? People who saw themselves as superfluous and in the way, who lived hidden on the fringes of civilization, as if hoping everybody else would forget they even existed.

Now that such a thing had happened right in her own backyard it was even more incomprehensible and abstruse to Marta. There was no sense to that mode of warfare. Only ogres and witches kidnapped children, only fairy tale characters born of humanity's deepest and darkest primal fears. Now she too, like Esther in those last days, felt the tug of a senseless urge to run away, to leave everything and flee someplace where war was never even mentioned. Into an African jungle, to a Pacific island or the heart of an Asian desert.... She wished she could fall into a long sleep and wake up years later after it was all over and even the memory of war had been lost. As in the Dutch fable about a man named Rip who had done just that and awakened many years later to find the whole world changed. It was Caleb who had told her this story.

When his family was still living in Rome just before the war, Caleb had abruptly quit the university, interrupted his medical studies, driving his parents to despair. "I can't read that stuff anymore. I can't do it, I just can't.... Nobody really knows anything about human beings and how our bodies function.... Medicine is all a sham!" He had always read strange books and told Marta he wanted to take up some Jewish profession like watchmaker or antiquarian. During those conversations he became attached to her, almost in desperation, as a drowning man clings to his rescuer. In response a strange kind of pity took root in her, as if Caleb too was a "poor soldier," about to be sent away to die at the front. Thus he became the first man in her life. Arturo had been the second.

She felt like the protagonist of an epic begun in her childhood when the Italian front collapsed, a story whose end was nowhere in sight. She simply didn't understand what was happening. One thing, however, was certain: her own sense of loss and confusion was now universal. Even this villa at the edge of a tiny village, where Signora Esther had felt secure and protected for years, had not been able to guard her secret. From now on Marta would never feel safe here either, never truly at home.

Instead she'd live with a constant weight upon her heart, always aware the Germans might return at any moment, hoping those who had been taken away would come back but knowing it was unlikely. In fact in recent months, when Haha used to come by, he had talked of people crowded into cattle cars in long trains that passed during the night on their way to unknown destinations in Germany and Poland. Sometimes scraps of paper, notes scribbled in the dark with a pencil stub, would fall onto the tracks. Thus the sinister rumors were true and another face of the conflict had appeared: the Germans had declared war on the Jews and the Gypsies too. But how? And why? And what were they going to do with them?

Haha went down to the river and collected the tools of his trades — he was both tinker and weaver of baskets and wicker furniture — and brought them back to the house, along with whatever else he could salvage from the caravans. The horses were still whinnying piteously so he untied them and led them to the tenant farmers' barns. He treated them with special tenderness as if they were the only surviving members of his family.

When Baldo came home from one of his canine excursions, nose covered with mud and snow, he jumped up on Haha as if to ask where Elias was, for Haha's grandson was Baldo's favorite playmate. From that day on Haha never spoke of his family again. He was visibly ill at ease living in a house, eating at a table, sleeping in a bed set up in a room. He kept to himself in the villa, choosing the smallest, most inconvenient spaces. His habit of wandering about was still strong and he often went off through the woods or visited nearby villages, always quiet and taciturn, but alert to whatever news or rumors could be gathered.

He was the first to tell the two women about the resistance movement being organized in the mountains to fight the Germans. What had happened in the forests of Slovenia and the rest of Europe was now taking place here too. The guerrilla fighters who took refuge in the woods and hid among the rocks and trees like Robin Hood's merry men had arrived in their neighborhood. But so had every other aspect of the war. Further north the mountains teemed with deserters from the disbanded army, young men who didn't want to surrender to German command, ignoring the official threats posted everywhere on walls and buildings.

Although he continued to fulfill his former role of news reporter, without his family, his caravans and his old way of life, Haha was lost and confused. Everything that had given meaning and order to his life was gone. He roamed about in his sheepskin-lined jacket, or split wood in the farmyard or played with the dog, as if he was trying to be both himself and Elias at the same time. He helped the tenant farmers with their winter chores, repairing tools for planting season or weaving baskets and bags. Once in a while, he took the dog and went down to the abandoned caravans, empty now and white with frost, their doors gaping open. Baldo would begin to howl. Being a mere dog, he alone was unashamed to vent his bitter grief for the missing gypsy band.

"Why must you always be wandering about? Why do you keep going off and leaving us alone?" Marta asked. "The way things are now, we've only got each other."

"All right, I'll do what you say," promised the old man.

For Marta, her responsibility as guardian of the villa and its contents implied a duty to restore everything to Esther when she returned. But meanwhile, if the three of them were going to survive, they should be able to use whatever supplies were on hand. Each day meant a struggle simply to make sure there was enough to put on the table at noontime or supper. Since the peasants tended to keep everything for themselves, she often had to resort to tedious arguments to get them to pay their rents in produce. But that wasn't all. Now that the last vegetables in the garden had frozen and there was no more fruit on the trees, she was forced to sell some of the Heshels' household possessions, just to keep a little money on hand. This meant appealing to the peasant's avarice, by trickery and subterfuge if necessary, until their eyes reflected the sparkle of the gold and silver objects she dangled before them. It was a case of necessity, she knew she had to do it, but her heart bled. In all that bargaining, all the prolonged quibbling to save a few pennies on the price of a couple of eggs or a few spoonfuls of flour, she was dispersing and dissipating all that remained of two reserved and thoughtful lives, entirely dedicated to music and art.

# Ivos

By now the guerrilla war against the Germans was no secret to anyone. It went on openly in plain sight. Partisans even appeared in the villages because the Germans didn't dare cross into Carnia, nor did they have enough men to attack an enemy so widely dispersed, in this double war they themselves had provoked: one at the front and one in the mountains. The guerrillas held all the mountain villages and valleys, and armed partisans circulated freely, quite ready to defend themselves. People knew they were organizing under commanders with oddly picturesque battle names, like Bora (North Wind), Saetta (Arrow), Sonia. Some of the soldiers were indeed women. Women, it seemed, had stepped out of their traditional roles as full-time housewives and mothers and taken up arms to fight alongside the men. One might say there was almost no distinction between the partisans and the local population — they were continuously identified. Of course certain individuals belonged explicitly to both groups and moved back and forth between them. One such person, a big strapping yellow-haired boy named Ugo, was as tall as a telephone pole and afraid of no one, not even the devil himself.

Marta, living in the villa, didn't know much about the partisans, and tried not to imagine what lay ahead. The future was too frightening. She'd had no word from Arturo for a long time now, no letters, not even a postcard. Little by little her thoughts in that direction faded behind a veil of mourning and resignation. True, a few men had returned from Russia, but not Arturo. Even thinking he might be found among the extremely small number of survivors was a luxury without parallel, and she knew her own destiny denied her any such hope.

One evening Baldo was unusually restless, barking constantly, not loudly, but more as if he were worried or distressed. Distant gunfire and a faraway rumble of explosions suggested the Germans might be preparing something, maybe even a full scale battle with the partisans. Once in a while Marta and the others could distinguish the sound of a single hand grenade or a burst of mortar fire. Next came the compact roar of Flying Fortresses, faint at first, then louder and louder as the formation passed far overhead, going north as they always did.

Marta took Baldo on his leash and went out, following one of the paths that circled the villa. These were hardly suitable times for an evening walk, but summer had returned and the weather was inviting. The mountains were dark gigantic forms and she wandered this way and that, deep into the woods until she came to the spring hidden by the bushes and beech trees. This was her personal place, absolutely her very own, even though it was surrounded by legends as old as the dawn of history, or at least from pre-Roman times when the Carnic Celts who had given their name to the region dwelt here. She felt more alive than usual, and happy in a strange sort of way, akin to Baldo and the trees and to the animals scurrying away into the dark forest. Thoughts flooded into her mind: that life began as a spring, a kind of bottomless well from which all living beings drew energy. Despite the unfortunate contingencies of war and all her present troubles, there was a secret harmony in the world that filled her with a fresh and nonsensical joy. She was as vital as life itself — it couldn't be possible that one day she would no longer exist. Life would continue, even if she were no longer there. In a way she too would go on living as a part of that continuity, because life was, after all, eternal.

She followed a path along the river. Now and then Baldo would bark softly, so softly it seemed as if he were merely asking her where on earth she was going. They came upon an old abandoned mill, where several small white ducks were swimming silently in the stagnant water of the millrace. A housewife had apparently spread out her wash on the grassy bank of the stream and then forgotten to take it in. The clothes, now damp with dew, shown white on the dark grass, like an enigmatic signal aimed at the stars. Despite the dangers and uncertainty of the future, Marta was happy, mysteriously happy.

She'd have liked to play with Baldo the way Elias used to, but a pang of sorrow reminded her she knew nothing whatever of that poor little boy's fate. Anyhow since there was no one else there to share her happiness she started to run about with the dog, then stopped and hugged him like a long lost friend. All at once Baldo began to bark loudly and lunged toward the mill, tearing the leash from her hand. "Baldo! Baldo!" she cried, running after him into the mossy dampness of the old building. She caught a glimpse of a man pointing a pistol at her in the dark.

"Call off your dog," he muttered.

"Baldo, come here. Stop it now!"

The dog ran toward her but before she could catch hold of the leash he dashed off toward the man again, barking and jumping at him but in a friendly way, in enthusiastic greeting. Marta wondered if Baldo wasn't always the first to size up strangers, then welcome them to his community. That's what he'd done with Elias and old Haha. The man conceded with a smile and put down his pistol on the low wall where he had been sitting. Marta took a closer look at him. The moon was now bright enough for her to see that he was thin, very tall, and his face was sad. Like Baldo, she felt an instant sympathy for him.

"Are you hungry?" she asked.

"Well I should be. All I've had to eat for two days is wild berries."

"Come with me. We live nearby."

The man stood up, but with a stifled groan of pain.

"You've been wounded?"

"My leg, but it's nothing much...."

"It's easy enough to get yourself shot nowadays," said Marta.

"That's for sure. All you need is a bit of bad luck."

"Here, you can lean on me."

"No need. I've made myself a stick."

Marta took him back to the villa. In a way she was pleased because here was somebody else she could devote herself to. The wound wasn't serious because the bullet had gone right through the calf without damaging arteries or tendons. She cleaned it, applied some tincture of iodine, then covered it with gauze and a makeshift bandage. She kept track of his temperature but luckily he showed no sign of fever. He gave his name as Ivos, but Marta couldn't decide whether Ivos was his real name or if he had already taken a battle name. He had come up from the hill country and had crossed territory under German control in order to join the partisans up here and hasten the end of the war. He had already served in Greece and in Russia and everything that could happen to a soldier had happened to him. He had had enough.

Marta listened intently. Wounded, hungry, returned from the front, Ivos was the model of her "poor soldier," in need of all she could give him — protection, food, care, assistance in general. He had triggered that instinctive response, the urge to help, in which she recognized the nucleus of her own character. For her, Ivos, if indeed that was his name, had emerged from a veritable odyssey, driven this way and that by the irrational forces of the war. The expression in his intelligent eyes reflected it all in silent contained sadness. He had fought on many terrains, rough, arid or covered with snow. He had seen places where water mixed with blood in puddles on the ground, and watched his comrades die horrible deaths.

The multiple hardships, the things he had seen and endured at the front, had penetrated his very being. This became even clearer when, after a few days, as his wound began to heal without infection or complications, he started to talk. His manner was sober, probably because in the meantime he had found out Marta's fiancé was in Russia and felt she'd be better off without false hopes. He described the siege and the fall of Nikolayev, the interminable march of the retreat, how his shoes had fallen apart and he had ended up wrapping his feet in rags like the picturesque beggars he remembered from childhood. The Germans had trucks, at least some of the time, but Italian soldiers who tried to hitch a ride with them risked being shot.

In his voice she seemed to hear the wind of the steppe where the Don, the Donets and the Volga rivers flowed. She thought about the winds she had known — in the Natisone Valley, in Trieste, Rome, wherever she had been in her life thus far. They were mere weak insipid little brothers to the relentless gale that howled over the steppe until whoever heard it was sure it was the only sound left on earth and it would never cease to blow.

He told her about the Cossacks who lived in their *stanitsy* along the rivers, about the vast spaces of Russia, how during the retreat they sometimes marched a day and a night and then still another day and night before they glimpsed a distant plume of smoke from an izba. But sometimes the joy of finding such a village was as vain and empty as a mirage because the izbas, far away and buried in the snow, turned out to be deserted. The inhabitants had either fled in the hope of escaping the war or been massacred by the Germans. Sometimes the sight of a truck ahead gave them a momentary thrill of hope, which vanished when they got closer and found its tires punctured or slashed and the driver machine-gunned.

Ivos spoke in low and even tones, and Marta sensed in him a kind of antique wisdom, quiet and profound, untouched by hatred or anger, despite full firsthand experience of the vicissitudes of war. It was as if he had not really come back, part of him was still there in the Greek mountains, or beside the rivers of the steppe and the Cossack lands. Esther and Aaron used to talk fondly about those places because they actually came from a small city in that region. Anita would have liked to interrupt this new guest to ask about her brother. But the expression in Marta's eyes forbade it. It would have only increased her own grief. Arturo hadn't returned, they had had no word from him for two years and they needed nothing more to sketch the outline of his fate.

It was easy to guess what had happened to him. They might wonder how he might have died but there could be no doubt he was indeed dead. Had he begun to wander in circles in the delirium that precedes the so-called white death and just before he froze into immobility seen a ghostly image of the rooms of the villa and Marta and his sister? Had he too ended up as a statue of ice? Or died of gangrene from extreme frostbite? Or perhaps a merciful bullet had ended his nightmare retreat. Anita didn't want to believe Russia had taken her brother. She couldn't accept the truth and kept hoping, beyond the limits of common sense and despite all the evidence, even though she didn't dare say so to anyone, especially to Marta, for fear of a sharp reprimand or a disapproving glance. But she was not prepared to accept his death until she saw his name on a wooden cross in a military cemetery overgrown with sunflowers.

Marta tried not to think about these things, but she was always defeated. Arturo had never come home. He must have died there in the *Chernozyom*, the fertile land of the rich black earth, or in some unknown place on the steppe.

Ivos' wound healed quickly. He could already walk without effort but his face still looked gray, and his manner remained silent as if he were preoccupied with hidden worries. Anita, Marta and the old gypsy were becoming used to him. For them he was now a member of the household. The villa was a singular place, thought Marta. The people who had bought it and owned it were gone, replaced by others simply because of random events.

Ivos was waiting for one thing only, to be well enough to move about as he wished so he could join the partisans. Marta couldn't understand his haste because Ivos was a man without myths, his spirit oppressed by an ancient weariness. She was afraid the Heshels' villa would not house him for long and she was sorry because now that Arturo had disappeared in the vast Cossack lands Ivos had begun to fill the empty space in her heart. She watched intently as he made his preparations to leave.

"Do you really have to go away?" she asked on one occasion.

"Yes, I have to."

"But you hate war...."

"More than anything else."

"And you aren't deluding yourself."

"No, I'm not."

"Then why are you so eager to go off to the mountains?"

"To shorten the war. Everything I do from now on will be directed to that end...."

The idea possessed him. To shorten the war even by an hour, thereby saving a mere ten human lives, was a goal worth the dedication of his entire soul. He was passionate in his conviction. Never again would he allow himself to be sent to a front to suffer cold and dysentery, without shoes and proper clothes. Never again as long as he lived would he take orders from deluded madmen led astray by childish dreams of great deeds and conquests. He knew now unequivocally that he had had the strength to purge himself of the entire world of military utopias. They would only transform themselves into disaster and ruin, once the real wars began. War was nothing but endless, senseless slaughter.

Marta realized that Ivos' iron resolve would lead him to the greatest sacrifice of all: to combat war he was willing to resort to the weapons and the ways of war, firing upon those who had willed it and threatening to go on fighting until it ended in total debacle. On this point he would not budge and any attempt to change his mind was futile, as useless as trying to stop the flow of a river with one's bare hands. His sense of purpose was so strong that it changed his weariness and revulsion into something vast and expansive, incorporating all his suffering on the fronts that had devastated half of Europe.

Still, he had been happy to stay at the villa. Every now and then he'd even forgotten that to put both feet firmly down on peaceful territory he had to take up his gun again and fight the last battle. He felt these moments were primarily due to Marta's presence. He'd watch her sometimes and her quiet beauty, her splendid rust-colored hair made him fiercely resentful that the war was not yet over, that he must leave this place and her. But his duty awaited and he had to finish the final task.

Sometimes he'd lose himself gazing at her round head and slender neck, her tall and shapely form, as she went about her work with a light and graceful step. She seemed to be following the motions of a kind of ritual dance, but spiteful destiny would leave him no time to learn its meaning.

He recognized his feelings as those of the returning veteran, but neither the house nor the woman belonged to him and he could only curse the cruel necessity that decreed he must leave. It seemed he had finally found out where he really belonged, and now he had to move on. Would it always be his fate to come home only to return once more into the thick of battle?

Yes, alas that's the way it was. The house and the woman couldn't really be his until the war was over. Marta had told him about Esther and the gypsies and her story only confirmed his convictions. Now and then he would see Haha going down to the bushes and stony gravel by the river. The empty caravans now looked more and more like all abandoned things, like the deserted izbas he had seen in Cossack territory, in fact all over Russia where the war had passed. His own arrival and the news he brought had probably diminished or destroyed any hope that Arturo might come back. But perhaps not. Marta might have somehow sensed Arturo's fate in advance so that Ivos had merely confirmed and expanded what her unconscious mind already knew....

Again and again he would say it was time to go, that he had already stayed too long. But even as he spoke a powerful almost magnetic attraction tugged at him and he'd find himself inventing one excuse after another to put off his departure. His irritable state was almost physically visible and the same was true of Marta. He knew perfectly well what was troubling both of them. She was full of compassion for the dead but still she knew they were at peace wherever they might be — in military cemeteries, in graves in the woods or in a field. For them the taste of the earth was the same anywhere — and so was its blessed protection and oblivion. But her pity for the living was much stronger. They were still lost in the dark Babylon of war.

One day Ivos seemed even more gloomy than usual and Marta asked him indirectly what was wrong.

"I had a thought," he said.

"Which is...?"

"Well it's this. We soldiers are destined to kill men who are already condemned to death by Nature itself. Isn't that insane?"

"You're quite right. But it's best not think too much in this world. You can go mad...."

Rather than waste time thinking, she preferred to act. It was as if the gypsy, Anita and Ivos were her guests (or rather Signora Esther's guests — right now she couldn't give her consent), and at the same time in a way her children, hers to care for.

"You've already risked enough. You've done your part," she'd say to Ivos.

"Not all of it. There's still something left to do."

"Stay here with us, in this peaceful corner. There's no war here."

"No, that's not really true. The Germans found their way here to take away your landlady."

He was moody and irritable partly because of Marta's presence itself and all it signified. Her words gave substance to an impossible dream but at the same time he had to defend himself from those words and the danger they implied.

"Well then, you'll be going. You've decided...."

"There's no alternative. I have to."

Troubled, Marta withdrew to her own room. Now she was convinced Ivos would disappear into the vortex of war, just like Caleb and Arturo. The old witch would carry him off, maybe never even return his corpse, just as she had done with Anita's brother. After making sure the door was locked in case anyone, even Anita, might happen to come upstairs, she threw herself down on the bed, and resting her head on her arm, gave way to silent weeping. Eventually she fell asleep for a while, from sheer fatigue, and when she awoke she felt like a new person. It was not the first time she had felt that nothing, neither person nor event, could ever defeat or subdue her, because unbounded energy and a will to live always welled up from the deep reservoir of life within her.

"So when are you leaving?" she asked Ivos.

"Tonight."

"No, not tonight, tomorrow. Tomorrow I'll let you go. I won't argue any more."

"All right then, tomorrow, if that's what you want."

Marta made some excuse to send Anita to sleep elsewhere and silently opened to door of her room to Ivos. He found himself filled with joyful oblivion and he too for a moment believed there was no war. War was something remote and improbable, vaguely unreal. Maybe the two of them had imagined the whole thing. After all the human mind does have a dreary tendency to invent its own torments. He stayed for three more days. The morning of his departure Marta barely stirred in bed, on sudden impulse feigning sleep. But Ivos wasn't fooled.

"I'm going now. But I'll be back. Back to stay."

Without answering, Marta ran her fingers over his face.

# The Golden Horde

Sometimes Anita and Haha would play board games — backgammon or "The Wolf and the Hunter," or card games like "Seven and a Half" or "Winner Take All," amusing themselves like carefree children. But then a sudden shadow would darken Haha's face and he'd toss the cards or counters aside and sink into gloomy thought, as motionless as a wooden idol. Anita would leave him to himself. She too was subject to sudden changes in mood. Forgetting Marta's advice, as well as Arturo's — now it seemed so long ago — she'd let her restless instinct lead her away from home and village, where men approached her along the road or path, attracted by her youthful figure and ingenuous manner.

She knew, of course, she shouldn't be doing this. Marta and Arturo were right, but it was so easy to forget. Those encounters were very pleasant and the men's flattering phrases were sweet as spun sugar. Marta didn't know what to do. How could she forbid to Anita what she didn't deny herself? Near the end of August the girl began to act evasive, like a child who's been up to some sort of mischief. Marta kept an eye on her, finally went through her things and discovered a set of woolen baby clothes in a dresser drawer. Anita had been knitting on the sly, like a mother cat or rabbit preparing a nest. In fact she had begun to emanate a kind of absent animal contentment, all her attention fixed on the baby growing inside her. She had realized she was pregnant almost more by instinct than by whatever vague knowledge she had about such things.

Marta was ready to tear her hair. "For God's sake what have you done? Having a baby at a time like this? What on earth will we do now?" The girl listened attentively, as if it were Marta who had gotten into trouble and of course it was up to her, not Anita, to figure out how to deal with the problem.

"Do you at least know who the father is?"

No she didn't. She'd been with woodcutters, partisans, soldiers who had deserted, refugees — in her own way she had acted just like Marta, moved by pity for one man after another. Except that, being more ingenuous than Marta, she now had to take the consequences.

"We're in a pretty pickle now, my dear. Do you realize that?"

"Oh yes, of course. It really wasn't the right moment...."

"Good God, this is all we need. You really don't have any sense!"

Anita began to sob softly. Now of course, when it was too late, she could see that Marta had been right and, worst of all, she had brought trouble upon her friends as well as herself.

"Come now, don't cry. What's done is done and we have to make the best of it. I'll arrange for you to see the midwife. Meanwhile your baby will have a roof over his head and us to look after him. That's not bad considering the times. And you, you must take care of yourself."

"But I'm worried...."

Marta had to laugh in spite of herself.

"Never mind. There'll be room in this world for your baby. Who cares anyhow, we'll manage!"

She gave way to a burst of merriment, not really sure why, maybe she didn't have any more sense than Anita. It might even be a good sign that this child was to make its appearance in the midst of so many misfortunes, so much suffering and devastation. Perhaps the baby's presence, announced so many months in advance, was a harbinger of happiness, a guarantee that everything was going to be all right, a talisman that would protect them all here in the villa, expanding its beneficence to the village and the whole valley as well. Now as never before, Marta recognized her role as a woman of the people, determined to persevere and overcome all obstacles, one by one, as they presented themselves, sure she would prevail in the end even though she was holding the worst possible cards in her hand. Her sudden joy was catching and Baldo began jumping around and yelping cheerfully as if his canine antennae had picked up a definite signal that this was a moment for celebration.

This event changed the direction of Marta's thoughts and awakened an impelling desire to be a mother herself. She identified with Anita, feeling the baby was partly her own. After all, hadn't Arturo entrusted his sister completely to her care? And Anita was so like a little girl herself she could hardly be expected to take on the full responsibility of a child. From now on life at the villa would be more complicated and problems would be more delicate and difficult to solve. And yet for all her worries she felt a breath of hope and a strong urge to get busy.

Even if everything went well this baby would be born a poor little bastard with a mother whose mind was still taken up with childish fantasies. But such a thought barely entered Marta's mind. And yet if by some miracle Arturo should return from Russia what would he say? She hadn't even managed to keep track of his sister for him. Best not to think about this either. Surrounded as they were with so much uncertainty it was better to live one day or even one hour at a time. Dwelling on all the things that might go wrong would only lead to paralysis. Anita calmed down almost at once, as if nothing had really changed and the only problem was preparing the baby's layette.

One evening Haha returned with the news that a trainload of Russians had arrived in the village. Russians? What Russians? Weren't the Russians and Germans bitter enemies? What was going on? This wasn't possible. Indeed it was more than possible because these were special Russians — to be exact they were Cossacks. The Cossacks had never accepted the revolution and, taking advantage of the hostilities, had joined the other side when the German armies arrived in their homeland, the vast plain bounded by the Don, Volga and Kuban rivers. To the inhabitants of the villa, especially Marta, this news was yet one more example of the futility of even trying to understand the intricate confusion of the war.

Their own former allies, the Germans, were now enemies because after the armistice the Italian army had gone over to the opposite camp. Now, certain Russians, former enemies, whose country the Italians, including Arturo, had invaded, had gone and joined the Germans. Thus they were still enemies, even having changed sides, because both sides had changed sides. It was enough to make anybody dizzy. But thinking about such things was a luxury no one could afford in times like these. Marta turned to God, for her a Great Unknown Being to whom she would pray once in a while, if only to maintain her sanity or keep her hopes intact. She'd been through so much, she'd get through this business of the Cossacks too. They came from the steppes and the *Chernozyom*, the very same place that haunted Esther and Aaron's nostalgic memories. Yet all things pass, the bad as well as the good. One just had to wait and hold on. Time itself would do the rest.

She tried to keep her mind on positive thoughts: Anita's baby, or Ivos. But she heard nothing from him. Apparently the grim necessities of guerrilla warfare had displaced all memories of her. He was thinking only of the overwhelming task before him. Still she was not discouraged. Ivos had joined the partisans because he wanted to shorten the war and his very determination gave her a sort of remote happiness. Sooner or later peace would return. Some day, not too long hence, people would once again be talking about cheerful subjects and making plans for the future. She clung stubbornly to these ideas, trying to imitate the simple turn of Anita's thoughts. Sometimes she would go down to the village to visit Alda, known as the prettiest girl in town. It was a pleasure to see girls in their twenties in the full bloom of youth. They reminded her of herself years ago, before the war and other complicated unlucky events had spoiled her chances. It cheered her to be in the company of young women whose prospects were still intact, who could look forward to an unknown but exciting future.

She liked Alda best because she was a proud and decisive girl who demanded respect. Alda's father had emigrated to Germany, been trapped there by the war and forced to work in an arms factory. But when men buzzed around her, no matter what their intentions, she sent them packing with a few dagger sharp words and no help from anyone, not even her mother. However, Marta was sure she wasn't indifferent to the idea of love and marriage — behind her combative pose she was jealously hiding a swarm of thoughts on those subjects. She remembered the last village festival two years before, when Alda and other girls her age from the entire valley had danced together in traditional costume.

How could she even think about such things now, with all this suspense and fear? Nobody knew what might happen from one day to the next. The Germans didn't dare venture into the partisans' territory and the partisans couldn't come out of the mountains, as if the world ended where the plain began. But now people were saying the Cossacks would cross these barriers.

For weeks now, more and more trains of cattle cars kept arriving from the heart of Europe, especially from Poland. It was soon clear the Cossacks were unusual troops. In fact they weren't actually troops, they were more like a people in mass migration, part of a whole population who had abandoned their homeland rather than surrender to the Red Army. They were bringing their horses, wagons, wives, children, old people, their Orthodox priest with his sacred objects, his vestments and icons — all in search of a temporary homeland where they could stay until they regained their own.

Rumors and gossip aside, if Cossacks continued to get off trains a few kilometers outside the village it was a sure sign the temporary homeland assigned to them was indeed Friuli. A breath of fear touched every village and valley. What kind of devilish scheme had the Germans come up with now? Did it mean the end of the war was retreating once more, despite the hopes of Ivos and others like him? Was it going to start all over again? In that case they might as well be in the Tale of Signor Intento where everything always ended up at the beginning, making a mockery of people's hopes. No matter what individuals might think, one idea was clear to all: their ordeal was beginning again in a different form and the end of the nightmare was further away than ever.

Once again the future looked dark and desperate, as it had when the Germans came down from the Alpine passes and the rumble of their trucks and motorcycles echoed through the night. People no longer even knew what to hope for. They waited, holding their breath. From one day to the next they expected to see columns of Cossacks with horses and wagons coming up the valley roads that led to the passes for Austria and Cadore. But they didn't. Nothing happened in any logical or expected way.

Ugo, the youth who went back and forth between the partisan camp and the village, went around telling people the Cossacks would never dare enter the Republic of Carnia. The Germans hadn't. Neither Germans nor Cossacks would set foot in their territory — they were both too scared the mountains would turn into a death trap. Others were less optimistic. It was said tens of thousands had come in on those trains. For three weeks now trains had been stopping at the little alpine station, letting off horses, wagons, women, children, soldiers, and old folks.

Haha had perked up, moved by a vague sympathy for the Cossacks. They were nomads, like his own people, except they had wagons and huge felt tents called yurts instead of caravans. He had already found ways to approach them in the meadows around the station and along the river banks where they had set up camp, and his first impressions were not negative. Where were they from? They were Cossacks from the valleys of the Don, the Volga, the Donets, the Kuban, the same places where Italians had fought and where Arturo had fallen victim either to a bullet or to the cold. They came from the Ukraine, from the steppes or from the fertile *Chernozyom*. Many came from even farther away — there were Siberian Cossacks from the shores of Lake Baikal, and from the valleys of the Ussuri and the Amur rivers. Their numbers were vast and their people were dispersed through the south of European Russia as well as Siberia. The Siberian Cossacks were known for their extreme loyalty to the czar, who had been shot by the Reds along with his entire family.

Marta listened to these accounts with a curiosity intensified by anticipation. Esther and Aaron used to talk about their native town in the Ukraine and though she recalled their stories only dimly, they still inspired the same fascination. The Cossacks stirred her Slavic spirit, the part of her that had made it so easy to learn Russian the moment she went to work for the Heshels, and she was eager for more news. But not everything she heard about the Cossacks was reassuring. Alda's mother reported something terrifying.

"You know they're nothing but savages!"

"Why? What did they do?"

"They're crazy. They took somebody's cow that was pastured in the field by the station and simply cut its throat. Then they skinned it right there on the spot with their scimitars — everybody knows how sharp those things are — then cut it up in pieces and set about roasting it over campfires down by the river. Laughing all the time they were and drinking carafes of tea...."

The bellows of the dying cow — it was probably skinned still half alive — had echoed through the mountain gorges and nearby villages, destroying the evening quiet. People were saying these Cossacks were nothing more than barbarians....

In Marta's mind, however, these reports underwent an odd revision. True, the Cossacks might be somewhat uncivilized, but in general she imagined them to be as ingenuous as children. She felt they had accepted a nomadic life to regain their freedom and the traditions of the past. They were surely tired, disheartened and hungry — victims of war, which always made life more complicated and terrible. She wanted to see them for herself. Leaving old Haha to look after Anita, to spare her any strong emotion, she hitched a ride on a wagon and went down to the station.

By chance she arrived just as a train pulled in, one of the last of the two hundred or more that had transported the vast migration. The sight cheered her because she found herself thinking that if the Cossacks had made the journey in cattle cars maybe it wasn't so bad Esther and the gypsies had gone off to Germany or Poland in the same kind of trains. What difference did it make? In wartime you traveled any way you could — everybody knew that. So why should she go on seeing cattle cars as such an evil omen?

She watched the Cossacks unload their enormous placid draft stallions, then the smaller more nervous saddle horses, then wagons covered by hides or canvas, like the covered wagons of the American pioneers. The men were dusty and disoriented. As they got off the train, they looked around, bewildered by what they saw. Many had yellowish skin, slanted eyes and gray beards. Some wore low fur hats pushed back on the nape of their necks, others had caps more suitable for the season.

She was sure their abstraction was increased by profound doubts about what sort of future awaited them up here in these mountains, among these meadows, rivers and roads. For a minute or two after they got off the train, they didn't know which way to go. Then they'd see where others were headed and quickly join the group moving like a column of ants down to the river. It seemed they were drawn to the water and the wide low river banks, which spread out for dozens of meters, their gravel and stones shimmering in the slanted rays of the soon to be setting sun. Some of the men were setting up their great circular yurts on the grass of the meadows sloping gently toward the river. Others, guided by an invisible logic, were separating into smaller groups and moving off in different directions. As she watched Marta realized each group was identified by the color of the stripes on the men's trousers — lines of wagons, horses, soldiers, women and children, all finding their place in a pre-arranged order.

People watched from the windows of the few scattered houses nearby, wondering what event had provoked this latest wartime expedient, the most bizarre yet. Children were fascinated by the scimitars and the crossed cartridge belts the men wore on their chests, like pictures of Mexican guerrillas. And the horses — they had never seen such gigantic horses. Even the old peasants regarded them with ill-concealed envy, thinking how magnificent they'd be for work in the fields. Two or three horses like that could pull as much as the tractors they had seen in American films before the war.

A young Cossack singled out a little boy standing at the edge of the road and invited him with a gesture to get up on one of the horses. The astounded child blushed and looked around in confusion, seeking his parents' tacit consent or disapproval. But the Cossack abruptly picked him up as easily as if he were a stick and placed him on the horse's back, steadying him with one hand. At first the frightened boy wanted to get down but then he began to like it, to look about and smile, proud as could be that he was the one who'd been chosen. His worried mother watched from a window. Other mothers had rushed out to get their own children and bring them safely inside.

After a couple of hundred meters the Cossack reached up to help the boy dismount, but now he didn't want to and would have ridden on in triumph all the way to the camp beside the river. The Cossack noticed Marta standing on the edge of a garden plot, smiled, then pushed his low fur hat back on his head and saluted her with his hand. She didn't respond, merely watched. The heavy stallions were sweating and occasionally they lowered their heads to crop a tuft of dry dusty grass. The Cossack children were ragged and dirty. Some whimpered, rubbing their eyes with grubby hands as they tried to adjust to the bright light. There were a few young women, proud in their bearing, dressed in embroidered skirts and blouses and leather boots with their black hair wound in chignons. The enormous hooves of the stallions struck the hard gray earth of the road in resounding blows. Sniffing the water they could not yet see, they raised their heads and whinnied. From the covered wagons came the high pitched sound of women's voices and the crying of babies.

A furrow creased Marta's brow. What she had heard was indeed true. This was no army, it was an entire population who had arrived to settle and take possession of Friuli. What was going to happen now?

She went down to the river and gazed from a distance at the seemingly endless encampment. The felt yurts extended for kilometers along the grassy river banks. Cossacks were wading knee deep into the river to water their horses and wash themselves. Some had taken off boots, jackets, and caps, entering the stream half naked with joyful shouts. She could sense their happiness at finally reaching the end of an interminable trip through unknown countries, a journey filled with hardship and discomfort. She could feel their elemental joy at leaving the train to find water and refresh themselves, at having at last arrived at a destination, whatever it might be. Some of them, the youngest, were laughing and splashing water at each other with the flat of their hands. Others on the banks were using heavy mauls to drive iron stakes into the ground to tether the horses. As they led the horses to be tethered they murmured, "Trrr, trr...."

Some of the men had the distinctly oriental eyes and drooping black mustaches typical of Mongols or Tartars. Tethered among the many horses were several camels, both Bactrians and dromedaries.

Realizing that it was getting late, Marta turned back and for part of the way followed the same path as the Cossacks. An endless line of wagons, horses and soldiers was moving along the hard dirt road, dusty now, but still full of holes left by sudden summer downpours. She couldn't help thinking that, like her own valley, the Gorto, Incaroio, Timau and San Canciano valleys must also be crowded with horses and wagons. After a few days of uncertain respite the invasion would surely spread out in all directions and no part of Carnia would be spared.

By the time she got home it was already dark and she felt a twinge of remorse at having stayed away so long, a remorse colored by fear the Cossacks might have preceded her and already taken possession of the villa. Haha and Anita were on the verge of becoming alarmed, unable to separate her absence from the disturbing rumors circulating in the village.

The Cossacks had not yet arrived there but people expected them from one hour to the next and everyone was tense. Then what? Would they engage the partisans in battle right away? Marta was worried, very worried. The war just kept on going — it had moved through Africa, the Balkans, Russia, Scandinavia, France and now here it was in Friuli. God only knew what was going to happen now. It was like a hailstorm — it just hit where it hit and there was nothing anyone could do about it.

The next day the interminable columns of Cossacks began arriving in the village. The men were silent, speaking only now and then to urge on the horses. They approached cautiously, keeping a suspicious eye on the watching villagers, but gazing more intently toward the distant mountains. These Cossacks were from the valley of the Terek, identifiable by the wide blue stripes on the outsides of their trousers. They were pleased with the beauty of the fields and meadows, the charm of the little village. Nonetheless they had already known, even before they left Poland or the Balkans, that this was dangerous territory, full of *partizany*, like all of Europe. You couldn't see them but they were up there hiding out in shepherds' cabins near the highest peaks, or in the forest or holed up in the cheesemakers' huts in the green alpine valleys.

Long experience had taught them that wherever they went partisans would fire on them without warning, then disappear underground like moles, only to leap out again when least expected and attack like wolves in the night. This indeed they knew from experience, but they had also learned that this land, like any other gift from the Germans, was tainted. Undermined and corrupted by treachery, it would be as full of rebels as a garden is full of worms.

They felt alone and abandoned in a foreign country, like the Italian alpine troops in Russia, hated and feared by the population. They tried to believe they had finally found a place to stay for a while after all this endless wandering through Russia and Europe.

They took comfort in the fact that their long voyage was over — for some of them it had lasted almost two months — and that they had arrived in the promised land. However, this promised land, like all the others before it, was already inhabited. When would they be able to return to the steppes and their own rivers? When would they finally succeed in banding together in one Great Cossack Army led by Generals Vlasov, Krasnov, Shkuro, Polunin, Domanov and so many others? When would they renew the struggle against the Bolsheviks? The war between Whites and Reds had been suspended when their troubles began and that was decades ago.

Vlasov was in Berlin desperately trying to persuade the Germans to bring together a Cossack army of liberation. After years of exile in France, Krasnov, the great ataman of all the Cossacks, had moved his court to a requisitioned hotel in a village not far from Lake Cavazzo. There he waited, bursting with impatience to resume that ill-fated and ancient war.

The horses whinnied, as their hooves rang against the cobbles of the village streets, and the jingle of their brass harness bells blended with the voices of their drivers. The Cossacks were settling in along the roads and in farmyards, in the piazza in front of the church and the *braide,* grassy fields behind the houses. They brought their horses to drink from the trough filled by the fountain in the village square, then washed and curried them as best they could. The animals grazed in grassy areas, or along the dusty edges of the roads, their heavy lips and strong teeth cropping whatever vegetation they could find. They moved slowly and clumsily, sometimes stamping their heavy hooves, every now and then bumping heads or bellies. Later on some of the men went into barns and stables and pulled down huge armloads of hay as villagers watched silently from their windows, not missing a single move. The Cossacks said nothing, gave no sign, simply took what they needed with no defiance — knowing full well no one dared oppose them. They acted as calm and unconcerned as if these were their haylofts and homes, their own *stanitsy* on the banks of the Terek River.

Their reasoning was perfectly simple. The horses had to eat and thus they needed the hay. Then something happened. An old man tried to stop them. "That's my hay," he muttered. The Cossacks abruptly pushed him aside with little notice and no violence, almost as if he weren't even there. Once the horses were fed, they began to consider their own needs. The Cossack always thinks of his horse first, then of himself. They set up camp in farmyards, in the village square or in the middle of the road, lighting fires under enormous copper kettles, then tossing barely plucked and carelessly cleaned chickens into the boiling water, or great chunks of mutton, which they pulled out of leather sacks or metal containers. They had brought entire skinned carcasses of sheep and young goats and seemed to want people to see they had plenty to eat and shouldn't be taken for gypsies or vagabonds, who never had anything at all.

The day passed quickly and a peaceful night, fragrant with the smell of hay and wild flowers, descended on the valley, as the mountains slowly changed into dark imposing masses. Stars shone dimly in the incipient glow of a not yet risen moon. Some of the Cossacks withdrew to their wagons covered with animal hides, took off their *valenki* — their leather boots — and went to sleep. But others had something else in mind. They pounded on the doors of houses with their rifle butts until people were forced to let them in. Once inside, they surveyed the rooms, carefully sizing up the space available for their own use. Clearly, all the young girls had been hidden away out of fear, and there wasn't a trace of a young man anywhere.

"Boys, all *partizany*?" they said sternly.

"No, not partisans, soldiers," people answered, "soldiers like you. Gone to the front."

But the Cossacks shook their heads, unconvinced. All European youths had joined the partisans and things couldn't be any different here. You had to be constantly alert, sleep with one eye open — there was always a chance of ambush. They'd have to set up rotating guard duty right away. They took possession of rooms that were either half empty or filled with tools and provisions, beans, grain and corn. Bringing ample bundles of straw from the stables, they announced, "*Kazak* sleep here." It was never a request, always an affirmation. They went about their business without asking anyone for anything, as if they were in their own homes. Their actions were measured and confident, like those of a long familiar ritual and indeed they were doing the same things they had done in many other European towns and villages. They needed lodging and they knew it was best to take what they wanted quickly with no preliminaries, to provide for themselves in the best possible way now and thus avoid future friction with the inhabitants.

## At the Villa

They swarmed over the countryside like a plague of grasshoppers, five or six in every house, divided into family groups. Once they were settled in with a roof over their heads, a fireside and a kitchen, their good humor returned and they were happy just to be alive. They laughed and joked and sang their epic *dumy*, or the traditional songs of the Terek Valley, as if they were not here, but somewhere else. They seemed to want their hosts to join them, winking and exclaiming, "Wine, wine!!"

"No wine. There isn't any," the villagers replied.

"*Nyet.* You *mnogo* wine — much wine. Hide. We find tomorrow. Wine for all...."

The day they arrived in the village one group of Cossacks found their way to Marta's villa as she, with a certain dread, had expected. She recognized one of them, the youth who had given the little boy a ride on his horse and this pleased her. He looked about twenty. With him was an older man, apparently quite serious and deliberate, a middle-aged woman holding a little boy by the hand and a colonel already graying at the temples. They came into the house together, greeted the occupants with a military salute, then looked around with wonder and curiosity. The youth smiled and took off his low fur hat, freeing a thick lock of jet black hair.

"Girei," he said, then added, "Gireikhan," to emphasize his importance.

Marta shook his hand. All them glanced around as if to assess what space would be available for the newcomers.

"Gavrila Ivanovich Bakazov," said the older man, taking Marta's proffered hand and barely touching it with his lips. But his real attention was directed at the house. Although Marta had long ago hidden rugs, tapestries, paintings and silver, the villa's spacious elegance was clearly visible.

"*Une belle maison. N'est-ce pas, madame?*" said the colonel.

"Yes, it is a big house. There's room for all of you," Marta replied in Russian.

Dumbfounded, the Cossacks crowded around her, curious as to how she had learned their language. She told them about living here with Russians for many years, emphasizing Signora Esther's sad fate, kidnapped by the Nazis and sent off to Germany in a train of cattle cars. She asked the colonel, who seemed to be the one in authority, if it would be possible to ask the German commander for information about Esther.

"Oh well, the Germans," he answered with an apologetic gesture. They were not on good terms with the Germans and he himself had never been able to get a civil response from one of them — just clipped irritable replies delivered with contemptuous looks, as if he and all the rest of the Cossacks were no more than a bunch of ragged vagabonds. And he had lived for years in France as an exile. He referred vaguely to work camps in Germany and Poland, where deported Jews were taken to do heavy manual labor on roads or railways, or in local factories.

He spoke in a low voice as if unwilling to pursue such an unpleasant and problematical subject. Who knows where such a discussion would lead? At least this was Marta's distinct impression, and one more veil of distance and apprehension fell between herself and her former landlady. How could she even imagine the poor lady dressed like a convict, slaving away like a common laborer, maybe even in the cold and the rain. No, she couldn't, and wouldn't. Perhaps they were keeping her in an infirmary of some sort, concerned for her fragile health. But as these thoughts passed through her mind she was overtaken by melancholy, an insidious aggressive permeating sadness that seemed to wrap itself around her.

The younger officer said his name was Urvan. Unlike the others he didn't pay much attention to the house, but showed more interest in Marta. Still there was nothing impertinent or insistent in his manner because clearly he didn't want to be labelled as rude or ill-mannered even though his origins were humble. He kept looking at her intermittently, obviously entranced by the round face framed by an airy mass of hair, her luminous expression, the well-modeled neck that emerged from her blouse.

Since everyone seemed to be waiting for her to decide, Marta assigned the rooms: one for the woman and child, one for Urvan and Girei, and a third smaller one for the colonel. She herself would continue to share her room with Anita and Haha would remain in his tiny cubbyhole at the edge of the household. All seemed satisfied this was a just apportionment, indeed the best possible, and heartily approved her decision. It was good to be settled under a roof, and especially to exchange their former precarious accommodations — a cattle car, a covered wagon and a yurt — for the comfort of a beautiful house.

The boy Luca, Girei's little cousin, soon found the door to the back yard and made friends at once with Baldo, who sensed a kindred spirit. The dog always liked children anyway because they were as playful as he was. Haha felt a pang of grief because Luca was the same age as his kidnapped grandson and from a distance the old gypsy's failing eyes might easily mistake him for Elias. Like him Luca had long black hair — the resemblance was all too close. Sometimes he'd call him Elias, then correct himself, caught in a sudden tangle of emotions, but then the knots would unravel and he'd give way to long sighs....

Until now Haha had been hard-pressed to find ways to fill his day, other than going to gather wood in the forest or stopping in the village to pick up whatever he could in the way of news, but Luca's presence made the time fly. He didn't even need to take part in the little boy's games, it was enough just to sit on a bench in the yard and watch him from a distance. In fact Luca seemed to have more or less the same effect on everyone. Lively, noisy, always running and playing, talking to the dog, he was changing the whole atmosphere of the villa.

One member of the household was rapidly learning Russian. Baldo. Luca's peremptory orders delivered in his own language would puzzle the dog for a moment, but then he'd dash off to carry them out. He'd retrieve sticks and stones, sit up on his hind legs, lie down on command or run up the slanting trunk of an old mulberry tree that had grown up crooked in the back yard. Baldo's momentary puzzlement showed he was used to receiving orders in more than one language. He had become a polyglot dog. His innate clownishness made him respond with joyful abandon to the silliest of commands: raise one paw, wag your tail, turn round and round. Besides he was a perfect match-up with Luca who was certainly a budding animal trainer. Girei had already made him a little leather whip, which he snapped skillfully in the air. Baldo heard that sound as a solemn command and he concentrated on deciphering it, for to disobey was sacrilege. His conscious allegiance to Luca was now complete, at least when the boy came out to play, though occasionally the woman Dunaika kept him inside because of a cold.

If Baldo learned rapidly to obey orders given in Russian, Luca was equally adept at acquiring Italian and Friulan. He picked up language as easily as a sponge soaks up water, evidence of a quick and active mind. His whole being seemed to be in constant motion. His raids on Marta's pantry left clear evidence of his passage where she had stored quantities of jams and preserves in fearful anticipation of even harder times.

Dunaika, nicknamed Babushka by the Cossacks, did all the housework for her compatriots. Girei, more or less the colonel's orderly, brought in rabbits, plucked hens with their heads dangling, or half-skinned still bloody young goats. He'd glance guiltily in Marta's direction, hoping to reach the kitchen without her seeing him bring in stolen animals. But he had to steal in order to survive. He knew he was acting according to a law everyone recognized and applied, although it was not spelled out in any language but imprinted by instinct on human nature. Dunaika cooked for the Cossacks in one corner of the kitchen, trying not to take up too much room. Here she reproduced as best she could the sauces and spices of Terek cooking, based on Tartar and Mongol recipes derived from the culture of central Asia.

Although the Cossacks rejoiced in these odors when they entered the kitchen, Marta and Anita had to make an effort to suppress their disgust. But there were some dishes that appealed to both groups, like pilafs, simple recipes based on rice and butter, tasty and pleasing to both young women. Haha didn't seem to care whether his food was eastern or western — he was quite ready to eat whatever he found on his plate. Taste didn't matter as long as there was food.

Now and then as Marta prepared a meal a few steps away from Babushka, she'd be taken with sudden amazement at the thought that she was sheltering allies of the Germans in her house. Did her failure to see anyone as an actual enemy mean there was something wrong with her? No matter how hard she tried she couldn't manage to grasp such an idea, much as she couldn't bring herself to understand the war itself. It was still unreal to her, a dark and bloody fable that somehow materialized in the world for reasons that could only be perceived as wicked and perverse. She not only found it impossible to hate the Cossacks, she couldn't even conceive of them as adversaries. Today's adversaries of course, because before the armistice that term was applied instead to the English, French, Russians and Americans. Now everything was turned upside down — former enemies were friends and former friends enemies. Nothing made sense.

She wasn't reacting to the effects of the war, the Babel of confusion, the chaos and destruction. It was the very concepts of war and enmity that couldn't seem to find a way into her head, but remained outside, abstract, abstruse and without meaning. Was it possible Urvan, Gavrila or Girei might one day shoot at Ivos and other partisans? And if they did how should she deal with it? She had no idea. She tried not to think about it and just hoped it wouldn't happen

Among the five Cossacks she had taken in, the boldest, liveliest and most ready to joke and tease was certainly Girei. He was very familiar with Urvan and always found excuses to make fun of him: he missed the point of a story or a pun, there was something wrong with his horse's belly or other such things.

"Just be quiet and eat, boy," the captain would say, "these days we've hardly got much to laugh about."

"Why? Am I supposed to be serious all the time like you? What's the use of going around with a long face? It doesn't help anybody."

Then, for one reason or another he'd give way to frenetic laughter. Neither Dunaika nor Urvan responded to his provocations, remaining quietly absorbed in their own troubling thoughts.

Gavrila was often absent. For good or ill, he was a former career officer. A lieutenant at the outbreak of the civil war, he had risen to the rank of colonel during his years in exile and was thus responsible for the local garrison. If he ever thought about it, he himself wouldn't have known whether he was a real colonel or merely a lieutenant grown old in exile. He had never lifted a finger to obtain that rank, but Krasnov had promoted him anyway, perhaps because of the twenty-three years spent far from his home and family. He had passed those years and grown gray at the temples managing a farm in Berry. By now he knew more about dairy cows and grains than he did about war. But here, in Carnia, he was in charge of the garrison and he tried as best he could to fulfill his role as colonel.

The cornerstone of his strategy was not to confront the *partizany*. Let them stay where they were, up in the mountains. The Cossacks would remain in the valley, using whatever means they could to avoid a battle. Nonetheless, to save face, and for prudence's sake, he had placed certain areas under constant guard, especially at night: bridges over the rapid mountain streams; high tension power lines, as well as those for electricity and telephone cables; and military barracks, where Cossacks had now replaced Italian soldiers. He put a watch on any place or anything he thought might be threatened by the invisible guerrillas.

Even Girei had to take his turn at night guard duty. Whereas Gavrila was full of doubts about his own worth as a colonel, Girei, scarcely emerged from noisy mischievous boyhood, was different. As soon as they had handed him a gun and a cartridge belt he hadn't the slightest misgiving — he was a select soldier of the garrison. Night duty was a bit tiresome. There was a sharp chill in the air and he was glad to have his fur hat, called a *kubanka*, as well as his heavy wool jacket and *valenki*. Although it was only the beginning of autumn you needed warm clothes at night. He heard the screech owls, the deeper hooting of the horned owl, the yelps of foxes who had dared come down from the woods. The village dogs barked once in a while and the moon shone on the alpine pastures and the dark masses of spruce on the mountains. He picked out the peaks whose names he had learned from Marta. Some were entirely green, whereas others had rocky outcrops and crests. He tried to compare them to those he used to see from his *stanitsy*, off toward the Caucasus — they weren't that different. As far as he was concerned all mountains looked alike, as if they were all patterned after the same model.

Some nights the wind howled and it too was like the wind that blew through the rushes of the Terek and the groves of maple and poplar of his native valley. Or if it was quiet and all he heard was the rippling of a stream or the rustle of a small animal in the leaves, he could easily believe there was no war. If it weren't for the occasional rumble of the Flying Fortresses high overhead on the way to Germany, or sporadic shots from rifles or Stens, the war might be nothing more than a memory.

Since Girei never saw or heard anybody, he felt as if he were standing guard over nothing and let his mind wander. His instinctive fear of the *partizany*, acquired when he was in Poland, led him to think of them as invisible bandits, too clever to catch, like the legendary Abrek marauders his great grandfather had told him about when he was a child. They used to come down through the valleys of the Caucasus Mountains to prey on the Cossack *stanitsy.* In the nineteenth century catching an Abrek was a glorious act celebrated for days throughout the entire village.

Urvan also often had night guard duty, but for him it had its pleasant side. He enjoyed solitude and liked the sound of nocturnal creatures, the smell of the woods and the last cut hay. But at the same time he was acutely conscious of being in a foreign country and his thoughts turned to past deprivations, including the events that had destroyed his family. While they were in Poland his wife and youngest son had died in an epidemic. Strong as they were, like most Cossacks, the hardships of the war had worn them out and they were too weak to fight off illness. His oldest son, who would now be almost Girei's age, had been killed by a stray bullet. For Urvan Poland was a cursed country. He perceived all places as either blessed or cursed, according to what happened there, and in Poland he had known only misfortune. He still couldn't come to terms with it all. Especially the stray bullet. Over and over he wondered who had fired it, where, and why. He knew that in wartime and especially war against *partizany* stray bullets are commonplace, fired off with no purpose, no target, no sense, by some heedless youth simply because in a momentary rage or euphoria he finds himself holding a gun in his hands. That bullet went off in the direction his son was moving and there the two met, thanks to the utterly bizarre will of destiny. And Urvan was left all alone.

Now all he had left to care about was his Terek people. They had become his family, the only object of his affections, and the real purpose of all this wandering from one place to another wherever and however the Germans decreed. He'd heard nothing from his parents or grandparents, his brothers, sisters or their children for years. They had remained in the *stanitsy* to cultivate squash and sunflowers. But he had come away with his whole family. The Germans had lured him with the mirage of reviving the conflict between Reds and Whites, the war he had fought in Crimea and the Ukraine with all his Cossack pride, at the age of twenty.

In those days he followed the atamans Krasnov and Kornilov with a blind and absolute loyalty. Whatever they did was right, and their orders were gospel. He had consumed his youth in the tumult of a senseless war that constantly fanned the flames of Cossack nationalism. Although he was young he had seen at once that the ardent thirst for liberty fundamental to the *kazak* was in no way compatible with the order the Red Army was setting up throughout the land. An unbridgeable gap divided the Bolsheviks from his own people. He saw the Reds as a people gone wrong because they had demolished everything that mattered to him — freedom, the past, tradition, ownership of land. Now they wanted the proudest and freest nation on earth to submit to radical change. In reaction to this absurd and outrageous presumption he had joined the Cossack Army of Liberation.

Like an almost imperceptible current the primeval instincts of his remote ancestors still trickled through his blood, or so it seemed to him. He understood perfectly the Cossack predilection for the hunt, for revenge, war, ambush, mass migration, for a free unfettered life.

Inside Urvan's very soul the ghosts of those archaic traditions still stirred like a long-faded memory rooted deep in past centuries, and his pride in belonging to the *kazak* nation was fully intact. As he stood guard at night over the leather-covered wagons he heard the whinnying of horses stabled next to the local farmers' cows, or the snorting of camels, and he felt as if he had ended up nowhere, left waiting on the other side of a wall for something obscure and unpredictable to happen. He no longer wondered why the Germans weren't sending the Cossack Army off to fight the Reds and liberate the land that had belonged to his people for hundreds of years. He went through the motions of daily life as though his whole being were coated with a kind of dust of weariness and distrust. His former hopes were now dimmed and draped with cobwebs.

One day Urvan, Gavrila, Girei and Burlak, a tall burly Circassian who had turned up among the Terek Cossacks, as well as others from the garrison, went out on horseback for a reconnaissance mission through the whole valley. They rode along silently at an even pace, often patting their horses' necks to keep them quiet and reassured. They encountered other villages and other garrisons, observing their surroundings carefully in order to understand that mountain landscape so unlike the one they remembered. Only Burlak seemed to feel at home because this country reminded him of his childhood home. He seemed actually to sniff the odor of future battles with the *partizany*.

"Why don't they show themselves? How come they don't attack?" he asked Gavrila.

"They have their own way of fighting. Blowing up bridges and railroads. They put dynamite between the ties or under trestles. They only come out when the coast is clear, like moles," the colonel replied.

"You should know them well by now. We've had to deal with them in so many places," added Urvan.

But Burlak and Girei couldn't accept that kind of warfare, and gave way to fits of impatience. Burlak drew his razor sharp scimitar and slashed the air, cutting cleanly through young hazelnut branches, which fell truncated onto the path. He couldn't stand the inactivity, this barracks war, this stagnant fruitless waiting.

The colonel's thoughts were far more tranquil. The reconnaissance had revealed nothing in particular and his assessment of the patriots remained exactly the same. The only notable fact was that they were camped out high in the mountains where it wouldn't be possible to get at them. Maybe a surprise attack would work, carried out in the old Cossack tradition, through the woods with the horses' hooves bound with strips of cloth to keep them from making noise. But the idea was distinctly repugnant somehow because he didn't feel as if this were really his war. He had no quarrel with the guerrillas, he had landed here solely by chance, by an unlucky destiny that had dogged his steps for decades. His war was against the Red Army. He wished it would really happen — he had waited half his life for it. But when, my God when? His patience was running out. Only two or three years ago that war seemed imminent and victory already close at hand, but then it receded again as things became more problematic and confused.

He too, like Urvan, had fought in the civil war under Krasnov's and Kornilov's command. He was only a lieutenant then, just a few years out of the military academy and engaged to marry the daughter of a local ataman from the Terek district. Because of the war they had had to postpone the wedding, but it never did take place. He had fled into exile in France and since then he'd heard nothing from or about his intended bride.

For him as for Urvan, the defining moment of his life had been the civil war. He recalled the smoke of artillery fire, the smell of powder, the neighing of horses, the battle cries of attacking troops, particularly Budyonny's cavalry. Budyonny, whom he and his comrades called the madman, was a Cossack who had forgotten his heritage and deserted his people to join the Bolsheviks. Gavrila's memories of cavalry charges with drawn swords were still so vivid it almost seemed his life had ended at that moment. The twenty-three years spent in France, some of them managing the *domaine*, counted for very little. He thought of them as a dream, a long reverie that had helped him pass the time until the war and his real life began again.

As far as he was concerned events in Russia since then didn't matter at all, hadn't even happened. He barely noted the cataclysmic changes that tore apart the society he had known, shredded the very fabric of his former existence. The clock simply stopped when the war was interrupted. The possibility of reviving their cause had set time running again, but only in a halting defective rhythm. Would the long awaited day ever come? The Germans continued to postpone it and he could hardly say he didn't know why.

In Berlin they kept putting off Vlasov with one excuse after another because nothing had changed. They treated him with contempt since for them the Cossacks were an inferior nation, barely civilized and useless in warfare. At best they might serve as guard dogs to keep watch over a few poorly armed partisans, who were already hounded like rabbits. In fact the German army was retreating all along the front and hadn't yet made up its mind to unleash the Cossack army against the Reds. The colonel couldn't keep these thoughts to himself any more and had begun to share them with Urvan, Girei, and when the opportunity presented itself, with Marta. He wanted her to know because he needed to confide his troubles to someone. Besides, Marta was kind and patient and ready to listen to anybody. Her presence, or just the thought of her presence, momentarily softened his torment and diminished his regrets, like a healing touch on his weary soul. In a way she replaced the women in his life, his Cossack fiancee, the woman he had had in France for so many years.... Marta's knowledge of Russian was another comfort and with her nearby his situation at the villa and the garrison was less tedious. As he talked with her he forgot her humble origin. In fact he was quite surprised to note that what had once seemed so important — whether someone belonged to the aristocracy, the middle class, working class, or peasantry — had dissolved into insignificance. Social class mattered very little. He felt perfectly at ease with Marta and talking to her seemed to help him come to terms with his life.

When he returned from an inspection tour he liked to sit down and collect his thoughts. He'd forget about his duties, absorbed in watching the colors of the precocious mountain sunsets. At such moments even he could forget the present war in this oasis of calm, comparing his surroundings to one of the mythical islands of the Pheacians, where these times were a distant memory and he could busy himself with pleasant tasks like grinding toasted barley or putting another log on the fire.

Once it got dark they had to make sure all the shutters were tightly closed because of the blackout. Neither the bombers on the way to Germany, nor the partisans in the mountains could be allowed to see even a sliver of light. Inside they might as well have been in a ship drifting on a calm and windless sea, completely separated from the world.

# The Metamorphosis

One of Gavrila's greatest pleasures was to tell Marta about his exile in France. Although he didn't realize it, France had become his second homeland, little by little replacing the first one. While he was there all he did was dream of returning to Russia to fight the Red Army, but now that he had left the French countryside behind he understood how profoundly it had affected him. He was no longer completely Russian, nor was he truly French. In fact he wasn't sure anymore who he was, what he wanted to do, or where he wanted to go. He missed the *domaine* in an odd sort of way, as if the castle-like dwelling where he had lived with the owners of the estate were calling him back. It was the same with all the aspects of his exile — he was nostalgic now for things he had not particularly noticed until they faded into the mist of the past. But he knew he couldn't go back, even if he wanted to.

He wished he could confide these secrets to Marta but thought her head was so full of present worries she'd hardly be interested. However she herself considered Gavrila a refined and gentle man and regarded him with the same mixture of sympathy and compassion she felt for everyone.

Sometimes she wondered how she could help him. Once she went and rummaged about in the attic and cellar until she found a copper samovar and a couple of Russian icons. They had belonged to the Heshels and she herself had carefully hidden them away. She left them in Gavrila's tiny bedroom to create an aristocratic and distinctly Russian touch. The colonel was both astonished and flattered, and Marta realized that she too was attracted by refined and elegant objects. Apparently living for so many years in a luxurious house with the family of a talented musician had marked her in a subtle but lasting way.

Still she was aware of the profound distance between herself and Gavrila when he talked to her about Russia. He told her the country was ruled by a band of fanatics and impostors who must be unmasked and driven out by force. Once the Cossack Army launched an attack on the Bolsheviks the Russian people would rebel and Stalin's regime would crumble like an izba built of rotten wood.

Furthermore he was convinced most Russians wanted the restoration of the czar. The massacre at Yekaterinburg was vivid in his mind, like a still-bleeding wound. At the very moment when they were finally sure they were safe, the entire Romanov family were slaughtered like sheep. They had trusted their captors blindly, just as they had always trusted their servants, never once suspecting the treason perpetrated by the Communists under Lenin's personal command. To Gavrila the affair was a repetition of the biblical Slaughter of the Innocents. The children were certainly guiltless: a sickly hemophiliac boy subject to frequent relapses, during which he suffered and sweated with delirium and fever; cheerful vivacious young girls, full of zest for life, always ready to laugh, so jolly they didn't even believe they were about to die when armed revolutionaries burst into the room. They thought these men with the guns had come to take them across Scandinavia to a secure exile in England.

Girei didn't know much about Russian history, but he listened gravely to Gavrila with the same astonishment he'd have felt upon hearing about some local catastrophe in the Terek Valley. He felt strangely pleased to think he was actually engaged in a struggle to return the throne to a princess he had never seen, who Gavrila said had miraculously survived the massacre and was now safe in France. Nonetheless the only thing that really mattered to him was the hope of recovering his homeland and his river, and for this he was ready to fight to the end. This hope was kept alive by vivid memories of his boyhood *stanitsa*: the infinite number of sweltering summer afternoons when he'd go down to the stony banks of the Terek and swim or fish for trout where the water meandered sluggishly through thickets of bamboo and willow; the calm surface of the river, sparkling with reflected sunlight as it flowed along, almost majestically slow. In some places the clay soil or sand was useless for planting crops and only scrub willow grew, or rushes with sword-like leaves so sharp they could cut your finger.

Even the sound of the church bells still echoed in his ears. When his mind turned to such thoughts he too felt like a wandering exile, and his homesickness was almost a physical pain. But the way things were going now, that long-desired return seemed dimmer and more distant with every day that passed.

As for the war against the partisans, which hadn't yet begun either, it wasn't his war — he had no quarrel with these rebels who wanted to chase the German invaders out of their territory, just as his own people had wanted to drive out the Red Army. Indeed he felt a touch of sympathy for the *partizany*. They were young like him and their war was not unlike the one the Cossacks dreamed of. But Girei's impetuous nature wouldn't let him linger on this subject and he'd soon be bursting with eagerness to test himself against these guerrillas, to smell the smoke and hear the din of a real battle.

With a sort of mystical obstinacy Gavrila tried to hold on to the hope that the Cossacks' moment would come, that their struggle was sacrosanct and fated to succeed. It couldn't be a lost cause. His belief in destiny shone like a halo around his every thought. His faith in Krasnov was absolute. As long as the general was alive and in command of the entire Cossack Army, hope could not die. Krasnov was a true charismatic —

there was something extraordinary about him that simply precluded any doubt or uncertainty.

His conviction was adamant but he couldn't explain it even to himself. Perhaps Krasnov represented a kind of pure idea, the very essence of the hope he had nurtured for so many years. On the other hand, Vlasov, who was still in Berlin negotiating with the Germans, was less trustworthy, in fact almost ambiguous, because he had actually fought on the side of the Red Army during the battle of Moscow. No one could be sure he wouldn't do it again. He was a suspicious figure for Gavrila — not once but twice he had joined the winning side.

Urvan noticed Gavrila's frequent conversations with Marta and his instinctive discretion kept him from intruding. He thought the two of them were establishing a general understanding based on refined and aristocratic behavior. It seemed such a relationship would exclude him. One day, stopping by Gavrila's room, he noticed the icon and the copper samovar and suddenly the whole situation was clear. He himself was only a commoner, completely without distinction either by way of birth or European exile. He was just an ordinary man from the steppe whose parents were peasants, even though he had gone to school for a few years and become a typographer.

Marta had a vague notion of what he was thinking — she was good at guessing what was on people's minds. Her intuition for hidden intentions, the magma of things not said, the motives that remain in the dark but bear heavily upon a person's life. Her enigmatic antennae, tuned to pick up the most basic impulses, had already provided her with plenty of information about Urvan. As a woman she had read his signal that he regarded her as someone he should keep his distance from. She knew he had analyzed the situation and concluded that if anyone was going to be allowed to have designs on

Marta, it would have to be Gavrila, who had lived in France, addressed her as "madame," and could tell her all about the *domaine* where he worked for so many years....

Thus Urvan had been quick to accept the division of labor at the villa and had taken on the humblest tasks with no hesitation, the same as Girei. For instance, he looked after the horses and went to the village to requisition hay to feed them, knowing full well the real meaning of the word "requisition." He took what the horses needed and the villagers would never be paid for it. Back in his *stanitsa* on the Terek he would have used other words to describe such actions — he would have spoken of robbery or plunder by an invading force. Unlike Gavrila he couldn't pretend not to understand the grim laws of survival. Men and horses had to eat more than once a day and since no one was giving him what he needed and he had no supply lines behind him the only thing he could do was steal from a population who already had very little for themselves.

By now the courtyard of the villa, like the village itself, was taking on the appearance of a Cossack *stanitsa.* Actually some houses, built partly of wood, were slightly reminiscent of izbas to begin with. On every street corner there were piles of straw or cornstalks sodden with manure from horses and camels. Inside as well as outdoors the same strong odors hung in the air — the smell of horses, of leather, of sweaty felt and wool blankets. Curved swords, old fashioned rifles, cartridge belts, and the Cossack *kubanki* were ubiquitous reminders of a presence halfway between the military and the peasant. Nobody thought to clean up the straw or manure in the streets. The babushkas, including Dunaika, left it where it was, to dry out and harden so that later when it was dense and desiccated they could collect it and burn it in their stoves, just the way they would at home.

"What are you doing?" Urvan asked.

"What I've always done...."

"But you don't need to do that here."

"Why?"

"For goodness sake, woman. There's plenty of fuel for the stoves and fireplaces right here at the house. Didn't you see the woodpiles? We aren't in our own village here. We have to do things the way the local people do."

"Listen to him now," grumbled Girei's mother, still holding the bucket of *kizyak* she had braved the cold and the wind to gather, because autumn was nearing its end and winter was rapidly coming on. But Urvan yanked the bucket out of her hand, walked over to the manure pile to dump its contents, then rinsed it in the frigid water of a nearby fountain. In fact Urvan was becoming sensitive about how Marta might regard him, and what she might think about his people.

And yet little by little the village was being relentlessly transformed into a Cossack *stanitsa*. It was a common sight to see Bactrian or dromedary camels being led to drink at the fountain, especially in the evening at nightfall, which came quickly this time of year. The first in line with his camel was always Akmekkhan, an old Russified Tartar who often came up to the villa to visit Urvan or Girei. Everyone brought horses to drink at the fountain twice a day. The town was littered with hay and straw, some even caught between the stones on walls of houses where men had brushed by them carrying armfuls of fresh bedding or fodder for their animals.

Shopkeepers were beginning to stock merchandise with the Cossacks in mind. They did have a bit of money on hand and, more important, they maintained deposits in the *Feldbank*, which kept its funds in armored strongboxes in various locations in Carnia and distributed pay to the various garrisons. Shop windows displayed caftans, blouses with Tartar embroidery for women and girls, colored ribbons, *valenki*, other minor articles of clothing at low prices, small Cyrillic Korans, rosaries with crude wooden beads, astrakhan fur hats in all sizes, but especially the low style worn in the Terek. There were *matryoshki*, sets of hollow wooden dolls that fit one inside another, which the Cossacks bought for their children, not to mention bridles of leather or rope, assorted harnesses for horses, clothing of dark flannel, icons, samovars, tea services that ingenious Friulan artisans had already begun to produce, hoping to derive some profit from the invasion. It seemed as if the characteristic colors, odors and objects of the Cossack homeland had been picked up all at once and suddenly spirited by magic here and throughout the villages and valleys of Carnia.

Urvan was deeply happy to see that the *kazaki*, after being again forced into nomadism by the misfortunes of war, had found a kind of temporary home, could rest for a while, get their strength back, and treat their wounds, especially the invisible kind he himself suffered from. He knew how tired his people were, how desperately they needed rest after all this adversity and wandering all over Europe. He was convinced the Cossack was strangely cursed, fated to be repeatedly driven out of his steppe and away from his rivers, as if somehow at the beginning of time he had been tainted by some obscure crime.

Yes indeed, an interval of rest and healing was exactly what the *kazak* needed. This was Urvan's major concern and he didn't give much thought to other considerations. Marta watched him attentively, this man with the sad face and hair thinning at the temples, who had lost his entire family in the war. It seemed to her that even more than Gavrila he had something of the ataman about him — he had to keep hope alive for his people, even if it were mere illusion. Without hope, the *kazak* simply couldn't survive.

The Cossacks were visibly satisfied and felt quite at home there in the village, whereas the local population was astonished and frightened. They felt as if they'd been robbed of something uniquely theirs. One local tavern was even selling a newsheet printed in Cyrillic characters, entitled "The Cossack Homeland" and printed at Krasnov's headquarters. Marta tried reading it. The articles were written with a disarming candor, full of rage against the Reds, Stalin, and the Kremlin and hope for the earliest possible return to their own countryside. It read like a publication aimed at elementary-school children.

The village was swarming with Cossacks all day long. Their laughter and exclamations rang from windows and farmyards, and the affectionate commands and endearments they addressed to their horses were clearly audible. The men had long Asiatic drooping mustaches. Stuck in their belts or colored sashes, they wore curved daggers, some decorated with the Muslim crescent, in copper-studded leather sheaths. The leather-covered wagons made their way along the muddy frozen streets or stood in courtyards or on threshing floors beside farm wagons. Now and then Cossacks quartered in other villages or even other valleys would pass through. Then the faces of the Terek Cossacks mingled with other faces: those of Kalmucks, Khirghizes and Circassians as proud and bellicose as Burlak. The valley had taken on the appearance of a mini-Kazakhstan, and the river seemed to have turned into one of the many rivers of the steppe, like the Don, the Donets or the Volga. At night the men's voices could often be heard in chorus, in loud and drunken celebration of their success at finding where their unwilling hosts had hidden their wine.

One evening Marta, Girei and Urvan passed by a house where a horse hide was stretched out to dry on the wooden terrace. The curtains were closed, smoke rose from every chimney, and from inside came the sound of singing. The three of them stopped to listen. The song told the story of a boy, Vassily, who returned home after several days' absence to find a terrible scene. The *stanitsa* was as silent as a graveyard — all the houses had been burned leaving only the stone parts still standing. Vassily couldn't find his father, mother, brothers or sisters. He had been left as alone as the single tree in the middle of the farmyard. Obviously the Russians had been there, killed all the men, kidnapped the women and set fire to the village. Desperate, the boy sat down under the tree. His eyes wandered to a stone shed and he noticed that his balalaika was still where he had left it, miraculously intact. He picked it up and began a wailing refrain, "*Ahi, dai, dalalai!*" the only way he had left to pour out his grief and anguish.

Girei stood there transfixed and when the song ended he wiped away his tears with his coat sleeve. He identified totally with Vassily, with the memory of that terrible event so far away in a Terek village. The song had deeply affected Urvan as well, for the Cossacks were an emotional people, their very souls imbued with mysterious insatiable yearning.

"The song tells a true story," said Urvan.

"So I guessed," said Marta.

"Cossack villages were often raided. If it wasn't the Abrek mountain tribes, it was the Russians from the plain. And everything was always burned and destroyed...."

"Just like the Germans have done to us."

Marta too was troubled, not so much by the song itself but because it stirred up a whole complex of feelings. The war, always the war, coming closer all the time — how, if ever, would it end? And Arturo who had disappeared in Russia and she would never see him again. And Caleb's cruel death and the way Signora Esther and Haha's relatives had been taken away to Germany in cattle cars. And she herself deprived of the chance to marry and have children, the hope of any young girl. These were personal subjects, hardly as far-reaching as the fact that entire populations had been driven out of their land to become homeless people with no future. And Ivos who hated war had felt obliged to leave her and go off to the mountains to fight. Everybody was being swept along in different and disastrous directions by the invisible forces that govern the world, forces that are never still, always moving like the wind blowing clouds this way and that. She thought of Urvan's family, the stray bullet that had killed his eldest son. She wondered about Gavrila's intended bride — had she grown old alone in her little city on the Terek, waiting for someone who would never return?

Thus Marta, like her companions, felt the tears well up in her eyes and would have willingly joined her voice with the soldiers' sorrowful refrain. She thought about Gavrila's false hopes, his apparent failure to realize that during his twenty-three years in exile the force of events had completely changed Russia. Life there was now terribly different from what he imagined. Nor could she forget Urvan's attachment to his people, his tenacious conviction that they were absolutely unique.

Urvan was a tall and handsome man, his dark hair grown thin at the temples, his face marked by the sorrow and weariness of these past years. Now that winter was upon them and the roads and trails were covered with snow he habitually wore his *chekmen*, a long coat that reached his feet, open at the neck and with a front closing bordered by a leather strip decorated with silver. He kept a dagger in a leather sheath stuck in his belt. When he was not on duty guarding whatever the partisans might damage, or off in search of food or fodder for the horses, he was content to sit and chat with Marta or Haha in front of the stoves he himself kept stoked with firewood. Often he listened as they told their stories. Haha described his people's customs, how they elected their king or queen, the assemblies when they all got together, marriage and betrothal ceremonies or celebrations for the birth of children. Custom and ritual were all there was to discuss since the gypsies were a rootless nomadic people who lived outside time and history.

Urvan himself would tell about the Cossacks. He knew their history mainly through the *dumy*, epics in which poets recounted heroic deeds of ancient times, like the bits of Greek oral poetry stitched together to form the *Iliad* and the *Odyssey*. According to the *dumy* the Cossacks were descended from Asian pastoral tribes who had emigrated to the Ukraine in the fifteenth century and established a homeland there. However, their collective memory of long migrations remained alive. Marta's finely developed intuition for the past made her wonder if this memory of nomadism might not be the defining characteristic of the *kazak* nation.

Urvan pointed out that the word *qazaq*, which evolved into *kazak*, actually meant "nomad." They, like the Khirghiz, were nomads and they were indeed fated to wander. Yet even here, so far from their homeland, they maintained their traditions and social structures. They were subdivided into military communities called *arteli* and into guilds according to occupation or trade. But those distinctions didn't count any more — war was the only job, everybody's job. Now and then they would come together in assemblies called *Rada* to discuss their future. But for Urvan the future looked too dark — he preferred to talk about the past. For instance about how during the civil war their generals — Wrangel, Kornilov, Denikin and Krasnov — had temporarily held off the entire Red Army and been a dangerous thorn in their side.

He also recalled that shortly after the Germans arrived in their territory something auspicious happened. A Cossack division was formed under the command of the German general Helmut Von Pannwitz. A student and admirer of

Slavic and Cossack culture, he was the only German who did not regard them as an inferior race. But the illusion soon faded and the Von Pannwitz division was relegated to a reserve unit for the Germans, a tremendous disappointment for the Cossacks.

Really, Marta wondered, how could the Cossacks have possibly believed those deceitful Germans? Hadn't they already renamed Friuli *Adriatisches Küstenland* before they rechristened it *Kosakenland*? Both names were as false as counterfeit money. Friuli was not the Asian steppe, the American prairie or the Australian outback — it was a densely populated area. So how could the Cossacks think it could be theirs? They might as well believe in fairy tales.... However, she was sure the Cossacks didn't want to think about all this, that for them it was a taboo subject and they were doing their best to keep their minds off the future.

Urvan, at least, avoided such thoughts, knowing it was useless to lose yourself in a labyrinth of unknown possibilities. But he was more sensible and realistic than Gavrila.

Marta felt sorry for the Cossacks. True, she felt compassion for almost everybody — soldiers risking their lives at the front, partisans freezing to death in the mountains, prisoners, refugees, people who were lost or missing. But the fate of the Cossacks pained her most of all because they no longer had a homeland or a future. Once again she found herself sinking into a vortex of reflections on a war that seemed more and more sinister in an almost supernatural way — a relentless sequence of events that left no room for pity or hope. Like the trains that had taken the Jews to forced labor camps where they disappeared and no one could find out anything about them....

These were terrible times, lawless and chaotic. Everything was upside down and backwards and what once seemed outrageous was now commonplace. Many villages in the mountains as well as in the hills had been burned by the Germans because the partisans used them as bases. And now there was word from elsewhere that Cossacks had driven people out of their homes and moved in as if they meant to stay there permanently. Local people were terrified. Their original good will and understanding disintegrated and deep and atavistic fears revived. Now they saw the Cossacks as a barbarous medieval horde.

As for the Cossacks, they harbored a dark and cavernous hatred toward their supposed allies, the Germans. A number of different sentiments intensified this emotion. They felt the Germans were treating them as inferiors, refusing to help them or supply them with provisions or arms, forcing them to live by plunder and thus pitting two populations against one another with murderous results. They hated the Germans for saying they had given them this land when it was not theirs to give and was plagued by deadly partisan warfare. It was as if one Cossack told another Cossack he could have somebody else's horse or wagon and the recipient of the gift was then obliged to steal it or take it away by force. They realized more and more clearly that Friuli and Carnia were false gifts. They themselves had been pawns in German hands, exploited and treated as servants. Hatred born of wounded pride continued to smolder until sometimes the accumulated tension ignited like a spark and exploded with savage consequences.

One night two Germans on a motorcycle, after riding for hours vainly trying to find a particular village, lost their way completely. It was a bitter cold and snowy night with a strong wind blowing, and the road was little more than frozen ruts as hard as stone. They kept consulting their map by flashlight, and at a certain point a sudden gust of wind tore it out of their hands. One soldier jumped off the cycle in pursuit, but couldn't catch it before it flew straight up over the hazelnut bushes, flapping like a pair of wings, and disappeared. For a moment he thought the howling wind had bewitched the map and carried it off through the valley on purpose, to play an evil joke on the two of them. His companion, still sitting on the cycle with the motor running, waited anxiously for him to return.

"Did you find it?" he asked, when he caught sight of the other.

"Find it? I ran like crazy. No use. It's gone."

"That's impossible. We can't get along without it."

"I tell you it's gone, swallowed up by the night. It just vanished."

The other began to shout and swear. Without a map they were as helpless as a couple of blind kittens, or two moles driven out of their tunnels by force. Always used to traveling with a map, constantly checking the names of towns with the road signs, now they couldn't have felt more lost in the midst of an Asian steppe. And the partisan threat was so palpable they could almost smell it — the very ground under their feet crackled with danger. They imagined armed figures behind every spruce or beech or filbert. Cursing their fate, they took off at high speed, shivering with fear as their wheels skidded on the icy road. Obsessed with terror, all they wanted was to get away from those mountain valleys and slippery roads, to flee this veritable den of wolves.

They tried to get their bearings by looking at the mountains but couldn't see very well. Furthermore, the shapes were unfamiliar and the two men perceived them only as huge menacing forms hovering over them. They had never paid much attention to the landscape — the map had always been their reference point and their salvation. One desire kept time with their rapidly beating hearts: to finally catch sight of the well-known surroundings of their own garrison. But all they managed to do was to go up and down and round and round, often seeming to return to the point they started from, hopelessly lost. Convinced that all local people were either partisans or friends of partisans, they didn't dare ask anyone for directions. A request for information meant admitting they were lost and would put them in enemy hands.

Increasing terror matched their breathing with the wind wailing through the valleys. Round and round in circles they went. The roar of the motorcycle reverberated for miles, suggesting to local residents barricaded in their houses that this might be one of those damned and cursed nights when the Germans came out of their dens and rounded up and arrested people with horrifying speed, according to plans long meditated in offices hung with swastikas.

Hence no one dared go out, and nearly everyone was afraid to look out the window to see what that roar of motorcycles going back and forth like an echo was all about. The two men crossed through the village, slowing down, then found themselves in the midst of a Cossack *stanitsa*, or so they thought from the sounds made by horses and camels in the stables. Their rage and fear intensified — they felt as if they'd ended up in a barbarian encampment. They didn't know what to do, whom to blame, how to get out of this crazy labyrinth made up of a hundred roads.

Then they spotted a Cossack patrol in the distance, commanded by Burlak the Circassian.

*"Stoi! Stoi!"* he shouted at them in Russian. *"Dokumenty!"*

It was obvious to Burlak as well as to his men that these were Germans, but they pretended to mistake them for *partizany* in disguise. The age-old hatred between their two nations was still strong and so was the Cossacks' urge to avenge the many recent humiliations they had endured under German command.

"*Sie schmutzige Kosaken! Weg, weg*!"

Arrogantly the Germans tried to push past them, but Burlak wasn't going to let them get away so cheaply. He galloped forward with his whip raised, splattering them with mud and slush thrown up by his horse's hooves.

In a burst of anger the Germans grabbed the revolvers they wore in holsters on their chests, but Burlak and his companions just as quickly drew their scimitars, always the favored Cossack weapons. Trapped by their own arrogance and fear, the two men on the cycle opened fire. The shots reverberated across the night, and inside multitudes of darkened houses people started in terror, the ancient perennial terror of war. The echoes bounced back and forth again and again, through every gully and ravine, until finally they died away and people sighed with relief and slipped back into sleep, thinking whatever it was, it was all over now. But it wasn't over. A young Cossack had been wounded and Burlak raised his scimitar and fell upon the Germans, followed by the others. Stifling the shout of savage rage that rose in their throats they hacked the Germans to death. It was a scene never before witnessed in those mountains, but perhaps it resembled historic cavalry charges, for instance during the Napoleonic wars when the Cossack horde attacked the French at strategic river crossings. For Burlak and his men, this was an atavistic response hidden deep in the Cossack soul, which, when triggered like an earthquake, produced a kind of brutal release.

Moments later the Circassian made a decision.

"These two never came through here!" he said to his men.

"Right. Nobody saw them, nobody heard them," replied one soldier.

"No one heard the motorcycle," Burlak pointed out.

"There were no shots and we never took out our scimitars," replied the soldier, cheerfully adding his support.

They set about the business of getting rid of the two bodies. The motorcycle was completely dismantled, reduced to little more than nuts and bolts, the larger pieces buried with those who had ridden it. As for the tire tracks, the current heavy snowfalls would take care of them. The entire Terek garrison found out what had happened and reacted with a crude elemental enthusiasm, as they would if an ambush or an assault had gone particularly well. It was almost as if two Abreks who had come down out of the Caucasus Mountains to raid and burn the *stanitsy* had been killed with a bullet between the eyes. Their jubilation evolved into a unanimous desire to celebrate. "Wine! Wine!" they demanded, but the frightened inhabitants could only think of the expected reprisals, which the Germans would not wait to carry out. *"Schnapps!"* the Cossacks kept insisting, as if expecting a deserved reward for their valiant deeds. Inside their houses, completely dark from outside, oil lamps burned and they sang songs of war and chanted their *dumy* well into the early morning hours.

Days turned into weeks as the villagers waited for German retaliation. They had not forgotten the burned town at the summit of the valley. The inhabitants up there were still camping out and the roofless blackened abandoned houses were a grim reminder of those terrible days. The village buzzed with rumors that this time no settlement in the entire area would be spared and no one, not a single person, would escape the vendetta. But things turned out differently. The Germans came up from their headquarters in cars and trucks to look for their missing comrades. They searched along the roads and trails, the shores of the river, then took the shortest route back to their base — it was obvious they were not in friendly territory. What had once been the Republic of Carnia was now the Cossack Republic, and it was full of partisans hidden like mushrooms in the woods. It was far healthier for Germans to keep out of their way, wherever they might be. They did, however, make some inquiries about a missing motorcycle with two riders, but the response was always a shrug or a negative shaking of heads. No one had seen or heard anything. The two soldiers must have taken a route through some other valley and perhaps fallen into a ravine somewhere. Or they could have been captured by *partizany* or even joined them. These days anything could happen.

Old Haha was the most fearful of all. He kept wandering back and forth through and around the village in a state of constant anxiety. He was sure that sooner or later a flash flood or a mudslide would uncover the two corpses, or the motorcycle wheels or the body of the sidecar and it would suddenly be clear what had happened. Then the wrath of the Germans would fall like a bolt of lightning over the whole valley. In his restless peregrinations he ended up one day where the empty gypsy caravans, snow-covered and buffeted by the wind, were beginning to rot away slowly. A painful sight it was. But nothing of what he feared came to pass.

This valley as well as the other valleys in Carnia was looking more and more like a miniature Kazakhstan. Men on horseback or horse-drawn carts moved constantly back and forth through every mountain hamlet and along the roads of the lower valleys. Friendships developed between the officers of the different garrisons, as well as among the women and children dependent upon them. Cossacks from the Don and Donets, identified by red stripes on the trousers of their uniforms, mingled with their Siberian counterparts, who wore yellow stripes. They greeted one another effusively, with embraces and offers of drinks, or invitations to sing or dance. Despite everything their inherent youthful cheerfulness was never far beneath the surface. If they managed to get hold of some wine they were quick to share it. But underneath it all was a kind of dull weariness, the moldering residue of too many misadventures, too many reverses, and there was still no end in sight. Their conversation returned again and again to the places where they had settled temporarily, but only and always to fight the partisans instead of the real war, the one that mattered most. They also mentioned the names of *stanitsy* abandoned far away on the steppe or in the fertile *Chernozyom*, and perhaps most often they spoke of their lost rivers.

On all festive occasions Akmekkhan was ready to celebrate. Although he was well along in years he was in splendid physical shape, lean and wiry, and full of energy and good humor. The young people called him Uncle and he was indeed a lively witty mischievous uncle, clever and quick in every way. He had a bloodhound's nose when it came to finding out where the locals had hidden their wine. No disguise, no double door, no subterfuge could fool him. He kept his eye on his hosts like a hawk watching its prey. No suspicious move, furtive gesture, or evasive act escaped him. Sooner or later he'd find the small bottle of wine or the big bottle of brandy or the salami hidden in the straw. He got the best of everyone.

Uncivilized at best — and even his pointed features recalled those of a fox or a ferret — he was absolutely unrestrainable once he got hold of wine or grappa. Possessed by an urge to revelry he'd seize the nearest guitar or accordion and break into song or begin to dance in traditional Cossack style, arms folded, legs extended, bouncing on his heels, until everyone else succumbed to his exuberance. The wood floors of kitchens resounded under dancing feet, houses filled with song, echoing from cellar to attic. But after a while the lateness of the hour or the wine itself began to dull the levity and taint it with melancholy.

Akmek himself, seemingly cut out for nothing but merrymaking, found himself sinking into gloomy reflection. Rancor showed in his eyes as he pursued his thoughts. The *kazak* had nothing but enemies: *partizany*, Germans, Reds, Allied forces, sickness, lice, hunger. And everywhere he went people stalked him or shot at him.

Now and then the demon wine got to Urvan as well and at a certain point he'd sink into a morass of doubt and sadness, and bitter thoughts would stir in his mind, like wolves coming out in the snow. One evening during yet another of this succession of drinking parties, he was struck by a sudden idea. Perhaps the Cossacks should never have left Russia. Maybe it would have been best just to stay instead of abandoning the steppe and the river. Whatever destiny had in store for them, they should have faced it right there at home. If they had to fight, that's where the fight should have happened. If they'd died they'd have been given funerals in their own churches and been buried in their local cemeteries. It seemed to him this thought had been laboring within him for a long time, like a mole digging a tunnel, and now it had finally come out in the open.

Yes, he was sure now. The Bolsheviks in Russia were to him an evil. But they were an evil of his own country and a domestic evil is always somehow lighter than one encountered on foreign soil. If he had it to do over again he would never have chosen to leave his river and his *stanitsa* and to wander aimlessly from one place to another. Now, unexpectedly, he felt as if he'd done everything wrong, from the beginning of the war to the present, and his mistakes had destroyed his family and left his people in a state of terrible uncertainty. A vague feeling of discouragement swept through him and turned into desolation as vast as the desert between the Caspian and Aral Sea. His was a Slavic and a Cossack soul with infinite capacities for enigmatic regret and never-ending nostalgia.

Each time he filled the wooden ladle with wine from the bucket on the table, his sorrows and regrets expanded.

But something else was troubling him — was he indeed some sort of traitor? It was bad enough to have abandoned his homeland, but he had joined forces with the Germans, with the same army that had invaded his country, sowing death and destruction everywhere. He and his comrades had changed sides, allied themselves with invaders who held the Slavs in contempt. Meanwhile the Bolsheviks, who were his real enemy — or so he had believed since his youth — were completely out of reach. He hadn't seen them for years and there was no possibility of engaging in combat with them. He might as well have fallen into a whirlpool where a man could drown without even noticing, sucked in by the deadly force of events. And yet here he was, uncomfortably aware he was in the wrong place, getting drunk on stolen wine instead of attending to his duties as second in command of the garrison. Again his mind went back to his village on the Terek. If he hadn't left, his family might still be alive....

He could see it all clearly now, leaving Russia was an error. If the Cossack's destiny was to make war, it was much better to do it on his own ground, in his own territory. He tried quietly confiding his sentiments to Akmek, but the Tartar contradicted him at every turn. The point was they had followed their atamans and thus there was no error — people had to follow their leaders. Back in Russia the Reds were in command and if the *kazak* were to rebel he'd be crushed immediately. And when the *kazak* was defeated he always abandoned his lands and went elsewhere. That was his custom and tradition. Even the women, who were more attached than the men to the land and to the izba, even they had wanted to leave. Such had been the wish of Urvan's wife herself, now dead and at peace, buried in a Polish cemetery. And the wishes of the dead are sacred.

But Urvan was not convinced. Doubts had begun to gnaw at him from within, like a weevil inside a piece of furniture in the middle of the night. About one thing, however, he had no doubts — his vow to stay with his people no matter what happened and to share their fate to the end. Admittedly there were many ways to be a *kazak* . For instance the Tartars and Circassians were less civilized than the others, more prone to orgies, plunder, and random destruction. But they too were *kazaki* and he regarded them as brothers. All Cossacks from the many distant and varied regions had something in common and he felt himself to be an advocate for the entire *kazak* people, a sort of embodiment of their collective soul.

He was happy in his comrades' company, enjoyed the wine and the singing, but he also liked to be alone. When his turn came around to go on patrol or make an inspection he didn't mind. He welcomed the chance to examine his own thoughts, to take notice of his feelings, and he discovered that by far his strongest purpose was his commitment to the entire *kazak* people, including those now dispersed through the valleys of the Republic of Carnia, sleeping at night on straw mattresses in barracks or cobblestone houses. The *kazaki* had for some time given up their old nomadic ways in exchange for settled lives as peasants, woodcutters, and hunters. But the war had forced them back into nomadism. Sooner or later the *kazak* was fated to mount his horse, hitch up his leather-covered wagon, load it with his copper pots and pans and set off again to wander.

But his comrades didn't care to hear his melancholy reflections. All they wanted was to drink and carouse and sing, to ladle out the wine from the bucket and cheer up the old man they'd taken it away from. Why shouldn't he join their noisy party? Burlak was the most insistent — he wanted everyone to be loud and exuberant and kept urging the old man to drink more and more. For Burlak the excitement of the recent carnage had not abated. His joy at the thought of the two motorcyclists hacked to death by Cossack swords still resounded within him. A bloody vendetta was especially pleasant to a Circassian warrior. Burlak's greatest ambition and keenest desire was to cut to pieces any enemy who refused to surrender. Thus what had happened a few days earlier made him profoundly happy.

He was so implacable in his desire for revenge that even the other Cossacks regarded him with a hint of fear and none of them would wish for any reason to cross swords with him. For some mysterious reason he regarded attack and vendetta as his peculiar duty — one might think he had read it in the Koran itself. Even in the midst of merrymaking with all his excesses of wine and song, he seemed to be on the lookout for an imminent assault or major battle, so impatient to join the fight he was almost sniffing the air in anticipation. His wide nostrils trembled with expectation as he burned with desire to go after the *partizany*, to take on those leaders whose names were constantly whispered throughout the whole area: Bora, Sonia, Saetta and now also Vento. Everyone re-membered their acts of sabotage, their surprise attacks carried out with deadly accuracy, but they themselves remained as elusive as ghosts.

Girei hung around Burlak, served him wine and watched him with admiring eyes, always hoping the Circassian would notice him. Without realizing it, he imitated Burlak's gestures and echoed his raucous laughter. He was dazzled, enchanted, his own identity completely lost in the reflection of the other's forceful personality. His eagerness to model himself after Burlak did not please Urvan one bit. He felt responsible for Girei, who might have been his son. In fact he felt responsible for all the others and couldn't wait for the party to end so he could take the boy home and send him off to bed.

# The Babushka

The party was suddenly interrupted by the sound of explosions. Bombs, and they weren't far away. Everyone rushed outside. To the south beyond the mountains toward the village where Krasnov's headquarters were located flares streaking in all directions lighted up the sky as bright as day. Every now and then a new series of explosions muffled the steady dull roar of the airplanes and jolted the Cossacks dispersed along the snow-covered road. These were certainly American planes from Italian bases and with every bomb that burst something in their hearts tore and bled. Whether by reason or intuition, they realized their own garrisons were the targets.

Each man was acutely aware of his own helplessness. With the arms they had — antiquated rifles, a few Stens or Russian submachine guns, hand grenades — they couldn't even lift a finger against the massacre of their compatriots. They all knew the ***kazak*** was once again doomed to die on foreign soil — this was just one more episode in a series that began ages ago.

The next day reports reached them from the area that had been hit. There were so many dead it was nearly impossible to find burial space in the tiny village cemeteries along the lake. Only two solutions presented themselves: hastily dig an enormous mass grave with picks and shovels or bury all the bodies in the lake. The second way would be easier. One had simply to tie a heavy stone to each body with a strong rope and the problem was solved. Krasnov, who had looked death in the face himself, opted for this alternative. It was quicker and he knew the sight of so many unburied dead would ultimately demoralize all the troops stationed on the lake shore.

These reports moved like a funereal wave through all the valleys of Carnia, touched every Cossack garrison, even the most distant and isolated, and wrapped each ***kazak*** man and woman in an invisible black veil of mourning. The old babushkas gathered in the village square by the fountain as if for a pre-arranged meeting and to commiserate with each other. The substance of their discussion was simply that war was terrible, terrible for everybody. Among them were a few Friulan women old enough to remember the other war, who, like Alda's mother, might have carried food or even bombs to soldiers behind the lines up in the mountains. The two groups managed to make themselves understood in a minimal way at least on the most important subjects: food, and life and death. Girei's mother Dunaika was also there. Tall, robust, a bit overweight, with a black kerchief on her head, she looked older than she was because of the hardships of war. In fact she so closely resembled the Friulan women of her generation that from a distance she could easily be taken for one of them.

Leaning on the fountain, she addressed the woman standing next to her, "War no good for anybody."

"None of us wanted it," said a village woman.

"So why did it happen? War doesn't just break out by itself. It's the leaders who wanted it. The leaders and the generals," said another.

"But when the war began everybody came out in the piazza to cheer and applaud...."

Alda's mother rummaged through her memories and discovered this was true. On the day war was declared people had welcomed the news with great enthusiasm in the streets and piazzas of all the nearby villages. Maybe after a certain period of peace and tranquillity men forgot how horrible war really was and when it broke out once more and they saw its true face they were astounded and unprepared. It made them think about their leaders, about the idea of destiny, or cosmic forces, all those things that influenced human history, made things happen. Dunaika bowed her head in resignation as if she knew in her heart there would be lots more pain and trouble before the war decided to end.

Now that she had been living at the villa for several months, she was increasingly conscious of a secret affinity between herself and the local women. Like them, she seemed to have been born to work hard, but most of all to shoulder the weight of misfortune, to carry on with infinite patience. Her husband had died in Poland too, like Urvan's wife, but he had been killed in a *partizany* ambush. She had only Girei now and her little nephew Luca, who had lost both parents. More and more frequently the Friulan women and the Cossack babushkas intermingled in the little village shops, the dairy store, or by the fountain in the piazza. With a certain effort, in heavily accented speech they managed to communicate their thoughts about the war and the daily problem of trying to find enough food. The subjects never varied — the conversation always took the same route, as predictable as a train on a track.

"Will this war ever end? How much longer can it go on?"

"It seems like it started a thousand years ago."

"And most of all, it's forgotten how to stop...."

Dunaika somehow liked the idea that the war just kept going, stolid and imperturbable, by force of inertia. It had lasted five years now, already longer than that other one everybody had thought unbearably long at the time. It was as if the winter on the steppe or the taiga had forgotten to end, the animals forgotten to come out of hibernation, the snow and ice to melt and the sun to rise above the horizon and bring back the spring.

Asking herself why she had ended up in this chaotic and bloody situation made her head spin and she preferred to avoid the whole question. Thinking about it was a waste of time. The only thing to do was try to repair a little of the damage, treat the wounded, wash the soldiers' clothes and cook their food, look after them if they were sick or their wounds got infected and more than anything else, pray for them.

In fact Dunaika belonged to the sect called "Old Believers" and she had arrived with a great many icons in her cart, enough to take up considerable space in her bedroom. Under them she lighted whatever candles she could find and afford in local shops — sorry looking yellowish objects at best. Even when she was doing her housework or serving a laboriously prepared dinner, she never stopped mumbling prayers under her breath. She was convinced the only thing that really mattered was religion. The state, the law, wars, even though they might turn the world completely upside down, were only secondary and insubstantial.

She tried to explain all this to Girei, who was committed to other modes of thought and trembled with eagerness to fight. But he also had something else in mind and in fact spent most of his time stubbornly pursuing Alda. He had, of course, noticed her right away and she was rarely out of his thoughts.

"You should stop hanging around in the village and wandering off by yourself," said his mother.

"What am I supposed to do then? Keep holding on to your apron strings?"

"Listen to me now, I'm telling you. In times like these it's better to be careful."

"You act as if I were a little kid. I'm grown up now, old enough to live my own life. And I'm sick of looking at icons all day. It suits you but not me."

"You like war better?"

"I like what men like. I'm a man now even if you'd still like to think of me as an altar boy."

He was always ready to abandon the villa and run off to the village, or down further into the valley, roaming here and there, attracted by what he thought were properly virile activities. Even the dreadful news about the massacre of the Cossacks in the lakeside villages and the problem of the victims' burial seemed to him to be men's business, events about which he ought to be well informed. If such things were happening his place was with the group of men who made decisions. His mother never talked about things anyway. She merely endured. With her long Circassian braids, she looked the very embodiment of resignation and acceptance. As for the victims of the bombs, all she did was pray for them — constantly — crossing herself over and over again. She had been quick to assimilate this new misfortune and add it to the infinite number of others that filled the bottomless well of her Russian soul.

She felt deep compassion for her people, subjected to this long Calvary of suffering, and particularly for the atamans, who had to take responsibility and make decisions. All her life, both in Russia and elsewhere, she'd done nothing but work all day long, but for her it was a privilege, especially now, because having so much to do took her mind off her troubles and she could forget them for a while. No housekeeping task was too hard or too distasteful for Dunaika. She had even cleaned and tanned the skins of goats and lambs, staining her work clothes with blood and grease. Her tasks had gradually evolved as a complement to Marta's and the two of them now managed the entire household in perfect cooperation.

But even when she was absorbed in her work her underlying anxiety about Girei persisted. She lived in terror he might fall victim to an ambush, be shot by the *partizany.* In her imagination she saw the mountains and forests as swarming with guerrillas aiming weapons at the men in the garrison, despite the winter and the snow. She never wearied of warning Girei to be careful, whispering to him in a barely audible tone, as if her words were yet another prayer before her icons. If no one was around Girei was patient with her, controlled his temper, and even let her run her rough work-hardened fingers, full of cuts and scars, through his jet black hair, for at heart he really was dependent on his mother. For him she was the ruler of her household and things went along in the smoothest possible way simply because she was in charge.

Actually the partisans were making their presence known more often and more insistently. There had been another surprise attack in the Gorto valley. One evening just as the light was fading, gunfire rang out from the woods, rifles firing from all different directions at a patrol. When it was over all the men and all their horses lay dead on the ground. The Cossacks now lived in day-to-day fear of such ambushes. Partisans might pop out of nowhere at any moment. They probably followed deer trails down to the village to spy on the soldiers' every move and set up deadly traps. The Cossacks were convinced the partisans were incredibly astute, and they judged themselves unprepared to deal with such en enemy. There was no way they could set up enough sentinels or send out enough patrols, and the typically Cossack bravado that often led them to underestimate their adversaries was now downright dangerous.

It was above all the women who felt this way, especially the mothers. Dunaika was sure the men in the garrison were as ingenuous as children, compared with the *partizany,* like bear or wolf cubs. She worried constantly about all of them. In fact everyone was a bit on edge. Sooner or later there would be another attack — they could feel it in the air. But so far it was only a possibility, a vague but ever-present threat. Like an approaching storm that never seemed to break.

Dunaika felt a strong feminine solidarity with Marta because they both hated war. Her own intense nostalgia for peace and the lost rivers never lessened although she had no idea how her people would ever be able to return. And yet she held onto a thin thread of hope — she didn't know where it came from or why. She somehow believed that things might work out in the end, like a snarled-up skein of yarn that little by little gets sorted out and untangled. The obsession with war rooted in men's minds would finally wither, the urge to fight and kill that had hardened their hearts would crumble and fall away like an old coat of paint, and they would once again wish for peace. This hope was her favorite subject when she talked with Marta.

Marta's energy and will to act was beginning to influence Dunaika and she found herself imitating her. Besides it was a great comfort to be able to converse in Russian, a secret source of consolation that in a small way made up for all the hardship. Fate had driven her into this mountain valley, a place she'd never heard of and she had found a young woman who spoke her own language fluently. And furthermore Marta was a pleasure to talk to and work with because she never let anything get her down. She was like an old friend or neighbor of many years. Actually Marta had this effect on everyone — as soon as people got to know her they felt they'd always known her.

Dunaika liked to talk while she worked and Marta was happy to hear what she had to say. It cheered her to listen to almost anybody because she was naturally open-minded and because she simply couldn't deny her impulse to reach out to others. She was especially drawn to Dunaika because there was something ingenuous, almost astonished, in her voice, which Marta imagined as an echo of the vast Russian countryside she had left behind. And Marta's proximity produced an unaccustomed optimism in Dunaika, a diffused sense of well being.

The Russian woman was also intensely interested in Anita's pregnancy. She gave her advice, told her what she herself had been told when she was young and pregnant, with Girei and with the other two babies who had died when they were but a few months old. She suggested herbal teas made with lime and mallow leaves to thin her blood. These would be good for the baby too because the blood would flow quickly into its growing body, like tea or vodka. But Dunaika's favorite pastime by far was to light the candles under her icons and recite her special infallible prayers, which she asked Marta to translate and write down in a notebook.

Every now and then something curious happened. Living in the same house with two young and attractive women stirred a flicker of feminine feeling even in Dunaika. She started paying more attention to her appearance, and tried to look as neat as possible. Sometimes, seeing herself in a mirror, she felt a quiver of excitement and wondered if she was still woman enough for some man to notice, at least momentarily. Perhaps it was true because lately Akmekkhan had seemed almost attentive in his way, paying her compliments as crude as rough hewn stone. She rejected him rudely, interrupting him and castigating him for daring to say such things to a respectable widow like her. But beneath her apparent indignation she couldn't deny a glimmer of satisfaction.

"Did you hear what he had the nerve to say to me, that miserable old sinner?"

"Oh well, it's just that he's thinking about you, he can't get you out of his mind."

"Marta, what on earth are you saying? I'm surprised at you!"

"All right, but it doesn't surprise me at all. Akmek lives alone and he hasn't forgotten about women. I don't know very much about this world, but there's one thing I am certain of. Men and women are made to live in couples."

"Hmph, fine advice you're handing out."

"It's not advice. I'm just saying that's the way things are."

"You talk like that because you're young. But I'm just an old lady and for me it's all over...."

"Oh come now, you're not old."

"How can you say that? I have a son old enough to go to war!"

Of course she was right. Her life as a woman was over and she ought to be thinking only of Girei, trying to keep him out of trouble and danger, seeing that somehow he got through this terrible morass of war alive and intact. Indeed sometimes as she performed her daily tasks she let herself hope, as if forgetting about the war would make it go away. Or she turned her thoughts to the future, after the war, when life would return to normal for the Cossacks and for everyone else too. Then she'd remember and more by intuition than analysis she'd realize there was no way out for them, and surrender with a shudder to her fears. Her longing for a return to normal life convinced her that people were meant to live in peace, to follow the humdrum of daily routine undisturbed by violence and conflict. Didn't her thoughts always come back to this subject, even involuntarily? But how could this war end for them? How could they ever untangle the hopeless complications of their situation?

Her leather-covered wagon stood under an overhanging roof in the courtyard of the villa and Girei's horse was stabled in the tenant farmer's barn. All her household possessions — pots and pans and cutlery, copper cookware, linens, blankets, icons — all had been brought inside the house. Everything was accounted for: her dresses, blouses embroidered in the Tartar style, colored belts with brass studs, *valenki* or *chuvyaki*. These modest treasures she'd managed to hold onto during all her peregrinations allowed her to think of herself as completely removed from any threat of total poverty.

Sometimes she would try on her most elegant dresses for Marta, not really because she was vain, but because she wanted to show she was not a mere vagabond and wanted Marta to understand that when she used to live in the *stanitsa* she had a certain status, lost now because of the war, but still visible in her possessions.

Occasionally when Marta offered her food she accepted. The Cossacks had to live by stealing and she knew it but she hid her shame, pretending not to notice evidence of slaughtered animals — bloodstains on the kitchen floor and hides thrown away here and there, which local people would salvage for their own use. A secret sense of dignity drove her to deny that aspect of her people's history, as if they hadn't been forced to live this way year after year, wherever their wanderings took them. She was mortified and tried to forget.

Marta was delighted to have so many living at the villa, diverse though they were, because she enjoyed the company of others. But every now and then she was reminded of her guests' hopeless plight. The most she could do was give them fragile temporary safety. She tried not to think about the future, concentrating on present complications, there were certainly enough of them. She continued secretly to sell gold and silver objects and trinkets, or to exchange them for food. As long as the Heshels' small treasure lasted she would be able to manage. But if it ran out before the war ended? No, she mustn't think about that. Anyhow even if it did some saint would provide for them. Her instinctive optimism prevailed and she was sure these problems, like all problems, would be solved, one at a time, as they arose.

That same optimism and her natural sociability led her easily in other directions. She watched over Anita's pregnancy and found time to play with Luca and Baldo. But then everyone did that because Luca himself was so lively and full of fun. He was deeply attached to Dunaika and Girei, but he had come to regard all the residents of the villa as his family. Marta was an aunt, Haha a grandfather, Urvan an uncle, a little bit older than most uncles, and Gavrila, who was around fifty, a sort of combination uncle and grandfather, although Luca himself couldn't make up his mind which.

He seemed to fill the household with his exuberance, always running around, inventing games, shouting and laughing. No one could continue to brood or worry in the presence of this lovable tyrant. Actually he had a kind of histrionic talent, at least for clowning. He definitely enjoyed showing off, playing jokes, inventing skits. When he set about repeating the stories Dunaika had told him he would create the characters by imitating their voices: the prince became haughty and pompous, the thief clever and sly, the peddler extolled his wares, and the jolly vagabond would break into song.

He had a particular passion for dressing up. He put on Marta's shoes with their thick cork heels and Dunaika's Circassian blouse, which came down to his knees, or try on Urvan or Girei's boots, though they reached all the way to his groin and he could hardly move them along the floor. He'd make friends instantly with anyone who came by, Cossack or Friulan. Friendship was a like a magic plant for him — it took root and grew in a flash. He recognized all the villagers, knew their names, where they lived, what their occupations were, etc. He had even formed a close relationship with the Orthodox priest — in fact he seemed to have a special predilection for the trappings of religion. One of his favorite games was to dress up like a priest and pretend to say Mass.

He was quick to go outside into the courtyard, then he'd head for the path and end up in the village. Dunaika had a hard time keeping him at home and insisted on wrapping him up in scarves and woolen hats that came down over his face because he had a weak chest. Marta made him a miniature lambskin hat with the hide of one of the many animals slaughtered by their Cossack guests. Dunaika had tanned the skin more or less crudely, but Luca was quite proud to have his own *kubanka*. In fact if he sensed any hint of impending festivity he'd begin tossing it in the air just as he'd seen the soldiers do so many times.

He was as quick with language as he was with learning who people were. He already knew numerous Italian and Friulan words and quite a few Tartar ones taught him by Akmekkhan, who in his sly and surreptitious way delighted in creating a veritable Babel of languages in the little boy. And Luca was an apt pupil, rattling off his new words as he bounded through the hallways or the courtyard. He tried them out on Baldo, in all sorts of different tones, to order him about and the dog obeyed at once. Thus for Luca his Tartar phrases not only expressed his own jolly good humor, they seemed to be endowed with some sort of magic power. Of course he would use them to greet Akmekkhan every time he saw him.

Despite his immersion in this Babel of many tongues, Luca managed with ease. Except for his native Russian, he transformed whatever language he might be speaking into a kind of comical stage dialect, distorted in form and pronunciation. No one who heard him could resist the humorous effect and all worries would be forgotten, at least for a moment.

But Luca's greatest love was animals, to whom he was joyfully, even gloriously, devoted. Not just Baldo, his preferred playmate, but the goats and lambs in the barns, the pig Marta and Anita had raised, or even a turtle or porcupine he discovered in the garden — he adored them all. Lately he had also developed a passion for horses and any observer would have to conclude: "There's no doubt. The boy is a real *kazak*." Luca had absolutely no fear of horses. He would dodge in and out among them as if they were trees in the courtyard, walk back and forth under their bellies with complete confidence they would not move or hurt him in any way. In particular he fell madly in love with Girei's horse. He'd climb up on his manger, hug his head and kiss him on the forehead as if he were human. He delighted in adorning the animal's ears and mane with colored straps and ribbons pilfered from his aunt's bedroom. Even here he expressed a taste for decoration with a kind of innate comical logic derived from his heritage.

# Girei's Exploits

One of the people Luca liked best to visit in the village was Alda. Perhaps without knowing it he too was attracted by the young girl's splendid beauty. Girei encouraged these visits, sending Luca ahead as a kind of scout, then following him to Alda's house as if to keep a protective eye on the boy in case of danger. This maneuver did not escape the girl's notice. She'd let Luca into the house, then slam the door in Girei's face, as if she hadn't noticed him or else wanted nothing to do with him. This irritated Girei but he persisted in keeping track of Alda's every move. He sensed she was ignoring him in a way too obvious to be sincere — something in her behavior didn't quite coincide with total indifference. In fact, after he tried approaching her just a few more times, and she closed the door in his face she did so with a particular glance that seemed to say, "Why do you keep coming around? Leave me alone. I'm not meant for somebody like you!"

He began to greet her in Friulan, "*Mandi*," or in polite Russian phrases, as if both languages had a kind of official validity between the two of them. Alda said nothing at all and continued to look as unmoved as a piece of wood. She seemed to be committed to obeying her mother's rigid instructions, or perhaps she was reacting with an atavistic feminie wisdom that told her not to respond to young men's advances, never to encourage them in any way whatsoever. Men were not to be trusted and even a single phrase might open the door to unexpected consequences. Besides Girei was a Cossack and for Alda, her mother, her aunts, and all her other relatives this meant he was some kind of uncivilized vagabond. One day he'd go off with his horse and his wagon who knows where, just the way he had showed up here. What's more he was tainted as an invader and a potential enemy of the young villagers who had joined the partisans up in the mountains. But to Alda all these misgivings were vague and unspoken.

Girei also was well aware that one day he'd be obliged to leave and any rapport between him and Alda would have no roots and no future, like a flower that comes up in the midst of a dirt road. Nevertheless a force stronger than his own will kept driving him back to Alda's house. She smiled and welcomed little Luca, gave him licorice candy or a cooky, picked him up and swung him around in the air. But all the while she'd be glancing at the window toward the street because she knew Girei was out there. Sometimes she pretended to open the window just by chance, to get a breath of fresh air or see what was going on. As soon as she caught sight of him, on foot or on horseback, she closed the window with noisy vigor, as though to shut him out of her life. But then, irresistibly, she'd find herself pushing the curtain aside to glance out and see if he was still there. He was, of course. Artillery fire wouldn't have kept him away. Often he came by on his shiny black horse, perfectly groomed like an animal from a fancy riding stable. He'd keep looking stubbornly upward as he passed.

Sometimes, when the street was deserted and free of snow, he'd suddenly burst into view at full gallop. As soon as he reached the front of her house he'd spring off his horse, run alongside holding on to its mane for a few steps then leap back in the saddle with the skill of an acrobat. She'd watch the whole show from the window, wide-eyed in admiration and secretly proud he was doing this for her benefit, in fact actually risking his neck. Once he didn't quite make it when he tried to get back on his horse and he ended up sitting down in the street. His face expressed total surprise and distress at this failure to perform an exercise he'd done a hundred times, a trick every young Cossack mastered to perfection on their native steppe. It was too much for Alda.

Wrapped in a purple woolen shawl, a red ribbon in her hair, she opened the window, leaned out and burst into laughter.

Girei looked up at her, miffed at first, but then he too began to laugh — something told him her intense amusement implied she liked him. What did it matter if she laughed at him and ostentatiously closed the window or the door in his face? He was sure Alda, the most beautiful girl in the village, was attracted to him. When he led his little cousin by the hand to visit her and Alda smiled at Luca and invited him inside and showered him with kisses, it was really Girei she wanted to kiss. He knew it now. Sometimes Luca went to see Alda by himself and she fed him homemade cookies and put a small silver coin in his hand. He wandered about the streets as if they were his element, like a fish in water.

Luca had a special place in his heart for Anita as well. She often played with him and those moments made her forget her troubles. She never thought very hard about anything, as if afraid to get lost confronting the unknown. For example she had never made any effort to understand the context or the course of the war. It was too abstract, too demanding for her limited imagination. Instead she let her mind drift to other more congenial subjects, losing herself in daydreams and fantasy. For instance she still hoped Arturo might return from Russia, although for years now very few survivors had come back and those who had insisted there was simply no point in people deluding themselves about the fate of the others.

She often returned to her former belief that the war was soon going to end like a bad dream. One morning she'd wake up and people would rush to tell her the war was over, no one knew how. She pictured another armistice and bold headlines in the newspapers, which by the way she never read, announcing the definitive cessation of hostilities. But this time it would really be true, not like that other time when instead of ending, the war had started all over again, more vicious and evil than before. Or else she abandoned herself to a fantasy about finding a young man who would marry her despite her condition and they'd have a wedding in a church all decorated with flowers. She wouldn't even care if he weren't rich or important, as long as he was young and handsome and in love with her. She'd even marry a Cossack without thinking twice, no matter what the future held for them.

She watched these Terek Cossacks with their black mustaches and slanted oriental eyes. She even had an eye for Girei, such a handsome youth. Of course he never looked at anyone but Alda, though he must secretly think her a witch and a devil, since she always pretended not to see him, acted as if he didn't exist. The truth was Anita herself couldn't really distinguish between friends and enemies because all men were the same to her and when they were young and good looking she was hopelessly attracted and easily seduced. She yearned for certain occasions the war had swept away, like the village festivals and religious holidays, which more than anything else reminded her of the town she and Arturo had left when she was only a little girl. Seeing her sad and thoughtful Marta asked,

"What are you thinking about?"

"Do you really want to know?"

"Of course."

"About the feast of San Martino. When will the church bells ring again for the Eve of San Martino, for the whole evening long? Or for the feast of the Madonna in August?"

"Who knows, Anita? Maybe soon. Maybe sooner than we think...."

"Remember what a great time it was? You came here before people stopped celebrating all those holidays."

"I remember perfectly well. How could I forget...."

And Marta had to admit, different though she might be from Anita, she too greatly missed the endless pealing of the bells that announced the eve of the major festivals. She wished she could go back to when those bells belonged to free citizens of a happy village, when there were no occupying armies, no Germans, no Cossacks, no partisans, just people living in peace, their lives not torn apart by trouble and fear.

She looked thoughtfully at Anita. True, she was beginning to show her pregnancy, but she was the same southern girl, a little wild to be sure and not exactly refined, but still very pretty.

Sometimes Marta found herself wondering about the area's prehistoric inhabitants. She knew they had lived in caves or in houses on wooden pilings at the edge of the same lake that had now been turned into a cemetery for hundreds of Cossacks. Despite all her responsibilities and worries, she liked to give in to her habit of reflecting on the past, so dense with mystery and full of shadows. Once she had taken Gavrila to visit a nearby cave to see if he could tell her whether the marks on the stones were actually prehistoric drawings.

"It's possible," the colonel said.

Wandering thoughts mingled with bizarre images carried Marta far away, in strange directions. She saw time as solemn layers, but the history she sought to know had nothing to do with major political or military events. She didn't care about the battles and the victors, she wanted to learn about the suffering, the day-to-day hardship and labor of ordinary people, the destiny of all humankind. People's private lives, whether lived out by the edge of the lake in houses on pilings or in houses made from stones taken from the river — family life, that's what she wanted to know about. And the perennial threat of invasion and destruction that people faced now just as they had during the Middle Ages.

In February the weather turned bad, and the wind howled constantly through the valley, giving even Marta the shudders. Every time she heard it wail the thought of Arturo frozen to death on the Russian steppe came back to her. That tragedy had played itself out two years ago, or maybe more. Yet for Marta, and to a certain extent for Anita, it hadn't ended, would never end — there was something fated and enigmatic about it. Urvan, reflective as always, approached Marta and with an awkward gesture of his hands asked her what was the matter.

"Old ghosts that keep coming back," she said

"Is it the wind that brings them?" he asked.

"Perhaps."

Urvan said the wind also reminded him of Russia, which people around here thought of only in terms of winter, snow, and ice. But there were other seasons too and in the *Chernozyom* springtime was beautiful. The air was full of fuzz from cottonwoods and birches and the fruit trees were covered with pink and white blossoms. Because he knew about Arturo he had guessed what Marta was thinking. He explained that in Russia village women, *babushkas* as well as girls always willingly offered shelter to anyone caught outside in frigid cold or in a snowstorm. They'd invite the stranger into their house and share a glass of vodka or plate of potatoes roasted under hot ashes. It didn't matter who he might be, he'd be rescued and warmed by the terracotta stove and he'd feel restored and alive again. Urvan's words brought comfort to Marta. She felt the old open wound of grief begin to heal, fade into a mere scar. If she could make herself believe that Arturo had not died alone out on the frozen wastes, but instead inside an izba, warm and cared for, if she could believe that she could finally resign herself to his death.... Yes, all this was very important, if Arturo had not died desperate and alone, frozen into a statue of ice in the dark night of the steppe, like a scarecrow wrapped in rags and blankets — if he hadn't been devoured by wolves but instead been buried in a village cemetery surrounded by a wooden fence, his name engraved on a wooden cross, then he would not have remained a total stranger in the endless vastness of Russia. The *babushkas* couldn't help but be hospitable and compassionate, weren't they all like Dunaika or even herself? After all Marta was the woman who always looked out for the "poor soldiers" who had been scattered in all directions by the winds of war, their lives ruined. She compared herself to the medieval women who always helped their men pick up the pieces and start life over after the passage of foreign armies, in the wake of disasters, fires, all kinds of destruction. She was, in a way, sister to women who had been raped by barbarian invaders and then, when the soldiers had gone, gave birth to the children of Huns, Lombards, Hungarians, and went on to raise them like their own husbands' offspring. Perhaps because of her strange sensitivity to the past she identified herself as not simply this Marta, here and now, who had been overwhelmed by war the first time when she was only five years old, but as a timeless feminine type whose eternal destiny was to take care of the victims of war as best she could. She had developed an odd notion of having already committed herself to a perennial task, marked out like a furrow in a field, the duty of beings like her who were capable of being inside and outside the war at the same time. A hazy intuition told her that in these times there were no more islands of happiness beyond the fiery fallout of war and although the war was completely alien to her she was hopelessly immersed in it. For her the men who fought, winners and losers alike, invaders and the invaded — all were defeated, all of them lost in weird and baseless illusions. She had known this for a long time, but the men didn't know it. And who could say how long it would be before they finally understood....

She regarded Gavrila and Urvan more or less in that light. They seemed lost in pursuit of ridiculous hopes, devoid of clear motives. But she also sensed that since she had come to know them they had begun to change, to see things more distinctly. The course of events had demanded that they adjust the focus of the lens through which they looked at the world around them and the images they saw had changed. She realized that both felt a peculiar need to spend time with her, as if her presence added substance to their vague identity as homesick wanderers.

"Have you ever been in France?" Gavrila once asked her.

"Hardly, Colonel. Ever since I was a girl I've worked as a domestic servant."

"Well, you could have gone there with your employers."

"I suppose...but the only traveling I did with them was in Italy."

"If you do go there sometime you'll see what a *domaine* is. The French countryside has lots of them."

"Wouldn't a *domaine* be like a big farm, with tenant farmers and so on?"

"Yes, but with a villa or a castle in the midst of it. Like a small feudal estate, a fief you might say, and rather sad and mysterious...."

Accepting Gavrila's attentions permitted Marta to conceal her stronger interest in Urvan. Gavrila poured her wine, held her chair for her at the table, spoke to her about the hopes he had treasured so long ago. She listened and pretended to approve with a nod, but she knew Gavrila was a beaten man, that time and events had already turned his dreams into vain illusions. He was only a survivor, still anchored in a world that had disappeared decades ago. To some degree he realized this himself — indeed he admitted that once again the new war between the Reds and Whites had been postponed. After twenty-three years of waiting he had thought the time had come, but he was wrong. All the evidence pointed to yet another lost opportunity. Hence he'd probably end up going back to France for another exile, with no end in sight....

He talked more and more frequently about France and in more detail. In fact in his conversation the Terek of his youth had been completely replaced by the Loire. It seemed as if the man who once dreamed of regaining his native land was moving aside to make room for another more current Gavrila who yearned for those years in exile as if France had become his real home. The renewed war against the Bolsheviks was only a mirage and his former hopes were like moldy old furniture covered with dust that grew thicker with each passing year. It took effort even to try to believe. He had waited too long and his youthful enthusiasm, his faith in the future, had simply burned themselves out. He was too tired, far too tired even to focus on the struggle. An opaque veil now hid his dream and he wasn't sure he could recognize it any more. If he put his mind to it, it wasn't even clear what he was doing here in Carnia. It seemed he had been carried here by the irresistible currents of war, driven into his present circumstances as the result of a series of events, none of which he understood, but each of which had caused the next. None of them really had anything to do with him. But fidelity was one of his strongest values and he would see the adventure to its end. He was committed to follow the orders of his atamans, whatever they decided, and his loyalty to Krasnov was absolute.

During those months in which the war was drawing to an end Marta kept thinking Gavrila was present in body only — his soul was far away somewhere, bereft of the illusions that once sustained it. To her he was more a man without a country than the others because he continually dreamed of other places: France, Berry, the Loire and Terek valleys. Perhaps now he had but one hope left, that the war would rumble rapidly on to its end before it burst into open conflict with the partisans. Although his were unusual soldiers in a singular situation he felt he couldn't really lead them any more since he no longer believed in the war itself.

But this hope that things would stay the same, remain in a kind of suspense until the end, didn't last long. It too was a mirage. The partisans continued to blow up bridges, barracks, and power lines. They attacked without warning, firing from ambush behind trees or clumps of hazelnut bushes. The result was always the same: Cossacks lying dead in the woods and their comrades' increasing resentment and desire to confront the enemy openly. A growing notoriety surrounded the partisan commanders: Saetta, Bora, Bora's lover Sonia, and most of all Vento. It was said Vento was sly as a fox. He'd get his men to spend the night up in trees or put on fishermen's hip boots to wade in streams from one place to another so they'd leave no scent to be picked up by dogs. Some insisted he never slept twice in the same hut or dairy shed and he kept his group constantly on the move, like the wind, which was of course the meaning of his name. It was rumored he, exactly like Urvan and Gavrila, hoped to avoid a direct confrontation between Cossacks and partisans. He was content to sabotage whatever might be useful to the Germans and thus extend the war. Saetta didn't agree. In fact he regarded Vento with hostility because he himself wanted the opposite, an out-and-out battle with the invaders.

Urvan, though he wasn't in command, had a much more comprehensive view of the situation than the colonel because the fate of the Cossacks was always his first priority. He realized with each passing day there was less, in fact no, possibility of returning home — the steppe was forever lost to them. But was it really? Maybe not. Maybe when the war finally ended everybody would be so sick at the thought of more blood, more acts of revenge, more firing squads, that there'd be a general amnesty and pacification, and they'd be able to go back....

But in general his instinct wouldn't let him follow these thoughts any further because they concealed a trap of desperation. People suffering from incurable diseases sometimes fall into the same kind of trap, believing they are not really sick, marshalling all the occult resources of their unconscious minds to convince themselves they are well and strong. Urvan knew any hypothesis to the contrary was assurdly impossible, completely at odds with reality. All scenarios were doomed to failure — the *kazak* was caught in a hopeless tangle of circumstances and there was no way out. Yet there had to be something to live for, to hope for. An entire people couldn't give in to despair, they musn't lose all faith in themselves and their future.

At present the future held only one prospect: the imminent war with the *partizany* desired by Saetta and by the Cossacks themselves. Trembling with lust for revenge, they sharpened their swords and prepared to fight. Their very honor was now at stake. Every day from all different areas of Carnia came new reports of Cossack soldiers left dead in the forest, Cossack blood staining the snow. Urvan and Gavrila's former project for a sort of non-aggression pact with the partisans, a tacit armistice more or less, was dissolved and discredited months ago....

"I'm afraid when spring comes there will be a blood bath," said Urvan to Marta.

"Don't go out on patrol. Nobody will attack you in the village."

"That would be cowardly. It would mean giving the partisans free rein, admitting defeat...."

"So who cares? The partisans are mad at the Germans."

"They're mad at the invaders. And we're invaders too."

"Then why don't you all desert together and go over to their side?"

Urvan was really struck by this thought, but he didn't want to admit it. Women! They were regular witches. They had more tricks than the devil and somehow they always managed to have the last word. Girei was right about them. Strictly speaking, desertion was a plausible alternative. The guerrillas had organized to fight the Germans. That was their primary objective. The Cossacks had ended up facing half the partisans of Europe simply because the Germans used them to divert the hatred of the local population away from themselves. Still Urvan didn't believe the Cossacks could change sides again. Everyone would think of them as professional turncoats, ready to adopt a different flag whenever things went wrong. It was a matter of honor for the *kazak.* If they reversed themselves again they might ruin their image permanently. Oh what a sad and complicated predicament! Some day poets who came after them would recount their adventures as nomadic warriors in the most melancholy *dumy* of all. Anyway it wasn't up to him to decide whether surrendering to the partisans was a valid idea. That was up to Krasnov, Shkuro, Domanov, Naumenko, Polunin and the other atamans. Besides it was rumored that the partisans, those extremely clever fighters no one could catch, were mostly Communists and no accord would ever be possible between Cossacks and Reds....

But where on earth were these *partizany*? Out in the snow, among the rocks, in tunnels, hideouts, or underground along those trails he'd heard about, supposedly dug by soldiers in the other war? He studied the heights through his binoculars, focusing on the alpine huts, the dairy sheds and the summits themselves, but all in vain. Probably with the winter cold most of them had come down to the villages and mingled with the local population. Maybe there really was no difference between the townspeople and the *partizany* and everyone helped them, being on their side. Perhaps the partisans were an unstable army, who came together sporadically for particular actions, commanded by Bora, Saetta or Vento, then disbanded and went back to their homes.

Thus once again Urvan began to look at the villagers with acute suspicion. The *partizany* were so hidden and mysterious that anything was possible. In fact the Cossacks were beginning to regard them with a strange and unfamiliar terror colored by an elemental fear of death or an unknown future.

Up to this point not one single guerrilla, identifiable as such, had materialized and been recognized. All they could see were the results of sabotage or the bodies of Cossacks killed by sudden unexpected machine-gun volleys. The partisans themselves were like spirits in the air, invisible, elusive, like elves or trolls, but they fired weapons and they killed. Once in a while a Cossack soldier would disappear and after ten days or a couple of weeks they'd find him, deep in the forest, his head buried in the mud or snow, his body already gnawed here and there by rats or the foxes the men sometimes heard yelping near the village at night.

It was hard for Urvan and Gavrila to convince their soldiers not to try to ambush the *partizany*, not to set out at night on horseback up the mountain toward the highest pastures, the alpine huts, the woodcutters' cabins, the dairy sheds used by cattle herders, where they thought they might surprise the partisan units. After all they were men too. They didn't have wings and it ought to be possible to take them by surprise and capture them. Still Urvan and Gavrila remained immovable, hoping to find some way to keep on good terms with the local people. This was their temporary home and for the moment, they had no place else to go.

News reached them that in one of the furthest valleys there had been a major ambush and a group of Cossacks had been cut to pieces. This time, however, some partisans had also died, since the ambush had turned into a full-scale battle. For once then the guerrillas had sustained losses, a small consolation after so many disasters....

Meanwhile a cloud of regrets at having left Russia was overwhelming the Cossacks. It penetrated the thoughts of the older people like damp cold winter fog, starting with Dunaika. One evening, worried because Girei had not returned home, she remarked to Urvan, "We should have stayed there. We should never have left our villages, not for any reason."

"You're forgetting about the Reds."

"I'm not forgetting anything. But maybe the Reds were only a passing phase, and the land is eternal...."

"We didn't think so then."

"We were wrong."

"Everybody thought the war against the Reds would start over...."

"That was a real blunder."

"All right, Dunaika, let's say it was. What would you propose to do now?"

"I don't know. But I do know that we took the wrong path...."

Urvan bit his lip. His own secret remorse, so difficult to admit even to himself, was now a common feeling among his people, especially the women. Thus the ancient Cossack pride was cracked and crumbling, ready to fall apart completely. The *kazaki* certainly were no longer a nomadic people and they could not live without a homeland....

However, as far as Urvan could tell, the atamans and the generals seemed to be paying no attention to these matters, and he'd have given a fur coat to know what was going on in their minds. How were they planning to lead the *kazak* out of this blind alley? He did in fact believe they were capable of coming up with different and daring ideas, unlike anything his own poor spirit could invent. But if that were so, they weren't letting on because orders received expressed only the usual conventional military mentality: don't leave the initiative to the *partizany*, go ahead and counterattack. Such orders appeared to derive from a conviction the war could still be set right and turned to their own advantage.

Reluctantly Urvan and Gavrila prepared an expedition against a group of huts and houses partway up a mountain slope used for pasture, hoping to surprise a partisan unit. The men were awakened in the dead of night with no sound, no bugle or drum, to keep the mission secret. Noncommissioned officers went quietly from house to house to alert the troops and in a little more than an hour the column was ready to move out. They chose only black horses, or at least dark-colored ones, to remain as invisible as possible. Before leaving they ate their fill of roasted meat and pickled cabbage, with sugary tea and cookies for dessert. Then they set off in single file, like a band of robbers, cartridge belts across their chests, rifles and Stens slung over their shoulders. For a long while they rode through the winter woods — filberts, alders, and chestnuts, all leafless now in the cold. It hadn't snowed for some time and the snow had frozen into a hard crust, not snow anymore, but not ice either.

There was constant risk a horse might slip and break a leg, and the soldiers grumbled through yellowed teeth as they made their way cautiously, uncertain and anxious about this assignment, though it had broken the monotony of their barracks life. All were counting on the element of surprise. If there really were partisans up there, the best chance was to catch them asleep and capture them. Burlak had high hopes of getting his hands on one or more of the leaders, and was already rejoicing in anticipation. At last they were getting some action. At last the *kazak* had entered the heretofore inviolable domain of the *partizan.* At last they were challenging him on his own territory, like going after a falcon or an eagle in his nest....

The expedition had indeed gotten off to a very good start. The horses seemed to sense their masters' objective perfectly — not one had let out a single whinny or shied or broken a dry stick or produced any noise that might cause suspicion. But both Urvan and Gavrila were worried, troubled by a train of thought whose logic their men didn't understand. They realized this action would break the long truce with the local partisans, ending a sort of magic equilibrium. A new chapter in the garrison's history was now beginning. Henceforth they'd have to live in a perpetual state of readiness for battle and any plan to salvage the integrity of the Terek Cossacks and provide for their future became much more difficult and problematic. The two of them rode along slowly. There was no need to hurry, what mattered was arriving without warning, disposing of the sentinels and surprising the *partizany* in their sleep. They were certain they would find partisans. Burlak had searched the village for an informer and had turned up a dubious-looking individual who assured him the huts, hay sheds and houses of Madroias were full of partisans, thanks to a strange local character known as the *Salvadi*, who provided them with shelter and fresh meat.

Burlak was imagining the upcoming scene with pleasure. Most important he felt the *kazak* had shaken off the heavy burden of inaction, the onus of having to wait for the enemy to start something. Soon the whole valley, and neighboring valleys too, would find out who the *kazak* was. Horses and riders continued to climb along the sidehill trail, almost invisible in the thick forest. Sometimes the horses almost came to a stop, seeming not to see the trail, which was indeed hard to make out. Then the men would urge them on with a soft: "Trrr, trr!"

Some of them, like Burlak or Akmek, had fallen passionately into the rhythm of the action, with no thought for anything else. The mission had rekindled their ancestral identity and they felt like their great-great-grandfathers when the Cossacks' enemy was the Abrek tribesmen and surprising and killing one of them was an act of bravery, a glorious feat to be celebrated in every village.

Gavrila, on the other hand, was thinking that his sojourn on the happy and peaceful island was over and the useless endless Trojan War was beginning again. He didn't know why but he was seized by a melancholy notion that in these times Ithaca and the Island of the Phaeacians no longer existed. There were no more places for men to go home to because nowadays no man could see such places or hear them calling him. They had become mere mirages. Perhaps modern man, of whom he was a model, could no longer have a homeland, was destined to be a foreigner everywhere....

The horses were breathing harder from the effort of the climb and their hooves made a crunching sound as they broke the crust of frozen snow. There was a smell of the stable and sweaty leather that always accompanied the Cossacks. Burlak, who was in the lead, stared intently ahead, expecting from one moment to the next to see the vast alpine meadow and the huts and houses of Madroias, where people still slept inside, guarded by alert and suspicious sentinels outside. He was already thinking about choosing a comrade of his own sort to eliminate these guards with a few swift blows of dagger or scimitar before they had time to warn the others. For this kind of thing he had the skill and quickness of a panther. But most of all he was sure this expedition would explain other mysteries, for instance whether there really were secret passageways dug during the last war, or trenches and caves excavated in the rock that led from this place to who knows where else. Anyhow a good number of unknowns obscuring the partisans would fall to pieces and the truth would finally come to light.

As they approached the limits of the forest they got their first glimpse of the Madroias clearing. They tied the horses to the trunks of spruces and left them in the care of Akmekkhan, who knew all there was to know about horses and camels, even what they were thinking. The Cossacks quickly noted that in the biggest house, probably the Salvadi*'s*, there was a tiny light burning. Burlak swore under his breath in his own language. Then, holding Stens and rifles ready, the men fanned out in a circle along the edges of the woods to surround the houses. But as they did so several sheep dogs began to bark persistently and other oil lamps were lighted behind the windows. Surprise was now out of the question — they had to attack at once.

The Cossacks rushed toward the building shouting terrible battle cries but all they found were a few shepherds and the *Salvadi* already on their feet with quilted overcoats thrown over the woolen underwear they slept in. The attackers ran back and forth, searched every house, hut and hayshed, but all they found were the shepherds' families, the *Salvadi's* sheep and ample supplies of hay.

"*Partizany?* Where are *partizany?*"

"No partisans. Shepherds, we're shepherds," said the *Salvadi.*"

"Here *partizany.* We know all," said Burlak.

"So if you want to look for them go right ahead."

They began a tough and meticulous inspection. Burlak, stubbornly set on locating secret passages, tunnels or other devilish subterfuges, was disappointed to find nothing of the sort. No weapons, no clothing that couldn't belong to the shepherds, no extra straw mattresses or bedding, no evidence at all even to suggest the presence of anyone else but the inhabitants of the strange mountain hamlet, so far removed from all other settlements. Burlak did, however, make one discovery that might cast suspicion on the *Salvadi*: the quantity of sheepskins certainly exceeded the number of sheep the shepherds would have slaughtered to provide meat for themselves. He examined them one by one, directing meaningful glances toward the *Salvadi*, who continued to look on with perfect calm.

The *Salvadi* was an imposing figure, a tall robust looking man with gray hair and a short thick curly beard like the fur of a young goat. All in all he looked rough and unkempt and he smelled strongly of sheep and the stable. The many deep wrinkles that crisscrossed his face seemed less a sign of age than of stubbornness and authority. This solitary shepherd who lived up here, even in winter, with only a few families to help him take care of his vast herd was a brave man who couldn't be frightened. He seemed to have no end of answers to account for those dubious sheepskins. Inside the houses the Cossacks found old cast-iron Austrian-style stoves giving off a cheerful heat that reminded them of the izbas of their own villages. In fact the *Salvadi* might very well pass for a native of the steppe or of their mountains, or at least someone quite like them and Urvan felt an immediate kinship with him that he couldn't deny. Theoretically he knew he should trust no one but in reality he was quick to identify with certain people.

"You give sheep to *partizany*," said Burlak, regarding him with a sullen stare.

"I sell animals to whoever pays me," answered the *Salvadi.*

"To bandits."

"To village butchers. People are hungry."

"So then you very rich," said Burlak.

"That's my business."

Burlak didn't know whom or what to blame. His disappointment at the failed expedition was beyond all reason and he paced back and forth inside the hut liked an infuriated bear. Instinct told him the partisans had been there and had used those houses as they pleased, probably even making them their headquarters. It was simply a matter of unearthing the proof, going over every square inch with a fine tooth comb. Gavrila was also intrigued by the figure of the *Salvadi*, who he thought resembled a shepherd king from a Homeric epic. Then one young Cossack discovered a perfectly oiled military rifle, wrapped in a sheepskin and hidden under a pile of hay. Burlak was exultant.

"What is this?"

"It's mine," said the *Salvadi.*"

"Military rifle."

"So it is. A fleeing soldier left it."

"Why you keep it?"

"To defend myself. We're all alone up here and it's dangerous. Food is scarce and some folks try to steal my livestock."

"Keeping guns illegal."

"What do I care? I need the rifle to survive up here."

A shepherd king indeed, thought Gavrila. He himself was the law in his village. Defending his livestock and taking care of his tiny mountain realm were all that mattered. The rest — Cossacks, Germans, wars — none of them were worth bothering with. Burlak moved perilously close to the old man as if to arrest him, but the *Salvadi* refused to be touched and directed a questioning glance at Urvan and the colonel.

"He's broken the law. We should shoot him," said Burlak in Russian.

"In my unit we don't shoot anybody," answered Gavrila.

"Then you're also breaking the law, Colonel."

"In times like these everybody follows whatever law seems right. So do I. We've found nothing here. Therefore we're going back to our base."

Urvan approached the *Salvadi* and asked him about a scar on his cheek. It was made by the tusk of a wild boar. He had hunted them in his youth. Then the *Salvadi* disappeared inside a hay shed and returned a few minutes later carrying a freshly slaughtered sheep on his shoulders. The blood was half drained away where its throat had been cut.

"For you and your men, Colonel."

"Thank you sir."

Then the old man offered Urvan and Gavrila cigars and they parted friends. But there was an angry glint in Burlak's eye. He trusted no one and he was certain the *Salvadi* and his kin had been warned in time and the partisans had been able to erase all signs of their presence and disappear. Somebody in the village must be keeping the partisans informed about every move the Cossacks made.

They roasted the sheep outside in the barracks courtyard. Urvan gave the hide to Dunaika so she could make a white sheepskin hat, which he intended to present as a gift to the master of Madroias. This would constitute a high honor because all Cossack fur hats were black except those of the atamans and the princes, which were white.

When Urvan was on duty he often conversed with townspeople since he was unable to get along without friends. The subject was usually their daily lives. They were farmers, woodcutters, stone cutters, basket weavers, wagonmakers, slipper-makers — artisans and workmen who followed more or less the same trades as the Cossacks of the Terek valley.

The difference between invaders and invaded, plunderers and victims, couldn't cancel the affinity between the Cossacks and the local inhabitants.

Marta sensed Urvan's strong inclination toward family life, despite the war and his collective life in the heart of the garrison. When he returned to the villa in the evening he wanted to do ordinary everyday things and sometimes he seemed content just to watch Anita knitting baby clothes. Marta had succeeded in getting her some Angora yarn for the layette. Actually he watched Anita because he didn't quite dare gaze directly at Marta.

As the days passed he was increasingly weighed down with a weariness of spirit, and wondered how he had ever managed to believe the war against the Bolsheviks could ever begin again. It had been lost in 1921 and that was all there was to it. Even his voice sounded dull and muted, as if his misfortunes had fallen upon him all at once, and he had become nothing more than a lonely man whose family had been destroyed, in command of a troop of soldiers whose people had lost all hope. When he wasn't on duty he hung around Marta like a lost dog wandering forlornly around a farmhouse. Once he said to her:

"Friuli and the steppe are alike in one thing."

"What would that be?"

"There are lots of Italians buried in our cemeteries and lots of Cossacks buried in yours. A kind of pairing off with respect to death."

"Yes, that's true enough. I remember when our soldiers went off to Russia the bells in the towns tolled the way they do when there's a hailstorm or a fire."

She went on to talk about Arturo's departure. In a barely audible self-deprecating tone, Urvan added:

"I guess you could say we've both been widowed...."

"Yes you could. What's in that bundle?"

"Some stuff for Dunaika, undershirts and socks that need mending."

"Give them to me. I'll do it."

"Why should you bother?"

"Urvan, I've no use for idle talk. If you want it done I'll do it...."

She took up her needle and some darning wool and set to work at once. Urvan watched her quietly while flashes of thought lighted up his mind like lightning during a storm. He was acutely ashamed to be an invader and a burden to a hard-working and peace-loving population. It was the Germans who had created the shame but he felt it belonged to the Cossacks too, he wasn't quite sure why. Perhaps they too, like the Bolsheviks, belonged to a lost generation whom God or destiny had condemned because they had collaborated in oppressing other nationalities, like the Poles or the Friulans. Or perhaps they were victims of an innate curse, rooted in some mysterious necessity he knew nothing about. War and life itself produced tremendous complications that always went beyond men's intentions and purpose. For him there was something false and strident in the very fact that the *kazak* had come here to invade someone else's territory. Nothing good could come of such a thing. The twinge of conscience he felt at the very thought was proof enough, but it was only a twinge, like a fire that flares up in straw or grape twigs, then quickly dies down. His mind would soon revert to the habitual Cossack way of thinking.

Above all he realized that to keep his people foremost in his mind he couldn't afford to distance himself too much from the Cossack mentality. That would mean distancing himself from all that had happened. It would be turning his back on his people like a traitor. His sense of ethnic identity and solidarity was complete, yet he wanted to be both a *kazak* and a friend to the Friulans, who were farmers, artisans, workers and shepherds, just like his own countrymen. He was powerfully attracted to Marta but he controlled himself and his behavior gave no hint of his feelings. The war had made him even more taciturn and melancholy than he already was. He was afraid to treat her with the merest trace of familiarity and hardly dared look into her eyes. If in an idle moment he found himself thinking about her he stifled such thoughts as if in guilt about forgetting his people's problems even for a moment.

But for Marta things were different. Urvan had already triggered a mechanism within her that couldn't be stopped once it was set in motion. It was set off, as usual, by the aura of pity and attraction surrounding anyone who had been robbed and mistreated by fate. She was particularly distressed that history had driven Urvan and his *kazak* people into a sort of dark dank tunnel where the flower of hope could never grow.

One night Urvan returned to the villa with the beginnings of a cold and a particularly gloomy expression. He had insisted on taking guard duty at a bridge, just like an ordinary soldier, and had heard faraway rifle fire, not a good omen for his Cossacks. By now he reacted to all events with a pang of apprehension. Everything that happened seemed to imply a threat to the *kazak*. Marta was mending woolen clothes in the dim light of the kitchen lamp. The rest of the household had gone to bed and Urvan thought perhaps she was waiting for him. The room and the light held him prisoner and he couldn't make up his mind to go to bed. He kept inventing reasons for lingering. First he cleaned his *chuvyaki,* then looked around for some tea and not finding any made a fresh pot.

"How are you, Urvan?" Marta asked.

"Not good," he answered.

"These are hard times. Why not try to do what I do. Just live one day at a time...."

"It's different for you. You're in your own home."

"You sound as if you have a cold. Maybe a fever. May I?"

She laid her hand on his forehead and noticed it felt a bit hot.

"You should take better care of yourself...."

"That's just talk."

"You're not interested in talk? You want action? All right, how about this...."

Slowly, as if she'd thought about it a hundred times, she put her arms around him and kissed him. He returned the embrace, whispering:

"But Marta, what are you doing? Haven't you got any sense...."

"I've as much sense as I need. Don't worry."

"But what will this lead to? Nothing good. There'll be pain and grief for both of us...."

"Don't think about that. I told you. In times like these you live each day for itself."

Urvan tried gently to remove her hands and move away, until his *kazak* nature overwhelmed him.

"But what if somebody comes downstairs? Dunaika or the old man?"

"Nobody will. Don't worry about anything."

Marta was one of those women who turn everything upside down. She was attracted by Urvan precisely because of what he was not and what he did not have. Only one aspect of the situation seemed in any way odd, that she had ended up in Urvan's arms instead of Gavrila's. When they had first come she had been more interested in the colonel because of his refined and cultured ways. But then little by little Urvan began to occupy her thoughts and her interest in Gavrila faded until Urvan took his place.

It seemed quite natural she should become Urvan's woman, and yet at the same time it was incomprehensible.

She wondered if she were some kind of complicated woman, one of those always concerned with subtleties and intricate hidden implications. No, she decided, she wasn't. She was a simple, even elemental woman, who looked around her and saw men, just men, all more or less the same though they might speak different languages and have different ideas in their heads. But they were all worn out by hardship and war, displaced and lost in the chaos and darkness of this world. All were cold, hungry, thirsty, afraid they'd be sent off to die. Every one of them wanted a woman to comfort him and a refuge of his own. Maybe she was stupid or a bit out of her mind, or it could be she just wouldn't acknowledge a certain dimension of reality. Therefore she habitually saw herself as disparaged, diminished or at any rate somehow not quite like everyone else....

Now, however, she felt more complete. Before there had been something missing. She recalled with sadness the days she had spent with Ivos, and the longer periods when she'd been with Arturo or before him, Caleb. For those two fate and been less stingy with time. But for causes completely alien to her, war and violent death had snatched all her men away, and each time she had found herself back where she started from, all alone. But she didn't like to live alone. She was only happy when she had a man to take care of, who might indeed make lots of work for her, but would fill her days and make her feel really alive. She still mourned for those who were gone, but from a distance, because the dead were now at peace and needed nothing. She was concerned for the living. Grief and mourning were not real — they were an absence, a path that led away from the road she wanted to follow, was compelled to follow. She simply couldn't dedicate her life to shadows who asked nothing of her. She needed to devote herself to living men, to flesh and blood.

Urvan accepted their situation but only on the condition that she promised to let him continue to maintain his people as his top priority. He would not allow himself to stray from his purpose and let his private life come first. Thus he divided his time and his thoughts between Marta and the garrison. Now that he slept in her room (Anita had moved in with Dunaika and Luca), he felt more strongly than before that he should remain vigilant and make sure his Cossacks did not lapse into violence and plunder. Above all he believed it was his duty to make sure that if the *kazaki* were reduced to thievery it should be for one reason only, to survive. Furthermore they must not harass or terrorize the population, rape women or kill men. In wartime the temptation to abandon all restraint and give way to brutal primitive instincts was incredibly strong. This he knew and he knew why: the very essence of war was the destruction of all law.

Urvan was not capable of bland or lukewarm feelings. His emotions were intense, his nature as fiery as a burning izba. After a few days his relationship with Marta was obvious to everyone, even the villagers. At times he seemed to burst with a happy exuberance that had apparently lightened a spirit too long weighed down by sorrow and anxiety. He hugged and kissed Marta with vigor, showered her with Cossack gallantries, called her "my little dove" or "my dearest heart" or when carried away by passion, "witch" or "she devil." His style of courtship was a bit heavy-handed, his compliments unrefined, but they were genuine. His long and lonely bereavement was ended. Instead of mourning the dead he could now devote himself to expressing his love for a living and vibrant woman.

He seemed to want the other members of the household, even the local villagers and the men under his command, to share this remarkable good fortune suddenly fallen upon him. For her part Marta made every effort to make him feel he was now part of a true family. She took pains to create a homey and cheerful atmosphere, actually convincing him to take off his *chuvyaki* or *valenki* when he came into the house, to put on slippers, as was the local custom. She used Dunaika's recipes when she cooked for him, seasoning meats with abundant pepper, mustard, paprika, Tartar sauces, anything she could get that would resemble Cossack food. Like a proper wife, she always made sure to look her best when he returned to the villa after a day's duties at the garrison.

Although she had given Urvan a most privileged place in her life, this certainly did not mean she neglected the others, or the house itself. As always, she took care of everything, even the farm animals, but everyone lent a hand, even Luca, who made himself ubiquitous in the hope that Marta would overlook his age and think of him as important. For Marta providing them with enough to eat every day was an absolute imperative — survival was her guiding principle and she refused to compromise. They had to be more tenacious than the war itself and they must not give up before it ended.

Christmas drew near and it came time to slaughter the pig, but Luca, who was hopelessly fond of animals, burst into fits of tears. Ghirei had to take him away into the village to distract him, ending up under Alda's window, where the squeals of the poor murdered beast could no longer be heard. Everyone remembered how bitterly Luca had wept over the disappearance of Pronto, a dog who used to roam about the village. The dog's owners had named him Pronto in jest because whenever they called him he took his own good time to come home. He was in fact a perfect example of a phlegmatic type, the exact opposite of Baldo, who bounded into action at the slightest suggestion. If Baldo had mercury in his veins Pronto had some kind of thick honey. Hence he was always extremely slow in responding to any command, amazed someone would so rudely interrupt his perennial occupations — eating and lolling about. He had become so fat his poor legs could hardly hold him up and his body resembled an inflated balloon.

One day Pronto simply disappeared, but almost no one noticed since he spent most of his time stretched out invisible on a pile of hay in some farmer's barn, taking his after dinner nap. But Luca missed him because Pronto had joined the roster of his many friends. "Where's Pronto?" he went around asking, until one person remarked that since he was so fat probably they had made him into soap. Thus began a long season of tears for Luca. He was all the more resentful and inconsolable since he was completely familiar with all the stages of homemade soap production, including the breakdown of fat by a substance that would dissolve paper. Only with the coming of Christmas and the long series of holidays, was he able to direct his attention to other things. The inhabitants of the villa were in a holiday mood. The fact that Catholic and Orthodox Christmas did not coincide only multiplied the merriment by two, making it last much longer.

Marta was particularly receptive to Christmas traditions because she was endowed with a strong sense of the sacred and she revelled in collective joys. Urvan fell into the mood because of his Cossack heritage and his humble origins. In contrast, Gavrila was almost nowhere to be seen. He had retired from the scene, packed up his hopes in his knapsack and left the field completely free for his more fortunate colleague. The expression in his eyes was now even more pensive than before. Since he could no longer look ahead to the future he directed his attention completely to the past, calling up his memories of the *domaine* in France. Now it too was lost forever, exchanged for the false hope of rekindling an impossible struggle....

The enchanted exile was over and now he was afraid the present war was also lost. Starved for news about what was really happening at the various fronts, he became more and more certain the Germans and the forces of the Italian Republic of Salò were spreading outrageous lies about the actual course of the war. One of the technicians at the base had managed to install a more powerful radio receiver and had monitored broadcasts from as far away as Moscow. Thus he, Urvan and a few others secretly huddled in a tiny room of the barracks had been able to hear the *govorit Moskva,* the Russian news service. Gavrila had always believed the German and Cossack reports, and assumed the Russian news bulletins were shameless lies. The band of fanatics who now ruled Russia could hardly be truthful. Lying was an integral part of their style.

But this time he sensed a curious turnabout in his own attitude. All his former convictions seemed to have reversed themselves like stars circling the night sky. Things he had long suspected but tried to deny were now painful penetrating certainty. There simply was no possibility of renewed war against the Bolsheviks and the hope that had sustained him during his exile, half his life, had never been anything more than foolish chimerical self-delusion. There could be no holy war. There was only the present war, a cruel, perverted struggle totally alien to his hopes. The sole prospect remaining for the Cossacks was an all-out battle against the partisans, who wanted to drive the invader out of their territory. The *govorit Moskva* spoke of Red Army troops advancing towards Warsaw, Romania and Transylvania and his innermost thoughts now confirmed what he had always believed utterly impossible: the reports given out by the hated Reds were very close to the truth whereas all he had heard from the Germans and the Cossack command was only a pack of lies....

And he was now absolutely sure it was all over for Germany too.

In fact, the whole country was being systematically destroyed by terrible ceaseless bombardment. Almost every night he and his friends heard the continuous dull roar of Flying Fortresses going north at high altitudes over the mountains. They sounded like an earthquake in the sky. He had seen what they could do in the ***kazak*** encampments on the shore of the lake. Returning one night from a bombing run to Germany they had decided to get rid of a bothersome surplus of unused bombs by dropping them on a secondary enemy. And hundreds of Cossack dead had ended up at the bottom of the lake. Judging from that incident, which now seemed a long time ago, and from the persistent sinister muffled roar from above, anyone could easily guess the extent of destruction those formations were wreaking on Germany and what had become of their cities....

Thus Gavrila was convinced the war was going very badly indeed. The slow process of deterioration was now almost complete. His grand illusions had lasted for twenty years, only to vanish in a few short months like seeds blown away from a dry husk. Or like dead bodies that remain perfectly preserved as long as they are closed inside sarcophagi, then disintegrate instantly into a kind of black dust once they come into contact with the air. Truth was a terrible solvent, like the lye that had dissolved poor Pronto's fat, he too a victim of the war. Truth had nothing to do with his own war, the one he had dreamed of during exile, but it was manifest here and now in this dark parody of his dream war, this dismal celebration of a debacle completely alien to himself.

He would never return to his city on the steppe, never again see the rivers of the *Chernozyom*. He'd never be able to go back because destiny now excluded the very concept of a homeland. Modern man was fated to wander forever, to get lost among powerful illusions and fictitious ideas, never to attain any goal or purpose. Homeland, fatherland, whatever you called it, simply didn't exist. There were only pale substitutes like the *domaine* in France or Marta's villa here in Friuli, where kind-hearted women temporarily consoled transients like himself, men who had lost so much. Perhaps at this moment Urvan was inventing further illusions. But they wouldn't last because men could no longer hold on to anything certain or definite. As for himself, if he were to be lucky, very lucky, the most he could expect would be a return to France, and hopeless exile in the *domaine* in the gentle Berry countryside.

There was, however, at least one positive aspect to all this: the war was rapidly coming to an end. For better or for worse, things were being resolved and the situation was becoming more concrete. Even in this holiday season nightly gunfire and explosions were becoming more and more frequent. It was rumored the railway leading to Austria had been blown up but then someone reported it wasn't true. Some said the allies were rounding up and capturing vast numbers of Germans and Cossacks in the hill country, or rather a full-scale battle was raging over in that area. Nights were as anxious as troubled sleep itself and anything seemed possible. Up in the mountains small fires appeared at intervals, in triangular or rectangular patterns — they could only be signal fires lighted by the *partizany* to send messages from one mountain base to another. But what did they mean? Were they a trick, or were they setting up an ambush? Maybe the *partizany* wanted the Cossacks to think they were up there when they were really somewhere else. The men had all seen and were waiting in suspense, apprehensive as people always are when confronted by the unknown.

Even the animals seemed nervous as if they too sensed something strange and abnormal. Horses whinnied and bunted their heads against the bellies of their stablemates and camels were restless and noisy. The intense anxiety had spilled over from the houses into the barns.

Girei went down to the farm buildings near the villa to see what was the matter with his own and the others' horses. The animals were definitely agitated. To the Cossacks it looked as if even the horses had lost all their zest and were as tired and discouraged as their masters. They snorted and pawed the stone floors of the stable and whinnied mournfully as though recalling the rich pastures of the *Chernozyom,* the Black Earth. Perhaps the constant roar of the Flying Fortresses going back and forth on their bombing runs was disturbing the horses as well as the men. They do sense certain things more quickly and keenly than human beings.

Yet despite all this everyone was filled with the Christmas spirit, grownups and children alike. Marta and Dunaika went as far as decorating the interior of the villa, and Anita set up a tiny nativity scene on a little table in the breakfast room. For certain things she was partial to small dimensions, though it wasn't clear why. She put the table in a quiet corner out of the way where the minuscule figures were so inconspicuous they would almost escape notice entirely.

Marta made a traditional dessert of the Natisone valley, a kind of strudel with raisins, pine nuts and apples and seasoned with grappa. How she managed to come up with all the ingredients in these times of critical shortages was a mystery. Everyone agreed the result was excellent and they ate it with loud and appreciative exclamations.

On the Orthodox Christmas the local parish priest arranged for Stepan the Cossack priest to say mass in the village church so they wouldn't have to celebrate in the dreary squalor of the barracks. He may have meant to warm their hearts with a reassuring sermon, but instead his message sounded as cold and lonely and sad as a train whistle heard in the night. He spoke of their distant home and the harshness of the *kazak* destiny, of the empty stanitsy now inhabited only by sand and buffeted by the wind from the steppe. He said peace was not yet in sight and every kind of danger still hung over them. They must, however, keep their faith in God and pray for all their brothers wherever they might be: dispersed throughout Carnia, in German prison camps, in the Red Army or even perhaps in the stanitsy in the blessed Chernozyom. There was no end to tribulation for the immense kazak nation, scattered to the four winds as they were, like the wandering Jews. Nonetheless it was their duty to hold fast to their honor, abstaining from any act that might stain it and give people an excuse to say the Cossacks were uncivilized and violent men. And they were bound to defend their lives and their future. "Let us hope God comes to our aid," he concluded.

But to the Cossacks God seemed far away and for all they knew he might be looking out for their enemies. In church they sang psalms in Russian and crossed themselve repeatedly. But when they returned to their houses (actually the Friulans' houses they had occupied by force), they felt helpless and forgotten. Even their own atamans and generals now seemed distant and powerless, deprived of their former charisma. Uncertain what to do, unable to act, baffled by destiny, they too seemed to wait in a strange passivity for events to happen to them, not lifting a finger to ward off unwanted consequences.

The Cossacks themselves had lost the urge to sing the *dumy* about their glorious past, preferring melancholy ballads like the one about the boy who returned to his *stanitsa* and found his izba burned and his family slaughtered by the Russians, or another proclaiming the sadness of foreign lands far away from the steppe where the *kazak* could no longer hear the voice of his woman.

As usual nobody gave them anything and thus they had to provide for themselves if they were going to survive. But some of them stole with a sort of cheerful enthusiasm and unfettered commitment, as if remembering the faraway forgotten times when their people lived by plunder, or the years when the czar used them as guard dogs against the subject populations of his Empire. Burlak and Akmekkhan, for example, felt much more energetic when they were raiding barns and farmyards. They chopped off the heads of roosters, geese and turkeys with a single blow of their scimitars, and ravaged chicken coops like foxes or weasels. Their overcoats, so long they almost dragged on the ground, were always splattered with animal blood, and the women were kept busy trying to remove the stains. When they returned from a raid the two thieves boiled huge cauldrons of water over ridiculously large fires because they loved to do everything on a grand scale as they had in their native villages. Then they plunged the fowl into the scalding water several times to make the feathers easier to pluck.

One day Burlak showed up in Marta's farmyard looking for booty. This was absurd because she shared whatever she raised with the Cossacks who lived in the villa, but Burlak was seeking confrontation for its own sake without any rational motive. He went after a goose flapping its wings and honking as it fled from one corner of the barnyard to another trying to look ferocious. Marta happened to be alone in the house — even Anita and young Luca had gone out — and a sudden fear left her weak in the knees. Burlak saw her watching from a window but this didn't bother him a bit. In fact he appeared pleased to have her watch him commit robbery, to show her how it was done, and the expression in his eyes as he returned her gaze suggested the defiance of a raptor. Thus he pursued the poor squawking bird, keeping one eye on the window, and when he caught it he wrung its neck until it fell limp as a rag in his hands.

Marta was seized with a fit of trembling, a shudder of revulsion. But she didn't take her eyes off the Circassian for an instant. "For God's sake, go away and don't ever come back again," she thought. But Burlak didn't go away. He kept swaggering about with same expression he'd have if he were doing tricks on his horse to show off for the women at a *kazak* village festival. He seemed to be looking for something and after a while he found it. Luca had been playing in the yard with a small pillow and had left it on a washboard propped against a tub. Burlak, still watching Marta's window, took out his scimitar and with one quick stroke sliced the pillow in half. Then he laughed smugly, as if he had accomplished a remarkable feat, tucked the goose under his arm and went off. "You'll pay for this. You won't get away with it. I'll report you to Urvan and Gavrila," thought Marta. But later when they both came home she said nothing, restrained by an arcane fear of setting off dangerous rivalries. Instead she resolved to be extremely cautious, not to go anywhere by herself, nor stay alone in the house. She had no desire to find herself face to face with the wild-eyed Circassian.

It might be fun for Burlak and Akmek to live by plunder but it was mortifying for Dunaika and continual humiliation for Urvan. He was particularly worried the *kazaki* might be rapidly regressing, slipping back into their primordial instinctive behavior as wandering Asian nomads before they settled down on the steppe and the *Chernozyom*. He sensed the Burlak and Akmek were setting an example for the others, intentionally leading them astray. But now it wasn't just barnyard animals in danger, but young girls as well. Already several had been obliged to flee, screaming for help, then lock themselves in their houses. The Cossacks pursued them with raucous laughter, as in a game, but their eyes were dark with raging desire. And they went after clocks, watches, bicycles, as well as gold and silver with the same vehemence.

Gavrila and Urvan had to resort to public punishments in the form of whippings administered in the barracks yard for all to see. There was no other way to punish a *kazak*. It simply wouldn't work to lock him up in a cell. The Cossack was like a wild animal who couldn't be put in a cage because deprived of his freedom he would simply fall into depression or go mad or die. A dozen lashes or so he'd soon forget but he'd remember a month's imprisonment forever.

During the holidays Marta and Anita missed Esther more intensely. Marta was constantly reminded that the Signora had provided a refuge for them all, gypsies and Cossacks included, because the house was hers. Only she herself had been excluded and this was so bizarre and unjust that Marta couldn't come to terms with it. It filled her with anguished suspense. Esther ought to be returning soon, but instead she seemed strangely farther and farther away, a small figure on the horizon growing tinier yet as she repeatedly waved goodbye.

Little by little Marta's intuition was beginning to decipher the sinister features of those cattle cars with doors locked from outside and all other openings secured with barbed wire. Her thoughts found their way to the scraps of paper bearing messages scribbled in pencil that certain Jews had dropped along the railway to Austria. The dark meaning of these things only grew darker with present reports that Jews and gypsies of all ages and conditions — the old, the very young, the crippled, the insane — all of them had been taken off to concentration camps and none of them had ever emerged from those camps, except for the healthiest and strongest men, who were put to work in war factories or along the railways. What had become of the others? What was their destiny?

The evidence pointed to another reason for taking these people away and putting them in camps — a reason darker than the darkest night, an inconceivable, monstrous reason she dared not think about, for hadn't Haha said that beyond the wooden barracks of the camps heavy smoke rose day and night from mysterious chimneys? When she encountered the old gypsy they exchanged grief-stricken glances that spoke silently of the terrible enigma now casting an even more sinister shadow over the Germans' war. Haha's life was closed in by sorrow and grief. He gathered snatches of news and whispered rumors from other gypsies, wandering nomads endowed with antennae like crickets or stag beetles, which seemed to penetrate the most deeply hidden secrets of the war. A quiet madness tainted by horror appeared to have come over Haha and sometimes he went out to wander the frozen roads in the coldest weather, even at night. Nobody knew where he went.

Once Marta followed him without him noticing. He wandered aimlessly, then stopped near the cemetery and whimpered mournfully like an animal or mumbled something in his incomprehensible tongue. After this momentary bewilderment he headed for the wide stony shores of the river where his tribe had once camped among the bushes. It had been a long time since Marta had passed this way and she was quick to see the caravans were missing. All that was left were a few contorted pieces of iron. Since they were not being used, the Cossacks, or perhaps local people, had chopped up the wagons for firewood and nothing, not a single wheel, or window frame remained as testimony to their very existence.

Haha, having reached his destination, began to inspect the campsite with a kind of dazed intensity. He set aside an iron hinge, another smashed and unidentifiable object, a piece of tin, each with the same careful attention he would have used if he were gathering the unburied remains of his family. After a bit he stopped and sat down on a log in dejection, breaking into sobs that shook his poor old body. At that point Marta came out in the open and sat down beside him.

"They took them off to Germany to do away with them," he said in desperation.

"That can't be so," she answered.

"No it can't. But it is. They're all dead. And Esther won't come back either. She's dead too...."

"But why would they do such a thing? What did the gypsies ever do to them? What hindrance were they for the Germans' war?"

"No hindrance. Absolutely none. But that's how it is. They killed them in their cursed camps. They aren't work camps at all. Even if we've tried as hard as we could to believe that's what they are. Those places are extermination camps. Now, as we sit here, they are all dead, all of them...."

He fell silent, exhausted and overcome by his own words. Marta kept her hand on his shoulder but she knew he was right. All the rumors she'd heard came together in a single horrifying voice and the details and particulars added together formed a pattern whose meaning was unmistakable: the people who had been deported, whether they were Jews, gypsies, or partisans, had been massacred, every one of them. Even their bodies had been destroyed. It was incomprehensible and unacceptable but it was true. Train after train made up of cattle cars continued to enter the camps and nobody ever came out. Yes indeed, that was the truth, that and nothing else. Up till now she had known but not known, her grasp of the facts had wavered and hesitated. But the truth that had remained hidden for a long time was now unmasked and blindingly clear. Haha was right, beyond any doubt. There was no other reason for deporting old women or children like Elias except to remove them from the face of the earth, to transform them into a cloud of greasy smoke dispersed over the surrounding countryside. Those tall chimneys behind the camps had one purpose only, to carry off the exhaust from the vast ovens in which the Nazis tirelessly burned the corpses of their victims day and night....

Now Marta understood Signora Esther's despondence during those last days, when she wished she were only a crow or a frog or a grasshopper so she'd be left in peace, or when she wanted to dissolve into the air on a snowy night like the protagonist of a Russian legend, so she wouldn't have to go on living in terror. Esther knew about those camps because the rumors had reached potential victims. Marta put her arms around the old gypsy and they wept together as if linked by a mysterious kinship....

Oddly enough her realization of the truth about Esther and Haha's relatives did not depress her. Instead it strengthened her decision to survive at all costs and to hold out until the end. Life had to go on and she was ready to confront the long series of tasks that continued to accumulate before her without interruption. She accompanied Haha back to the house, then went out again to be alone for a while. Returning to her secret refuge near the legendary half-hidden spring that had created a pool of frigid water among the rocks and mosses, she noticed the astonishing state of her own mind. These dreadful things she had just accepted as certain beyond any doubt for her somehow still didn't exist, hadn't really happened, remained as unreal as folktales about witches and ogres. She was simply immersed in the current of her own existence, asking no questions about the causes behind events. All she wanted was to be able to go on living as she had, doing the things she'd always done, nothing more.

The soldiers of the garrison greeted the Orthodox new year with a lengthy celebration including dancing to the music of guitars and accordions. There was also a surprise, a Ukrainian singer who knew a number of arias from Russian and Italian operas. In addition one of the other garrisons sent a group of dancers from the Caucasus, all in traditional dress — astrakhan hats, brown uniforms with sleeves lined in red, silk shirts. They gave a long exibition of the *kazachok*. Squatting on their heels, they kicked their legs out straight, then leaped to their feet with a loud shout, the sound of their boots on the wooden floor reverberating through the barracks. The local Cossacks also took part in the dance. Excited by the wine, the dancing, the other men's singing, they didn't want to seem inferior, so they launched into a series of popular dances and songs so loud they rattled the barracks windows. They were ready to fight, with cartridge bands made of the same stuff as their uniforms crossed on their chests, and *kinzhaly*, silver-handled daggers, attached to their belts and bumping against them as they danced.

Every now and then they let out a savage howl, all together. Urvan was sure they had momentarily forgotten the war, the *partizany*, the Germans, the uncertainties of the future and were abandoning themselves completely to the joy of the festivities and their unrestrained passion for song and dance. Singing and dancing gave them an outlet for the powerful urge to live, not die, to express the desires of a people who still wanted a future, who yearned for their home villages, for a river in which they could swim and fish for trout. Song and dance were a spontaneous testimony to their immense vitality. Urvan could distinguish Girei's voice among the others in the chorus and he noted that the years seemed to fall away from Akmek as if the celebration had returned him to his youth. The Cossack people — Urvan could sense it — were crying out their desire to live, demanding their right to remain in this world, despite the war which had shoved them off on a siding. He realized his compatriots had completely forgotten the present situation as well as the reasons and circumstances that had produced it. Without realizing it they were demanding a place where they could live and work. Nobody could exist without a homeland.

Beneath the unfettered joy of the occasion Urvan and Gavrila detected another emotion, a sort of choking, burning desperation at their own fate, a blind, unconscious, but furiously angry protest directed against the Germans who had tricked them, the Bolsheviks who had taken their land, the partisans who shot at them from ambush, the Allies who bombed and machine-gunned them from the air, against the war that had turned out so muddled and vile for them or even against life itself, which had driven them into this blind alley of destiny.

When the singing and dancing finally stopped the Cossacks were left unsatisfied, still hungry for excitement and motion and revelry. They went out into the courtyards and began to fire their rifles into the air, with their perennial passion for weapons and noise. They bellowed like madmen and shot at the clear winter sky where the stars shone with twice their normal splendor. It was bitterly cold, like the nights on the steppe. Breath froze in an instant and the spruces, the roofs of houses, and the streets were covered with frozen snow, heavy as stone. They could hear the river nearby just beyond the bushes and the wide low gravel banks where Haha's caravans had been destroyed. The Cossacks' gunshots, numerous at first, resounded through the winding valleys, echoes bouncing back and forth and intersecting one another. After a while the soldiers began dragging people out of their houses, bringing them to the barracks or the piazza, insisting they join the festivities.

"For goodness sake, no. It's cold. We're sleepy," the villagers protested.

"So that's it. You're all *partizany*, you're spies, every one of you!"

"With this cold we'll catch our death...."

"No, no, not if you drink. Come on, everybody, have a drink with us!"

And they dragged them out, even the old who hung back and resisted. The young girls had hidden in attics and lofts, trembling with fear. Using copper ladles the Cossacks dipped out vodka or wine from small wooden kegs and, willing or not, the townspeople had to drink with them, all the while thinking of their young men up there in the mountains concealed in haybarns or cheese sheds. They wondered if drinking and celebrating with the invaders made them traitors.

Firing their weapons into the night, aiming at the stars or the mountains, had awakened old urges and desires in the men, a thirst for life, for conquest, plunder, pillage, the instinct for the hunt, the hunger for victory as in the days when they used to get into fights with every tribe they encountered on the steppe.

Girei was one of the wildest revelers. He felt completely adult and free, as mature as Urvan. The thick lock of black hair that emerged from his *kubanka* was an obvious sign he was unmarried and available for any girl. His uniform with its blue striped trousers had been perfectly washed and pressed by Dunaika and he had never felt so happy and proud to belong to the Terek Cossacks, convinced beyond any shadow of doubt that they were the best in the world. Or so it seemed at this particular moment. His joy reached its height when he noticed Alda, accompanied by her mother and two aunts who were closely guarding her, their faces stern and threatening as they made sure the young men stayed away from her. Marta had invited Alda personally and she was difficult to resist. Besides she seemed to create a kind of island or aura of safety around herself so it appeared there was no reason for Alda to be afraid.

Girei danced and sang for her benefit. Alda pretended to watch only the others, whereas she had really come because of Girei and every once in a while she couldn't keep from glancing in his direction. Girei felt a surge of energy — never had he been so happy and full of vitality. He achieved the impossible just to get her to notice. In all his life he had not sung and danced with such bold arrogance as he showed this night. Instinct assured him she was not only watching him, but among the dancers he was the only one she actually saw.

So many things had conspired to keep them apart — the war, the difference in race and religion, the uncertainties of the future, the fact that he might very soon be leaving for an unknown destination, that he was an enemy and should thus be vigorously repulsed. Actually Dunaika had noticed Girei's mood and was pondering how she could extirpate this crazy weed that had taken root in her son's mind. Overwhelmingly discouraged and worried, she shook her head. She was old and she knew the ways of the world, and certainly nothing good could come of that infatuation. Every possible aspect rendered it hopeless, except for one — instinct, or nature. Now and then Alda would look at Girei and her look clearly said: "I'm yours and I'm waiting for you, nobody else."

Girei had picked up her message and his reckless happy excitement was boundless. He was supremely satisfied with his uniform and his weapons. His dagger fitted into a studded leather sheath with a thin sheet of silver on the inside where it knocked against his belt when he moved. He had no lack of money because his father had left him plenty in the coffers of the *Feldbank*. Being a true Cossack, he felt he couldn't spend too much on military equipment and he never went about unarmed, even when there was no need for weapons.

His unusual skill with arms was due in part to Akmek's and Urvan's training, but instinct and atavism were also a factor. The same tendencies moved him to admire the Circassian mountain warriors most among all the Cossacks. He knew their legends and their war chants. Now, as the festivities continued Alda watched Girei furtively. Her female elders had told her a thousand times to pay no attention to the Cossacks, never to look any one of them in the eye, but rather to keep as distant as possible from them, because they were only interested in her body and they were even worse than other men. Indeed they were the most dangerous of all because they were uncivilized and besides they'd be leaving soon for parts unknown. Thus Alda's conduct toward Girei was completely contradictory. She acted annoyed when he looked at her or hung around in front of her house, yelling at him, "Stop bothering me! When are you going to leave me in peace? There are plenty of other streets in this town!" Nonetheless when he passed by she was always there behind the curtains, glued to the window and ready watch him go through all his equestrian tricks.

"Go perform for the Cossack girls, you worthless show-off!" she would say.

And he'd answer, "Not at all. I go where I want to go and I do what I want to do. The street belongs to everybody. If you don't want to watch, don't watch. Either close your eyes or close the windows!"

They both spoke mainly in their own idiom, but they understood each other perfectly. Although the gap between the two languages appeared to be unbridgeable, even their speech expressed an instinctive and undicipherable understanding. In fact there were some female Cossacks in the garrison, girls with long black hair, proud young women skilled at horsemanship, who wore the same *valenki* as the men, several of them strikingly young and beautiful. A few possessed the same degree of nobility as Gavrila and had been admitted to Krasnov's court. But Girei wouldn't even look at one of them — he had eyes only for Alda.

"Let me come in your house for a minute. I have to talk to you," he said.

"Do you think I'm crazy? An overbearing show-off like you who only wants to boast how great he is?!"

"What are you scared of? Your house is full of women."

"No. The answer is no, never!"

But her whole bearing, her slender agile figure, the expression on her face and in her eyes were always saying something else — she was his and would never belong to any other. Girei was being driven out of his mind. He remembered he was the invader and everything in this territory, including the women, belonged to him by right of conquest.

"I could enter your house any time I wanted to. I could requisition it and stay there day and night as the rightful owner!"

He knew this wasn't true, because Alda's house had already been requisitioned as living quarters for several rough, middle-aged, unmarried Cossack soldiers. All he could do was strut about under her windows like a turkey spreading its tail to attract a mate. But he knew in advance that his posturing was as useless as trying to talk to the wind. She would always say no. In a way he admired her for resisting him and saying no. But he could sense a barely perceptible offer behind all those denials. Her lips said no but her youth, her vitality, her instinct said yes. She burned with hidden desire, which she might have let come to the surface and fully express itself, if not for the war, the Germans, the invasion, these cursed times.... Girei was convinced she was secretly in love with him, sure his bachelor's lock had tickled her female nature.

Alda was proud of herself. This was the proper way to act toward an enemy, an invader, a mere vagabond. Thank God she wasn't like Marta, who was too easy and gave herself to men without thinking much about it. She liked Marta very much but on that subject she definitely didn't agree with her. Indeed Marta was the town scandal. Alda was a different kind of girl. No man had ever touched her and she blushed at the very thought of such a thing. Hence she was bound to keep saying no to Girei, no, no, and again no! She had to refuse his attentions and treat him with disdain. But Girei's intuition told him the avalanche of no's concealed a fundamental yes which cancelled them all and he reveled in secret happiness and satisfaction.

The day of Epiphany further confirmed what he had repeatedly guessed was true. As he passed by Alda's house she came out on the balcony to take in the laundry, frozen stiff after being out all night. At least this was her ostensible reason for appearing. But the real reason was different: she wanted him to see her in all the splendor of her beauty. She had apparently discovered, perhaps in some secret dresser drawer, a magnificent traditional costume consisting of a black skirt and black woolen head scarf, a purple embroidered bodice, white stockings and velvet slippers. She was wearing the whole outfit, along with a chain of gold coins, which glistened on her breast in the morning sun. Girei stood there enchanted. Never had she looked so beautiful and he realized she had put on the costume and the necklace inherited from some grandmother or great grandmother solely to dazzle him and leave him speechless. Nothing else had mattered to her, neither the risk of catching cold nor the chance of being seen by other Cossacks and arousing their desires.

He knew at once she was performing a kind of dance for him, as a peacock fans out its tail to display its maximum splendor. He swallowed hard from emotion and his amorous urges flared up with such intensity that he forgot everything. This was the supreme moment of his youth, he was in a kind of state of grace, of absolute and triumphant fulfillment of his years. His own precarious situation and that of his people, the tragedy and the desperation — none of these things existed any more — in his heart and mind her image had kindled a soft glow, the gentle light of hope....

# The Stolen Horse

Now Girei felt anything was possible. The war might soon be over and he and Alda could be married right there in the village church either by Stepan, the Orthodox priest, or by the local Catholic priest. How such things would come about he didn't know but they suddenly seemed possible. Anyway Girei wasn't much given to worrying about problems. He was only interested in immediate events, especially if they were exciting — he forgot the rest. In fact fairly often he even forgot the war, or if he thought about it he regarded it as perfectly natural because he was a Cossack and war was in his blood — every Cossack was born for conquest, born to spur his horse forward in a charge against the enemy. For Girei war was something cheerful and impetuous. He didn't really think about it otherwise, and although he deeply respected Urvan and Gavrila, their quiet troubled reflections on that subject had no effect on him. He was a bold and impulsive youth who launched himself into action like a galloping horse taking great breaths of air into dilated nostrils. He wanted to live life to its fullest, plunge into experience. Heroic deeds, passionate love, combat, adventure, danger, rage, whatever awaited him, he was ready.

It was almost an effort for him to control his reckless nature. He rode his horse furiously through the village or into the countryside to other villages and other garrisons. He had friends in all of them, which increased the intensity of his belief that he belonged to a vast nation whose destiny he shared. Urvan's mature and weary assessment of that destiny was the opposite of his own cheerful and vigorous enthusiasm. Often Girei had to stand guard over bridges or power lines with other young men like himself, or sometimes with mature soldiers. They kept fear at bay by pretending not even to know what it was. But Girei felt he wasn't meant to spend his time in empty guard duty, but rather to take part in furious cavalry charges like the ones Urvan and Gavrila told about during the war between Whites and Reds, before he himself was born.

He burned with the desire to scale the mountains with the Terek cavalry, to flush out the invisible partisans and confront them in open battle, to measure himself against them and show what he could do. He dreamed of shooting one of their famous leaders — Bora, Saetta or Vento — right between the eyes. Many years ago his great-great-grandfather had done just such a thing, killing an Abrek tribesman in a Terek River canebrake. He had returned in triumph to his village, where his elders and the women greeted him with smiles of congratulation. Ten times a day Dunaika would warn her son to be careful, not to go off on crazy excursions but to stay with the others in town.

"Of course, Mother. Don't worry."

"As far as you're concerned I can't help but worry, if you really want to know."

"No, no, you're mistaken. I don't do anything out of the ordinary."

"Don't do anything impulsive, just follow your orders."

"All right, all right."

"Stay close to Urvan and Gavrila. They don't go looking for danger. They try to avoid it."

"I'll do what you say, Mother...."

But sometimes he ignored all her warnings and went off on horseback along the mule tracks. One day he got lost and kept wandering aimlessly, at heart a bit scared, but still quite brave. He seemed to be a very far from the village, he could no longer see it. But he continued, urging on his horse with a secret hope of surprising a *partizan* and bringing him back tied up like a convict. He hadn't the faintest idea where he was and at a certain point he remembered with sudden terror what had happened to the two German motorcyclists who had lost their way. Still he kept going, sensing adventure in the air, like a colt who smells underground water even where the steppe is most arid.

At last he reached the old wooden houses in the Madroias clearing and his heart beat faster at the thought someone could fire at him from a door or window. At last he realized he had been reckless — his mother was right — but now it was too late. But there were no shots. Then the *Salvadi* himself came out of one of the huts, wearing his white *kubanka*. With him were a number of youths and armed men bundled up in coats and balaclavas. They looked at him, then smiled at each other, and some of them winked.

"I don't know you but I can tell you're a Terek Cossack by the blue stripes on your trousers," said the *Salvadi*.

"That's right," answered Girei.

"These are my family and my shepherds."

"Why are they carrying weapons?"

"We're afraid of thieves. Who doesn't carry weapons in times like these?"

"That's true enough. These are cursed times," admitted Girei.

"We're afraid partisans will come after our animals. They're hungry too, just like the Cossacks."

There in front of him stood the very partisans he had dreamed of confronting, but Girei didn't know it. His boyish ingenuousness acted like a blindfold. Even Vento himself was there, Vento the man who couldn't be caught, the cleverest mountain guerrilla of all, but Girei didn't recognize him because Vento was just a man like any other man, with no particular mark of distinction. He wore a quilted sheepskin jacket and there were a few gray hairs in his beard. He looked tired and sad. The other partisans exchanged interrogatory glances, then turned to Vento, who made an almost imperceptible negative gesture. He had decided to spare this incredibly innocent youth who hadn't understood a thing.

"We call this man the *Salvadi*," said Vento. "You can see his white hat like the ones Cossack princes and the most important atamans wear. Colonel Gavrila sent it to him as a token of friendship and esteem."

"I know," said Girei proudly. "They told me."

"Good. Now then go back to the garrison and tell the captain and the colonel the *Salvadi* and his shepherds send their regards. And say hello to Marta for me."

"Marta? You know Marta?"

"I know her well. Give her my very special regards."

"Why?" said Girei. "Why very special?"

"Let's just say because she's a beautiful woman and she's nice to soldiers. Say hello to Anita as well. Tell her the war will be over by the time her baby is born...."

"I'll tell her," Girei answered.

And he turned his horse around to go back to the village. It didn't take long because now he remembered the snow-covered trails he had followed on the way up. He hadn't discovered any *partizany* and he hadn't shot any one between the eyes. Yet he felt oddly happy just the same — in that unexpected place he'd actually met friendly strangers, and they even knew his own friends and asked him to give them their best wishes. But as he approached the village he began to realize there was something about his little adventure that didn't quite make sense. Why should those shepherds be armed to the teeth? And the one who sent a special message to Marta seemed to be in authority somehow. Why? He was no shepherd or family member, he was a partisan commander! It now occurred to Girei that he had in fact come face to face with the partisans without recognizing them. But if they were partisans how come they hadn't killed him on sight? What kind of crazy story was this anyway? And by the way, had they been making fun of him? And the one who acted like a commander, could he be Saetta, Bora or Vento?

At this point a curious change came over Girei. He had finally encountered the partisan enemy, but now that didn't seem to matter. The important part was talking to them as he would to any other men, or actually to his own friends. He was glad he hadn't shot and killed somebody, equally glad he himself hadn't been shot. Of course they were partisans, there was no doubt and he had been neatly tricked. But he was strangely happy things had turned out as they did. He couldn't understand why but he was pleased to have discovered the *partizany* were men like himself — they had friends, loved ones, women they cared about. The fact they hadn't killed him could only mean they weren't as bloodthirsty and terrible as he had been told....

By the time he reached the village he was sure he had outgrown his former self, as a result of a truly remarkable experience. He could never be as pessimistic as his elders — he was certain things would soon take a turn for the better. It wasn't possible the situation held no margin of hope for the *kazak*.

At that time there was an allied offensive in progress all the way from Holland to Switzerland. Metz and Aachen had fallen. On the opposite side of Europe the Russians had mounted a vast offensive stretching from East Prussia to the Black Sea. Forty-two Russian armies were spread along that endless front and every one of them included several divisions. Hundreds of thousands of men were involved. But the Cossacks knew nothing about all this. No one had told them, least of all the Germans. All they had was a feeling, a sort of premonition reinforced by rumors that reached them from the partisans and the local people. Even Urvan and Gavrila were uninformed about the exact situation because the powerful radio they had used to listen to the *gavorit Moskva* was broken and they had no parts to repair it. They only had a general sense of a vise slowly closing around them, or a trap that sooner or later would snap shut, when or how they didn't know. The Germans continued to talk of secret weapons and the coming victory and their own generals and atamans chose instead to ramble on about fighting to the bitter end and saving the honor of the Cossacks. The *kazaki* were uneasy, worried, tired and discouraged. They could even sense similar emotions in the voice of the priest when he urged them to trust in God and keep their faith intact.

Father Stepan was a tall heavy red-faced man, actually a bit apoplectic in appearance. He too was troubled and anguished about events. Like Dunaika he belonged to the sect known as Old Believers and he interpreted what was happening to his people as a sign they were soon to be plunged into extreme misfortune. The ancient doctrines influenced his mentality both consciously and unconsciously. For example for members of the old "Raskol" sect, religion itself and the religious hierarchy were all that mattered. The state was dangerous and treacherous and believers should keep their distance from it. Actually he was fascinated by all sorts of sects, including modern ones like the "Khlysty" to which Rasputin had belonged. No one had anything good to say about these people but Father Stepan recalled them with an enigmatic sympathy. About one thing he was certain: the state created by the Reds was truly that of the Antichrist and the situation in Russia was in fact the fulfillment of the prophecies of the Apocalypse.

His pessimism was becoming a kind of exhausting mystical passion which kept him in a continual state of agitation. He realized all was lost and the red hordes of God's enemy were advancing. He was tempted to cry out in his deep bass voice: "Get thee behind me, Satan!," to pronounce all the exorcisms in the liturgy, but he said nothing because he knew nothing would happen. God had turned his back and looked away from the *kazak* people, abandoning them to their destiny.

He kept his icons, vestments and liturgical objects in a tiny room in the barracks, but everything was worn out and degenerating into hopeless squalor. He himself was becoming a sorry looking specimen, ragged and hungry. The babushkas could no longer find ways to mend his torn and threadbare cassocks, the same ones he had when the long migration began, now completely worn out. Then the silver cross he had always worn around his neck disappeared. It was rumored he had exchanged it for cornmeal. Hunger was increasing in Carnia, which was besieged and completely surrounded by German troops who sought to prevent any supplies from crossing their lines. Occasionally some daring individual would get through at night with a wagon carrying a sack or two of flour scraped together on the plain. The Cossacks had run out of hay for their horses. Local barns and the nearest shepherds' huts had been almost cleaned out and people were now forced to slaughter animals not only for food but to keep them from starving.

The horses grew visibly thinner day by day. Whenever they were turned loose they roamed around restlessly, pushing aside the snow with their soft noses as they searched for a few blades of rotted grass to dull their hunger. Sheep and goats were increasingly rare and local herdsmen kept those few remaining carefully hidden, but when the Cossacks managed to steal one they roasted it in huge pots brought from Russia and ate as much as they could, knowing it would be a long time before they could hope to enjoy such abundance again. They had to take advantage of every chance they got. Life was becoming more precarious and nobody could tell what the next day would bring. Cossacks and local villagers were locked in a secret war of nerves, each group trying to outwit and trick the other in a struggle for survival.

The local people had launched their own counterattack and the invaders' horses and colts were starting to disappear. When Akmekkhan's mount vanished the Tartar was completely desolated and began to wander about looking for him. Deprived of his horse or his weapons a Cossack has no individuality — reduced to a pathetic nonentity, he becomes a drifting shadow on the face of the earth. Akmekkhan acted as if he had lost one half of himself and kept searching throughout the village, along the river, in nearby woods, calling out the animal's name, "Beluk! Beluk!" His shouts echoed dismally through the woods and countryside. The other Cossacks helped him, even venturing up some of the higher mountain slopes to call Beluk, keeping their guns ready in case of ambush. But in their hearts many of them were certain it was a hopeless search. The horse had been taken either by the *partizany* or the townspeople and by now Beluk had most assuredly been slaughtered and devoured.

Nonetheless the disappearance of a horse was an anomaly with ominous implications. For Urvan it was a premonition of even more trouble ahead. The temporary homeland they had found in Friuli was becoming uncomfortable, even beginning to bristle with hostility. It was time to think about harnessing the horses, hitching them to the leather covered wagons and moving on. But where? Gavrila was having similar misgivings.

Akmek's lined and leathery face, burnt by the sun of many distant summers, expressed a deeper gloom. It seemed as if the loss of his horse meant the beginning of the end for him and for the Cossacks. His desperate "Beluk, Beluk!..." had become a sob, a dull mournful lament. He regarded all the local residents with suspicion, trusted nobody, not even

Marta, Anita or Haha. Any one of them could have stolen his horse, or might know something they didn't want to tell him: they were all guilty, all in some way or other accomplices in the crime. A dark ugly hatred began to fester in his mind.

Two weeks later they found what was left of the horse, bones washed white by the river, reflecting the sun like shiny stones. Akmek was completely immune to any thought that other bones equally white, those of the sheep and goats he himself had stolen, might also be sparkling somewhere in the sunlight. For him the horse was much more than an animal — he was a friend, a confidant, a part of Akmek himself. Now he felt as lonely and bereft as a widower. Something changed within him. He lost his already thin veneer of civility, reverted to a crude instinctive ferocity, becoming vindictive, violent and predatory. He was as clever as a weasel and in his way practical and decisive. He no longer concealed his thoughts for the sake of prudence and good manners but came straight to the point as directly as a gunshot. When he saw Girei yearning for Alda, he burst into boorish laughter.

"What are you moping about for? You want her?"

"Of course I want her. But she has to want me too...."

"Nonsense. When a man really wants something he takes it without bothering with formalities, just like you steal a sheep or a turkey...."

"You're talking like you're drunk."

"Never been more sober. If you really want her, I'll get her for you."

"How?"

"Don't give it a thought!"

"You're crazy. You don't know what you're saying...."

"Is that right? Well, we'll see!"

Off he went, grumbling. He had plenty of memories of how Cossacks procured women in the old days, before the

Bolsheviks showed up. They kidnapped them, carried them off to the steppe on their horses, never mind all the niceties, and quickly did what they wanted to do. Sometimes young girls rebelled and struggled like cats shut in a bag, scratched and dug their nails into their tormentors' faces. But after a man had taken them at night to the canebrakes on the Terek, where the sand was still warm from the summer sun, then they turned docile as well-broken fillies. Moping and carrying on over a woman was the silliest most useless waste of time in the world. Nobody knew better than he did.

He recalled a lover he had when he was young, how he used to go to her room at night, making absolutely no sound so no one else would wake up. In the darkness he and the girl would recognize each other by touch and smell, then fall into a frenzy of love-making like a pair of enraged cats. He'd had a good many girls in more or less the same manner but never married because he was used to living as free as a falcon and couldn't bear the thought of anyone hanging around him to whimper and complain.

He continued to mutter and grumble. With age he'd developed a habit of talking to himself about whatever bothered or irritated him, and naturally there was a lot to complain about. Now that it was more and more difficult to get his hands on a goat or a sheep he frequently went hunting, using all different methods, a gun, nets, traps or snares. But there was very little game left either. Taking a wood grouse or a partridge was about as rare as a lunar eclipse. If he managed to catch a badger, a fox or a hare he regarded it as an extraordinary stroke of luck. God only knew when he'd get another such opportunity. When those hands of his, as dark and crooked as a chestnut root, took hold of an animal caught in a trap, when his fingers curled around fur or feathers he felt a thrill of pleasure and wrung the victim's neck with unconscious lust for killing itself. Then he would slit open the carcass and clean it with his curved knife and set about preparing a succulent roast flavored with basil, sage and nutmeg.

But after his horse was stolen a pall of mourning fell upon Akmek and dulled all his actions with muddled melancholy. Nothing gave him pleasure anymore. He moved about in a cloud of gloom as black as soot and everywhere he smelled death and decay. An odor of burned animal hair or bones permeated his very nostrils, or so it seemed. His face wore a habitual expression of general disgust and he acted as if the whole world were plotting against him and ready to knife him in the back. Sometimes when he was alone he'd be seized by a spasm of weeping, which gradually resolved into a hoarse primitive sobbing. He boiled with a raging desire for immediate revenge, but he wasn't sure against whom or what. In his lugubrious exasperation he pondered the possibility of playing practical jokes on the *partizany* or perhaps setting traps for them. His cunning intuition told him they too were in a tight spot and desperately needed food and arms.

"What about them?" he asked Urvan.

"There's no doubt. They can't be much better off than we are."

It was true, thought Urvan, the Cossacks, the local townspeople, the patriots and the Germans, continued to bark and snarl at each other, but everyone was hungry, perhaps even the Germans. All were caught in the same predicament and rendered similar by the universal disaster of war. Just poor unfortunate wretches at the end of their strength....

As for Akmek, he recalled seeing fires up on the mountains for several consecutive nights, fires that seemed to follow a regular recognizable pattern. At the time he hadn't understood what they meant but later he gave the matter some thought and now he believed he knew the answer. Along with Burlak and others of his own sort, he set out one night, climbed up to one of the high meadows and lighted a number of small fires. They didn't have to wait long. Very soon they heard the rumble of a motor and the dark shadow of an airplane began to pass back and forth above them, like an immense owl. Then it descended over the fires and a moment later, clearly visible in the moonlight, two parachutes opened beneath it. When they landed the men rushed to unwrap metal containers filled with every kind of goods: cigarettes, chocolate, coffee, tinned meat, powdered milk, weapons and more. They broke into loud cheers at the sight and Akmek was ready to burst into song and dance for joy.

They'd duped the partisans this time! Turned the tables on Vento, Saetta, Bora and Bora's lover Sonia, who was supposed to be even more beautiful than the famous actress Alida Valli. At least that's what the local townspeople claimed in wide-eyed admiration, adding that Sonia was also a ruthless executioner. Akmek, however, wasn't satisfied with merely stealing the supplies. He wanted to perfect his methods and go even further. Along with Burlak and the others he devised a plan to put all the booty together in an empty alpine hut and spread the rumor the stuff was there, hoping to ambush the *partizany*. The setting was ideal, heavy underbrush, hazelnut bushes completely surrounding the hut as if they'd been planted there with just this strategy in mind. The partisans would certainly show up sooner or later to reclaim their goods, because, as everyone knows, hunger lures the wolf out of the woods. They didn't tell Gavrila and Urvan because the garrison was neither ruled by rigorous military discipline nor governed by a rigid hierarchy. In fact the Cossacks weren't real soldiers in the usual sense, but rather a group in which everyone acted more or less on his own. Besides Gavrila wasn't a true colonel nor Urvan an authentic captain since the garrison generally followed the traditional laws of the horde, which decreed that the boldest and bravest should prevail.

The ambush was set up with great care by Burlak, who had been instantly taken with the idea, so much so that he tried to seize control of the entire operation, relegating Akmek to a marginal role, claiming he was too old for this kind of effort. But Akmek resisted. He didn't want to be forgotten. He wanted to remain active and take the initiative. After all it was his idea and he had worked out the overall plan. But the old Cossack sensed something sinister in the way things were being managed. Everything he did, everything that happened to him was tainted with foreboding....'

Saetta's partisans took the bait, because their leader was impatient. In a great hurry to reclaim what they saw as rightfully theirs, three nights after the drop they crept toward the hut. Only when they noticed the sentinels were not real men but uniforms stuffed with straw like scarecrows, only then did they understand they had been tricked. The Cossacks quickly sprang out of their hiding places and after a burst of gunfire four partisans lay motionless on the ground and four more were captured. The others fled precipitously as the Cossacks emitted triumphant yells. The prisoners, bound like criminals, were brought down to the barracks, shoved rudely along by the butts of rifles or Stens. Akmek's stratagem had functioned as perfectly as a well-designed wolf trap. The enemy who had remained invisible for so many months now stood there right in front of their eyes. It was the collapse of a myth.

At first the men from the steppe were choked with emotion, then they were overcome with primordial joy. Giving vent to savage howls that could have come from wild beasts in the forest, they slapped each other on the back with such force they all risked ending up in a heap on the floor. A fierce thirst for drink took hold of them and Akmek led them straight to Alda's door. As sharp-eyed and alert as a lynx, he had found out her household had not yet run out of wine. "Wine! Wine!" the Cossacks shouted. All at once they felt rewarded for the infinite failures, the vain searches, the expeditions gone wrong, the thousand mortifications inflicted upon their atavistic warriors' nature.

They overflowed with boyish happiness because the *partizany* were no longer elusive phantoms, only men like them, flesh and blood — men who could be grabbed and tied up like mummies. Standing there in front of Alda's house, Girei felt a faint tremor at the prospect of actually entering her home, but at the same time he was filled with boisterous, reckless euphoria. At last Alda was going to find out who he was and what he could do. She had underrated him long enough, now he'd show her!

Akmek flung open the gate to the courtyard and they crowded through in disorder like a drunken mob. All but Girei got off their horses. He was so exalted at the capture of the partisans, so excited to be part of a group of valiant comrades that he was ready to commit the most spectacular audacity. To show off to Alda he rode his mount right into the entrance hall of her house, while his companions burst into raucous laughter. The terrified women of the household scattered in every direction like hens at a clap of thunder. The idea of a horse in their carefully waxed and polished corridor threw them into helpless desperation. A horse in the house! This was unheard of even in local folklore. It was outrageous, completely beyond all limits....

Alda, forcing herself to control her fear of the horse and the shock of the whole bizarre situation, sent her admirer a withering glance. She was already engaged in figuring out how to make him pay for this. It began to dawn on Girei that in his strange excessive enthusiasm he might have gone too far and made a big mistake. Touched by a hint of remorse, he realized that without the company of his rowdy companions he'd never have dared to act like this. Such behavior might have reminded Italians of Rodomante, the boastful, boorish pagan knight from Ariosto's *Orlando Furioso.* He was suddenly embarrassed. What should he do now? What had gotten into him? He himself was confused and horrified at having brought his horse into a house so clean you could eat polenta off the floor.

But he didn't want Alda to notice his confusion. She should go on believing he was proud of his foolish bravado. He joined his comrades in drink and song while the women brought more pitchers of wine, one after the other, brimful, because they thought this was the only way to keep the Cossacks relatively quiet and inoffensive. As soon as a pitcher sounded empty when tapped Akmek shouted, "Wine, wine!" with the jolly conviction his voice would produce a miracle. They were all in a state of euphoria, but the one who seemed the happiest of all actually wasn't — Girei was embittered at having introduced a dangerous element into his rapport with Alda. But he continued to drink and sing at the top of his voice along with the others.

Then the entire garrison caught the exuberance of those who had carried out the expedition. They shoved the partisans, still tied and under close guard, into two wagons and drove off with them at full gallop. Meanwhile the heavy hand of a drunken Cossack set the local churchbells ringing out in loud cacophony, scaring all the horses in the barns. The wagons, guided by expert Cossack drivers, raced through the whole valley, stopping at every village and every garrison. Soldiers emerged from houses and barracks and the cheerful news continued to spread. The Cossacks had captured *partizany*! Everyone rushed out as if the wagons were transporting wild beasts from the heart of Africa, creatures never seen before, or perhaps Abrek tribesmen taken prisoner among the canebrakes of the Terek during the time of their great-great grandfathers.

At the end of the valley beyond the village burned by the Germans, the drivers turned back at full speed despite the risk the stones of the road might break their wagon wheels. They made their way through other valleys and everywhere they went the scene of triumph and victory was repeated. It seemed the obscure and mysterious enemy had finally been dislodged from his lair and sized up. Henceforth the struggle against the partisans would be entirely different, a fair fight in the full light of day.

But not everyone shared the enthusiasm. Gavrila and Urvan were worried. What were they going to do with those prisoners? According to the rules they should turn them over to the Germans, but for a number of complicated reasons such a step was morally repugnant to them. Thus they agonized over the whole idea while the wagons continued their triumphal rounds in order to give every member of the great Cossack nation a chance to thrill with pride at the success of this expedition. Again and again the same cheers rang out in each new village they visited and sooner or later some young man would begin to dance on his heels and kick his legs out straight with joyful energy, as if he'd just heard the war was over.

Since the Cossacks believed Italian partisans were all communists Burlak and Akmek proposed shooting the prisoners at once. They didn't like the idea of consigning them to the Germans either.

"Certainly not. It isn't an option. In case they take *kazak* prisoners we can arrange an exchange," said Gavrila.

"But the partisans don't take prisoners."

"That's not true. There have been exchanges elsewhere."

As the principal instigators of the triumph, Burlak and Akmek accepted his answer with clenched teeth. They felt they'd been belittled, and prevented from carrying their operation to its natural conclusion. They thought of all the Cossacks they had come upon in the woods or in the valleys — men with their mouths full of earth, their bodies already picked at by crows and foxes — and now their own prisoners were being taken away. A fierce inarticulate rage boiled up inside them. It was a bit like taking a hunter's wood grouse or partridge and putting it in a chicken coop instead of roasting it over an open fire.

# The Rag Doll

Day by day Urvan grew more weary of war and more discouraged about his own situation. His heart was heavy with memories of all the Cossacks who had died in a hundred different ways: some killed in encounters with Polish, Balkan or Italian partisans; others machine-gunned or caught in ambushes; still others victims of aerial bombardments or sickness. He couldn't rid himself of the idea that the *kazak* left a never-ending trail of dead behind him, so many dead that often there was no more room for them in village cemeteries, and they had to be dumped into lakes or buried in common graves. Paradoxically, he had begun to think of Friuli as almost a *kazak* homeland, since there were so many *kazaki* in Friulan graveyards.

When he overheard Dunaika and the other babushkas grieving among themselves he felt their lamentations as a reproach and the memory of the dead infused his daily life with sorrow. Once again he saw his people as blown off course in a never-ending odyssey, with no direction and no hope in sight....

Marta was his only distraction, the only source of relief from the constant tension. Every evening he came home tired and troubled and only when he and Marta closed the door to their room did he feel fate had allowed him a moment's respite.

"A rough day," he'd remark as he took off his *valenki*.

"Of course dear, but try not to think about it."

"To not think about it you'd have to be brainless."

"I know. But I have worries too and yet every now and then I forget about them."

"You're lucky. You have a cheerful nature."

"Really? Well, maybe you're right. Signora Esther used to say so. Perhaps that's just the way I am."

She felt Urvan's joy as each evening he rediscovered her generous body, endowed with the health and strength that so often derives from a mountain people's heritage. She was a spring that refreshed him, a balm that smoothed out his furrowed brow and let him forget. Marta knew she was able to tear him away from the torment of his thoughts, at least for a while, and this filled her with energy and revived her own spirits.

She realized her nights with Urvan were creating something she had never experienced with the men who had preceded him in her life. She was reminded of a plant taking root, putting forth flowers and fruit. As time passed her love for Urvan increased, became the most stable and durable she had ever experienced, although it was threatened, as her rapport with her former lovers had been. In fact this love was even more precarious because of the way things were going.

She often found herself returning to a single thought above all others: why were men so intent on killing one another when nature itself had decreed they all must die anyway? Actually it was Ivos who had given voice to such an idea and she had never forgotten it. Her close relationship with a Cossack did seem bizarre and if someone had told her it happened to another woman she would have found such a story perplexing and unbelievable. But here she was, drawn ever more deeply into the endless labyrinth of the Cossack soul, involved in all aspects of their culture: songs, *dumy,* proverbs, customs, food. Her life with Urvan appeared to be the material of dreams, as if she weren't fully awake. She felt like a sleepwalker who couldn't quite manage to return to reality.

Life was indeed strange and full of surprises. Sometimes she wondered if these things were really happening to her, they seemed so unreal and nonsensical. But she knew Urvan loved her more and more passionately. What had begun as a casual relationship with no thought for the future was now stronger than ever and she often found herself imagining bizarre schemes to rescue him from the final stages of this war. Yes, she told herself, she'd save him somehow. Perhaps she could hide him in a secret place in the villa where no one would think to look, or in a cave only she knew about. Urvan now dominated her thoughts — his fate was her most constant and anguished concern.

Toward the beginning of March, when the snow was beginning to melt, at least in the lower valleys, it was rumored the Cossacks were going to be moved once more to a different base, this time in Hungary. It was old Haha who brought this news to the villa. Urvan had already heard it, but done his best to conceal it from Marta so she wouldn't worry needlessly in case it might not really happen. Marta's first reaction was disbelief.

"Hungary? That's impossible. What would be the point...."

"It's just talk," said Urvan.

"But didn't you come from there? Why should they send you back now?"

"The Germans do what they want with us. We're like marionettes to them, we just go where they tell us to...."

"Which means your wanderings are going to start all over again. Off you go to meet the Russian advance."

"That was what we wanted in the first place."

"But it's madness now. It makes no sense at all...."

Then as vaguely as it had begun the rumor died down, and no one heard anything more about it. Marta recovered some of her peace of mind and her hopes revived with alacrity. Her optimism was like a mushroom that grows right back the next day no matter how many times some distracted walker steps on it and crushes it. She attributed the rumor to the increasing confusion, because as the war neared its end daily life seemed fraught with new pain and danger, like ever sharper stings and thorns.

Things were all coming apart at once. The war was lost for the Germans and the fronts moved closer as the armies steadily approached. It had to happen, it was inevitable — Marta had known for a long time now. For the Cossacks every day seemed to bring more hostile and discouraging news. The current rumor circulating throughout the valleys of Carnia held that the partisans led by Vento, Saetta and Bora had been joined by the "Stalin" battalion, made up of Russian communists who had escaped from Austrian prison camps — sworn enemies of the Cossacks. This meant the Reds were not only approaching from a distance as the fronts moved closer, but they were already next door in the mountains of Carnia. The Cossacks could almost feel their presence. Thus the boundaries within which they might maneuver to flee to freedom and safety were growing ever smaller, shrinking and shriveling up like an apple forgotten outside in the cold. The Red Army had already crossed the border into Hungary. At least one thing was now clear: the Cossacks could not be sent there.

Marta was obliged to spend more and more time bargaining with shopkeepers and peasants in her daily battle to make sure everyone had enough to eat and clothes to wear. In the back of her mind was a nagging doubt that the traditional misfortunes of past centuries had returned all at once — invasions, burned villages, famine, cruelty, summary executions, bitter continual strife....

Sometimes when she got up in the morning she was tempted to give up the fight, to let things take their course and stop trying to hold back the inevitable force of events. Whatever success she might have was ephemeral and she always had to start all over again with each new day. But those moods were temporary. Driven by the urgency of their situation and by her devotion to those who depended on her, she would become her old self again and take up the struggle with renewed vigor. She seemed to possess inexhaustible energy, tempered with immense compassion, although the source of these traits was a mystery. There were moments when she turned to Urvan for support but he was not much help because he had too many troubles of his own. She couldn't blame him, the way each day seemed to bring worse news than the day before. For example, it was unfortunate that the rejoicing over the capture of the partisans had led Akmek to Alda's house, where he had discovered and laid his hands on jugs of wine. It was indeed unfortunate that this rude and primitive Tartar, who thought of himself as Girei's guide and protector, should take it upon himself to make the boy happy.

Thus Akmek was irresistibly drawn back to Alda's house. Accompanied by Burlak and other rowdy companions, he knocked noisily at her door, refusing to stop until one of Alda's aunts finally came and opened it. The Cossacks who were quartered in the house came forward to watch, with malicious laughter.

"What do you want?" asked the woman.

"Wine! Wine!"

"More wine? But it's all gone...."

"No. Not all gone. You have *mnogo* wine — much wine...."

Akmek looked around, winking slyly at the others. He might be talking about wine but he was really after something else, something the woman pretended not to understand. Alda's mother and her aunts realized that having practically forced their way in, the intruders were not about to leave empty-handed.

"Wine, babushka, wine! Cossacks, no patience...."

"But I'm telling you it's all gone!"

"No. You tell story. Akmek smarter than you. We'll find wine now."

"All right, all right! I'll bring you what's left!" said one aunt and went down into the cellar. She returned with two full jugs, put them down on the table and served the wine in glasses to keep these barbarians from drinking directly from the jugs. She was mentally prepared to sacrifice much more wine, hoping thus to pacify the invaders and calm their strange brutish excitement. They all set about drinking but every now and then Akmek couldn't resist making a crude comment about Alda, noting how "Poor Girei" was so lovesick for her.... Every time he mentioned the girl's name the women shuddered, although Alda wasn't present. At the first sound of knocking at the door she had run to hide — the primary rule when dealing with Cossacks was not to let yourself be seen. "Thank God, Girei isn't with them," the women said to themselves, thinking of him as a possible danger to Alda.

They believed the wine would neutralize the Cossacks, hobble them like fractious horses. Settled down and sleepy they should give no more thought to Alda. But the more Akmek drank the more he talked about her.

"So why Alda not here?" he said, his face like a ferret's, his eyes peering at the women.

"She went to visit a cousin," said the girl's mother.

"In another town," added one of the aunts.

"Cousin...Ha ha! Cousin!" laughed the old Tartar as if the women had said something funny. "*Kazaki,* know where Girei's love has gone? To visit a cousin!"

"She'll be back. We'll wait here for her," said Burlak.

The women were worried. They kept bringing more wine but now they were beginning to wonder whether this was the right way to deal with these men. In fact not only had the wine failed to turn their minds away from Alda, but the drunker they got the less they could talk about anything else. The women exchanged terrified glances. Would they ever go away? How could they possibly get them to turn their attention to some other subject?

"Old lady, Alda should not go to cousin. Should stay here. *Kazaki* come for her," said Akmekkhan.

"But she's not here," said the mother.

"Not coming back," added an aunt.

"Coming back, yes. This her house. She come back. We wait."

They wouldn't leave, had no intention to do so. They were obviously planning to stay as long as it took to bring Alda out of hiding. What was to be done? Maybe they should send for Urvan or Gavrila? Alda's mother surreptitiously put a shawl over her head and started quietly toward the door.

"No! You stay here! You wait with us!" shouted Burlak in a terrible voice and began beating the furniture with his leather whip. The women, petrified with fear, no longer dared move a finger. Now they were sorry they had provided all that wine because instead of distracting the men it had made them vicious. Not only were they refusing to leave, sitting there the wrong way with their elbows on the backs of the chairs, but they were already impatient and suspicious they had been tricked. Akmek got up, unsteady on his legs, and began to look around intently and with distrust. He found a colorful woollen shawl and a pretty knitted cap.

"This Alda! Where is Alda!"

"Where is she? Where is Alda?" shouted Burlak and began hitting the furniture again with his whip. "Alda not go out. Alda here in house!"

Then the Cossacks began to move about in a more or less orderly way, as if in a planned operation against the partisans. One ran to bolt the front door and stayed there to guard it so no one could go in or out. Another went to do the same with the back door. Now the house was almost under siege and no one could escape.

"Now where is Alda? Still with cousin?" yelled Burlak in his terrible voice. As if obeying an order never given, responding to his angry tone, the Cossacks dispersed throughout the various rooms, searching every corner, every space big enough to hide her. Finally one of them found her, half dead with fear under a tarpaulin in the attic, desperately trying to pull handfuls of grain over herself to conceal her hiding place. With a shout of triumph he grabbed her arm and forced her down the stairs to the kitchen.

She was greeted by a simultaneous shout from all those present. Somehow in their minds a bizarre psychological transfer had changed the whole affair into a military action. They all rushed up and reached out to take hold of her. To Burlak, his eyes bloodshot with rage as well as drink, everyone who lived in that house was an enemy. He had always known the *kazak* had no friends, only enemies everywhere he went, enemies ready to trick and betray him. Here too, as usual, they had tried to get around him by lying.

Screaming in desperation, Alda's mother and aunts tried to pull her away from her tormentors. They begged and pleaded, even beat at the men with brooms. But the Cossacks were hunters who had succeeded in flushing out their prey. They ignored the women as if they hadn't even noticed them. At first they laughed at the brooms, but after a while, finding their efforts annoying, they knocked down two of the women and rendered them unconscious with blows from their rifle butts. Then they bound the third and gagged her with a dish cloth. Now they had a clear field with nothing to stop them. Their prey was in their hands, more beautiful than ever, still defiant but as frightened as a captured doe.

At that point they forgot Girei and all his lovesick yearning and reverted to the state of the primitive band with a captured woman in their power. Alda was a pretty toy and every one of them wanted a chance to play with her. Their atavistic urge for violence obliterated centuries of tranquil and ordered life in the *stanitsy* of the Terek valley as completely as a sponge wipes away a smudge. They turned into the terrible nomadic Cossacks of antiquity, the violent *qazaq* of Central Asia who had conquered the steppe and carried off the women of other tribes. Alda struggled and screamed loudly enough to be heard outside the house. Realizing she might rouse the whole village they tied and gagged her, calling her "witch" and "she-devil" and laughing like delighted children.

Tying and gagging her put them in contact with her rosy inviting body and their hands became greedy and avid. There she was in the midst of them and they took turns passing the little dove around and handling her tender perfumed flesh. Then, seeing no reason why each of them shouldn't take full advantage of such perfectly modeled feminine grace, they extinguished the lamps and threw themselves upon her, their breath fetid with wine and tobacco. Even though she was bound and gagged, she moaned and struggled, twisting and turning in terrible agitation. They called her a rebellious cat, punching her now and then or holding her down with extra force to keep her from moving. "Witch, hold still a minute!" they shouted angrily in Russian. She was a filly that had to be broken whatever it took and they'd never get a better chance than this. Although they were completely out of control, in the back of their minds they knew they mustn't do anything that would attract the attention of anyone outside, especially Gavrila, Urvan and Girei. This whole affair should go no further. It had to be kept hidden from everyone else, Cossacks as well as local townspeople. Even in their drunken state they were aware they were doing something no one else should find out about, now or in the future. It was best for the girl to lie quietly and give some sign of submission. With this in mind they doubled the gag and bound her twice as tightly and after a while she seemed to calm down. Of course they all thought there was no better medicine for impertinent and defiant girls than to bring them quickly to maturity by such means. It chased all the spirits and devils out of them and they acquired the quiet wisdom of experienced and expert women.

After a while they noticed that Alda's passivity was not due to submissiveness but to the fact she had fainted. She showed no more signs of her indomitable vitality. Again, as if obeying an unvoiced order, they untied her and took off the gags. But she didn't wake up or revive in any way.

"Well now, that's enough. She's settled down for good," said Akmek.

"Better than a well-broken filly," laughed Burlak. But his laughter sounded forced.

A vague uneasiness came over many of them, and they began to regret the whole escapade, wishing they could turn the clock back to the moment when it began. Suddenly they weren't drunk anymore but they struggled to recall why they were here, what had set off the whole course of events and how things had gone this far. Worried and vaguely frightened they milled around in the dark house, and then someone finally remembered the original idea had been to take the girl to Girei.

"Let Girei manage by himself. If he wants girls it's up to him to go after them," said Akmek.

"Right. That's his business. What's it got to do with us?" said another.

"If she's fainted she won't remember anything. She'll have forgotten it all," added a third. But they were still worried.

Things had begun all wrong, then gone from bad to worse and ended up in shameful stupidity. Their apprehension increased. Alda still lay unconscious on the straw mattress belonging to one of the resident Cossacks, her head awkwardly off the edge and her arms and legs spread out.

"Not much of a woman," said Akmek.

"Not like one of ours. They'd be on their feet yelling their lungs out."

"Well, it's easy to see the women around here are different. We'd better remember that from now on."

"Well, let's go. She'll come around by herself," someone suggested.

But they weren't altogether sure. They didn't think they ought to go off and leave her in that condition. They should try to put her back the way she was, and most important make sure she was conscious, even if she screamed and rebelled. With clumsy hands they began to adjust her clothes and shoes and pick the straw off her dress. Somebody had the idea it would be good to wash her off and comb her hair, but none of them would be able to do that because it was women's work. And out of the corner of their eyes they kept glancing at her head, still grotesquely turned on her twisted neck as if it couldn't return to its normal position. Their vague fear intensified, and rapidly overcame them. It was an atavistic fear, welling up from the depths of superstition, telling them they had violated a fundamental taboo.

Akmek, who was the oldest, felt he was in some sense the most apt to perform a woman's task and he began to sprinkle water on Alda's face, then to give her rapid little slaps and loosen the buttons on the chemise she wore under her sweater. He didn't dare pull up her rumpled wool stockings, or adjust her elastic garters. Fear tinged with reverence impeded his actions. Something strange had touched his primitive spirit. This man who had never had a wife, nor a relationship that was more than casual with a particular woman, felt mysteriously close to this poor unconscious girl, as if he were bound to her by a family tie.

"She's not coming to. What have you done to her?" he said to the men.

"I'd say she's faking. Women are great fakers," someone replied.

"We need some vinegar, or vodka, or strong smelling salts...."

Meanwhile others were doing what Akmek hadn't dared to do: taking hold of her as if she were a rag doll, they arranged her body and smoothed out all her clothes so no one could tell she had been manhandled. They tried every possible means to awaken her, but they only succeeded in making her head wobble limply. Finally one of them put his ear to her chest.

"I think this girl is dead," he said softly.

The words had a chilling effect on all of them because they articulated what each man had secretly suspected

"What do you mean, dead? How could she be dead if nobody killed her?"

"I tell you she's dead. She's not breathing."

Then all took turns placing their ears on her chest and no one could detect the reassuring sound of a heartbeat. Their fear intensified into an archaic primordial terror — western women, unknown creatures for them, could die for no reason? They had killed Alda without meaning to, maybe simply because they had tied the rag too tightly across her face. Because she had screamed and carried on like a wild creature they thought she was as strong as their own women. But she only seemed to be, she was really as fragile and delicate as a glass trinket. Now who was going to tell the lovesick Girei? And to think the whole thing got started because of the idea of doing him a favor.... Why did it change and go all wrong? And why did the girl die when so often you can't even kill somebody with a gun?

They all wanted to flee this ill-fated house, but it seemed as if as if the girl's spirit, moving restlessly about, kept them glued to the spot.

Finally they left, one at a time, silent and somber, being careful not to attract attention, and quickly disappeared into the night. Akmekkhan grumbled under his breath, beset by terrible disappointment and weariness at the seemingly endless series of deaths. Overcome by a kind of nausea, repulsion, and refusal, he gave in to a melancholy contemplation of this never-ending festival of death that added more and more victims with each day that passed. Meaningless senseless deaths. Deaths, one after another, like the drip, drip, drip of a leaky faucet that never never stops. Nobody wanted to kill Alda and yet she was dead and nobody knew how or why.

Akmek was now certain the Cossacks were afflicted by a curse laid upon them when they left their blessed *Chernozyom* and the steppe where their rivers flowed. Maybe it had all happened simply because they had abandoned Holy Russia. Yes, now he too agreed with Urvan, just like Dunaika and the other elders. So much had happened that little by little he had come round to their way of thinking, rejecting his former ideas....

It was a dark moonless night but the wind was blowing through the valley, shaking the last snow from the trees. Some of the Akmek's companions returned to quarters, threw themselves down on their straw pallets and fell asleep as though nothing had happened. Others who lingered outside thought they heard the meowing of a cat or the yelping of a fox just outside the village, or perhaps came upon a stray dog gnawing on a bone.

Then suddenly loud screams from Alda's house broke the silence. Her mother and aunts had regained consciousness, freed themselves from their bonds and discovered the lifeless girl. The mother's shrieks were like a siren that pierced Akmek's skull and he shook his head in defeat and humilation. What was he doing mixed up in such an affair? For him love had always meant happiness, song, carefree nocturnal excursions to darkened izbas, never followed by misfortune and lamentation. Here was another sign that things were worse than ever for the ***kazak***. Perhaps Alda's mother had gone completely mad and nobody would ever be able to restore her sanity. It might be a kindness to put a bullet in her head and end her suffering. In fact Akmek had lived long enough to be convinced that suffering always went on until death. Only in the grave could anyone find peace. For the dead all was finished. They were changed into the same earth as the sod that covered them and nothing could ever touch them or make them suffer again.

Alda's mother's screams and cries went on into the next day. The whole town was in an uproar and the murmurs of protest grew louder until they became a raging fury. If the Cossacks had killed a partisan no one would have said anything because war was war. Plenty of Cossacks had died at the hands of invisible guerrillas. But this was a different story. The bridge of tolerance and perhaps even secret understanding and sympathy, which had spanned the gap between the local people and the Cossacks now lay in shambles and nothing could put it back together....

It was increasingly evident the local people now saw these once picturesque strangers who had come from so far away with their horses and wagons only as cruel invaders. Urvan felt as helpless as the biblical pillar of salt. He had often feared something like this would happen, at the same time fervently wishing it wouldn't. He had maintained his hope of keeping the garrison in line — with their hands clean, their actions inside the law. And here was the result....

"It's horrible, just horrible this whole thing," he said to Gavrila.

The colonel nodded sadly.

"But in a sense," Urvan continued, "the Germans are guiltier than the Cossacks."

"How do you mean?"

"They're the ones who gave us this cursed gift. They told us, 'This is your land. Do what you want with it and with the people who live here.' That's what eventually led to the crime."

"Yes, you're right. The temptation was too strong."

"The Germans tempted and corrupted the *kazak*. They acted like the devil himself. But it's the *kazak* who will have to take the consequences."

"Exactly. You see things clearly, Urvan...."

But even as he spoke, Gavrila's thoughts were aimed in another direction. He was beginning to wonder what he had in common with his own people. He knew foreign languages, spoke fluent French and fairly good English, habitually greeted women according to formal etiquette, bowing and kissing their proffered hands. He now believed his obedience to Krasnov's appeal had been a mistake. No trace of the Cossack culture remained in his makeup — the spirit of the steppe was alien to him. His place was not here, but in the gentle French countryside, in a castle or *domaine* secluded among meadows and woodlands. He should never have left France. The war against the Reds was a nonsensical mirage and Russia was lost forever. He shouldn't have abandoned his French woman in exchange for an obscure hope of recovering his homeland. He too felt that Alda's death had destroyed something, and his future looked darker than ever....

Neither he nor Urvan knew what to say to Girei, or what to do to help him. The young man had simply closed himself up in mute and lifeless defeat. He wandered aimlessly through the house, the barnyard and the village like a lost soul looking for himself, with no hope left. The most intense and exalted moment of his youth had changed color, darkened into evil and grief. All his energy and enthusiasm had evaporated, leaving only a motionless passivity, like stagnant waters in a pond. He had no more desires, no more impulse to sing and carouse, no interest in wine, *dumy,* girls, no more dreams of rousing victories against the *partizany*, whom he had once encountered in a happier time without recognizing them. He would never again catch a glimpse of Alda's smiling face as she peeked out at him from behind the window curtains. If he were to go there now with his little cousin Luca, the child would receive no kisses, no smiles — those kisses and smiles Girei had believed were really directed at him through the child as intermediary.

Alda's funeral was held two days later, toward sunset. It had rained and heavy gray clouds still moved over the valley. Now and then they thinned out momentarily to let a pale dingy light show through. Marta, Anita, old Haha and all the residents of the villa were in attendance. The priest spoke only briefly, perhaps unwilling or unable to address a death so sudden, so unbelievable, even now when everyone was used to frequent deaths, a death whose victim was the last person anyone would have thought to be in danger. He said these were times of terrible misfortune and no one could feel secure or know where or how his own death might be lying in wait. A lovely flower had been torn from her roots, then crushed and thrown into the mud. All who heard those simple unembellished words felt a lump tighten in their throats. Despite the macabre celebration of ever more frequent deaths that had now lasted for years they had to admit they were neither completely accustomed to it, nor ready to accept it, not yet....

People directed spiteful glances at Girei. Hadn't it all begun because that rough uncivilized boy from such a far off place dared cast his eyes on Alda, who was not and never could be his? His stubborn insistence on hanging around her had been the first and ultimate cause of the tragedy. Even Urvan and Gavrila received accusing looks. They were the ones who should have prevented the disaster but they had proved incapable. The villagers' bitterness encompassed all Cossacks — they saw every one of them as an invader and they realized any invasion carries within itself the germ of a malediction. No matter how it comes about it will be corrupted by violence and bloodshed.

Girei remained gloomy and sullen, seeming not to notice what people were saying behind his back and equally unaware of the increasing cloud of resentment hanging over his people. In fact he didn't seem to notice anything. He was outside reality. When the others threw handfuls of earth over the coffin, he did the same, as if Alda were one of his relatives.

For a long time after the funeral he remained walled inside himself and wouldn't talk to anyone, not even Marta or Urvan. In fact he felt a sort of crude envy toward the two of them because they were alive, together and in love, whereas for him and Alda it was all over. He had just found out she cared for him when she'd been taken away and ruined and killed. If people tried to begin a conversation he cut them off abruptly, turned away and left the room. His heart had become like an expanding block of ice that closed him off in numbed isolation.

When his comrades got together to sing or just to enjoy each other's company he was never present. All such activities were poisoned for him — he'd sooner approach a serpent whose venom was fatal even at a distance. Gone were his illusions of being on the threshold of glorious events. His moment of grace, filled with hope and energy and promise, had ended as uselessly and ignominiously as fireworks that burn and fizzle in the sky with no color and little light. Nothing could induce him to perform his equestrian tricks, mounting and dismounting his galloping horse to amuse his little cousin and the other children. That was all over for him. On this point he was immovable.

However he still loved his horse. Now that Dunaika's scoldings were becoming more shrill and unbearable he spent as much time as possible in the peasants' barn where the animal was stabled. He never took him out, but he cared for him, curried, brushed and stroked him, bringing him armfuls of stolen hay. No theft was too risky to undertake for the good of his beast, whom he now loved better than any human. It was actually one day as he stood there stroking and brushing the horse's neck and flanks that his eyes first brimmed over with tears. "Lothar, go ahead and eat," he said. "It's stolen hay. We *kazaki* are fugitives and refugees and we have to live by plunder. It's our destiny. You understand, don't you Lothar?" The horse turned his head toward Girei and pricked up his ears, still rhythmically munching his hay. Girei was astonished at his own tears, at the fact he was talking this way to his horse, but he couldn't stop. He said all sorts of odd things, whatever passed through his mind. Meanwhile he found himself thinking he couldn't really feel any hatred for the Cossacks who had killed Alda, because too many Cossacks had been massacred, in all the places they had passed through, and they too would be exterminated. You couldn't hate somebody who was doomed to die very soon.

From that moment on Girei became fully conscious of his people's suffering, which he had hardly noticed before. No longer did he see war and conquest as glorious events that tested men's valor, but only as cruel and bloody instruments of murder.

Akmek, overcome with guilt toward Girei, began to follow him around abjectly like a dog whose master has turned him away with blows and kicks. Little by little he found the courage to talk to him and try to teach him things he'd learned by experience over his long life,

"Listen, young man. If fighting breaks out with the *partizany* or anyone else, throw yourself on the ground and stay there if you want to stay alive. Keep down, I say."

"Shouldn't I go into battle on my horse?"

"No more, boy. Horses are good from escaping or for covering long distances. But in a fight there's no better defense than the earth itself."

"All right, then. That's what I'll do."

"When a battle's going on, if you smell the earth instead of gunfire, you might survive."

"I'll remember what you say, Akmek."

"The earth will never betray you, my boy. It's not like men, who say they're your friends and then turn against you. The earth is your mother. We come from the earth and it's to the earth we return. We'll be buried in the earth when it's all over. The earth is the beginning and the end, and everything else is just stories."

But as he listened to the old man, Girei's thoughts were elsewhere. Here was Akmek seeking him out and telling him all this instead of talking about the one thing that really mattered, the fact that he had been with the men who had killed Alda. And they were planning to kidnap her and bring her to Girei himself. The boy no longer sang with the garrison chorus, nor went to their meetings, but he often spent time with Akmek. Together they played and sang the song about the boy who returned to his village and found it destroyed and the izbas burned by the Russians. The old voice blended harmoniously with the young one in the sad refrain: "*Ahi dai, dalalai!*" Girei was aware that this was the old man's way of confessing his crime and his own role was to absolve him because Akmek had never meant to kill Alda — her death was simply a cruel trick of fate. The boy realized that although Akmek was uncouth and primitive, he felt compelled to confess in that strange and oblique manner. Thus not a single word passed between them about the subject that constantly occupied both their minds.

Burlak also tried to approach Girei and, strangely enough, he too wanted to reinforce certain ideas — the boy should be proud of his *kazak* heritage and, most important of all for Burlak, he should resolve never to surrender. Girei began to feel himself pulled in two different directions. On the one hand his sense of identity as a Cossack and his pride in his heritage were stronger than ever. He neither rejected Akmekkhan and Burlak nor felt any desire for revenge against them, but was perfectly willing to let them approach him and talk to him. On the other hand he was learning Italian rapidly, in competition with Luca, and he was starting to feel closer to the people of the valley. He entered their houses with his head bowed as if he were ashamed, and remained silent except for an occasional word or two. But people were beginning to get used to his company. After all, they mused, he fell in love with the prettiest girl in the village simply because he was young. Nature itself had led him to that point because nature paid no attention to what was or wasn't possible and the fact that Alda and Girei belonged to two different cultures, at war or half at war with one another, didn't matter one bit, nor did the difference in religion and so on.

So what had Girei done that was wrong? Nothing. He had simply acted like any young man, like their own young men, and no one should blame him. The older villagers were the quickest to arrive at this conclusion. Even Alda's aunts were not completely opposed to such a point of view.

He began to spend more and more time with local families, often in the evening after the church bells had rung for vespers. He looked for ways to make himself useful, trying to guess what people wanted or needed just by the way they looked or acted. If an old person died he would join in the family's mourning, his face expressing the same sorrow he would show for one of his own relatives. He seemed to react to every funeral as if it were Alda's. That had been the moment when Girei began to be sensitive to the tragic side of life, to the finality of death, to feel as if he were wrapped in a heavy blanket of melancholy. Henceforth he regarded death with shock and disbelief. He found himself thinking about the loss of his father and felt more keenly than ever his duty to protect his mother and his little cousin. Luca, like Girei, was always wandering about the village.

Girei often sought out Urvan to converse with him. The captain wondered if the boy were trying to guess what punishment he would decide to mete out to those who had killed Alda. But Urvan, ever more troubled, knew the only proper punishment was to shoot them. He shook his head thinking about it. Shoot a dozen men? What would that do to the *kazaki* of his garrison and to all the other garrisons? He knew these were anything but normal times and that the laws one applied in peacetime couldn't be enforced in such a precarious situation as theirs. He felt as if there was no law of any kind. The original laws of their nation were no longer relevant — they had lost all force during the eternal migrations. He refused to recognize Bolshevik law and German laws had been the source of all their troubles. The ancient codes of conduct of the nomadic tribe and the horde had been obsolete for centuries. So what could he do? What decision could he make? He didn't know. He realized that in this case he himself, more than anyone else, was the incarnation of the law, and an immense responsibility lay on his shoulders. It wasn't simply a matter of applying whatever law he decided upon, but of bearing in mind the survival of the garrison, which was also his responsibility. As far as Alda's death was concerned he did feel the fault was his because his duty was to oversee the garrison and make sure his men respected local custom and stayed within the limits of civil behavior.

But he had not succeeded. He had failed. Now he would never be able to forget this incident that had introduced the germs of corruption into his garrison and extinguished all hope for the future, just as the Domanov affair had cast a shadow over the entire *kazak* people. A Cossack general serving in Poland had been murdered in mysterious circumstances and all rumors implicated Domanov, his second in command, who had indeed succeeded the general. The whole ugly business had plagued the Cossack army from its very formation. Time passed and Urvan still couldn't decide what to do. Making one man the source of the law was to assign him a task beyond his capacity. The load was too heavy to carry and he couldn't do it. Gavrila was no help either. He avoided the subject and absented himself from all garrison activities.

Urvan understood why. He knew the colonel had tacitly renounced his role as commander, leaving Urvan in charge. In his long years of exile Gavrila had given up his commission and career, had become a man of peace, a tranquil administrator, despite the fact that Krasnov had promoted him to the rank of colonel. Urvan was also a man of peace. He had been a typographer and had no formal military training, but he had to command the garrison because otherwise it would be left with no leader. Tormented by his overwhelming responsibility, he treasured those nights when he held Marta in his arms, nights that were still long there in the valley even though it was nearly spring. He sank into oblivion, forgot his troubles and became an ordinary man again — a man whose only worries concerned himself and his woman. It was important to make her understand certain things and he started to say....

Marta shushed him by putting a finger on his lips and changed the subject to planning his future when the war was over and people took up their lives again, as they had after their disastrous defeat in 1917 at Caporetto. She also wondered what she could do for Girei, who seemed so withdrawn. During pauses between her household chores she tried to talk to him, reminding him he was young and would forget his sorrow if he managed to survive this desperate situation. But it was Akmekkhan more than anyone who kept track of the boy. Since Girei listened so patiently the Tartar had convinced himself his own presence was indispensable to Girei and believed his words were building up lasting structures in his young mind.

"You mustn't be sad, my boy. That's for people who don't know what life is all about."

"You're a crazy old man...."

"I'm a wise old man. You should never let yourself brood, no matter what happens. You're young. When you're young you should be having a good time, living it up. There'll come a day when you suddenly realize you've gotten old and women don't notice you any more. Then it'll be too late. Your time is now. Don't waste it. When I was your age I had two or three girls who used to wait for me in the dark in the izbas. I didn't waste my time, believe me and I don't regret a single one of all those years behind me...."

But Akmek's voice betrayed his regret at growing old. His youth was long past and no matter where he looked there was nothing left to remind him of it. But a person could die young, as so many Cossacks had. Every day could be your last and therefore no one should put off living for the joy of the moment. Akmek spoke with passion and he was sure he had opened Girei's eyes to the imminent peril of losing his way in dark paths of melancholy. The Tartar could sense the pressure of events bearing down on them like a landslide. There was no time to think — life was closing in. He seemed to hear the approaching armies as the thunder of an immense cavalry charge.

Even in the general confusion Urvan understood their situation rather more clearly. Henceforth the Friulans would regard the Cossacks exclusively as violent invaders, just as violent as all those others who had occupied their land repeatedly throughout the course of history. Thus an undercurrent of tension made their situation even more stressful. The illusion of remaining in Friuli had completely evaporated. Now, thinking back, he realized he had never really believed in such a possibility. Something about it had never added up for him — the basic conviction that leads to certainty had been missing. It was a myth they had accepted because the idea of a promised homeland helped combat fatigue and desperation. It was, however, even less credible than the other myth they had clung to for such a long time: the dream of confronting the Bolsheviks in the midst of the Russian steppe and provoking a general uprising against them.

The truth was very different. After having suffered horrendous losses against the Germans and surviving a veritable avalanche of death and sacrifice, the Red Army was now advancing everywhere and would deserve most of the credit for a victory that now seemed imminent. What would become of the *kazak* people? The generals and atamans hardly seemed to notice what was happening. Suspended in a strange half-conscious condition like sleepwalkers who make no effort to wake up, they continued to talk about resistance and final victory, apparently regarding the *partizany* as their major enemy, and assuming that once they were out of the way all problems would be solved.

Not one order, not a single phrase that went out from headquarters, indicated a global awareness of the situation. When he read their dispatches Urvan was astounded. He himself, with his modest knowledge, could only see one possibility of saving his men: surrender to the English and the Americans, who were at the moment massacring them from the air with bombs and machine guns, as if the Cossacks were their most dangerous enemies. After the surrender when all the peace treaties were signed, wouldn't the Allies be able to come up with some corner of Australia or Africa or America, a piece of semi-arid land like the steppe where they could rebuild their villages and start life over? Going back to Russia was absolutely out of the question. The Reds would regard them as traitors and they'd end up being shot, down to the last man. There would be no mercy. That much was certain. Nobody would defend the *kazak*, who had rebelled only in order to remain faithful to himself and his own past.

And yet there was something elusive about his commanders' apparent serenity. Perhaps they were considering a solution too complex for a simple man like him to grasp. Maybe they had information about German secret weapons which would change the course of the war....

Urvan didn't understand, didn't know what to think. Every now and then his thoughts reverted to Alda's death, and how those who had raped her shouldn't be left unpunished. But what punishment might he invent that would be right? He couldn't put them in prison, having them whipped like thieves who had stolen watches or bicycles wasn't enough, and shooting them was excessive and would demoralize the troops. So what was left? It was always like this, here and everywhere else. There was no way out. He was lost in an endless labyrinth. The nature of war itself was chaotic and disorienting....

It was perfectly easy for him to identify the members of the group who had raped the girl. All he had to do was look a man in the eye steadily and he understood at once who had been there and who hadn't. They were as ingenuous as children and didn't know how to hide anything. He discussed the affair once more with Gavrila and together they decided to have the guilty ones whipped.

They took their punishment quietly, hanging their heads and saying nothing, except for at most an occasional hostile glance to protest the humiliation. They felt no guilt because for them the girl's death was simply a piece of bad luck, an accident. War gave the victors a right to possess the enemy's women, just as the hunter who kills a hare has the right to eat it.

Urvan wasn't the only one who understood their attitude in the context of its underlying causes. Marta also saw them in the same light. She considered Alda's death a fated event, so to speak, because when an invading army is imposed on a population this kind of thing inevitably happens. Being fully aware of the frequency of such incidents in human history, she knew that the capacity for brutality inherent in each and every man would always explode into violence if circumstances were right.

The Cossacks' destiny was now certain, there was no turning back. The truth that had wavered before their eyes from the beginning, the truth they had all pretended not to see, was now becoming more difficult to deny. It was still hazy, barely outlined, and each person tried to turn away and act as if it weren't there simply because that's what everyone else was doing.

But a current of acute anxiety began to wind its way through all the garrisons and villages in the Tagliamento, Gorto, Incaroio, Timau, and San Canciano valleys. The weather was growing milder and the colonels mounted their horses and met in a designated place as if for a council of war, but in reality none of them had any idea what to do.

Urvan was convinced that in their situation they had to try to find out what their commanders actually had in mind, if indeed they had anything at all in mind. Perhaps they were no better off than the colonels, captains, lieutenants, all the Cossack troops — or to put it in Marta's terms, they too were lost, blown this way and that by events beyond their control, just men who were dazed and bewildered, with no place to go, like shipwrecked sailors drifting on a raft.

"I was thinking about something we might do," he said to Gavrila.

"What would it be?"

"Ask for an audience with Krasnov. We've always trusted him, followed him with no questions asked. It's time now for him to tell us in plain terms what he has decided to do."

"Yes, my friend, I can only agree."

One morning they rode out on horseback through the valley, across the river and all the way to the village where Krasnov's headquarters had been set up in a requisitioned hotel. As he listened to the sound of his horse's hooves, Urvan reflected that nearby, only a short distance to the south was the lake into which hundreds of bodies had been thrown after the terrible air raids in November. Perhaps that lake was full of the restless ghosts of the unburied dead, like the Caspian or Aral Sea.

The officers at the hotel informed them Krasnov was not there but they could wait if they wanted to.

"Very well, we'll wait," said Gavrila. They wandered through rooms decorated with rugs from Turkestan, precious icons hundreds of years old, copper vases, silver crucifixes, antique banners which had known both glory and defeat in the civil war. Both felt a flicker of emotion thinking they might have followed those very banners in the Ukraine and Crimea during the far-off days of their ardent youth. For an instant they were transported back into times that now seemed infinitely long ago.

While they waited in these aristocratic surroundings whose sparkling decor resembled a country villa belonging to the czar or some Russian prince, a number of senior colonels and generals passed in and out. No doubt they had been with the Whites in the triumph of early days as well as during the final disaster. Urvan found himself thinking the at-mosphere of this place was somehow abstract, outside of time, a drifting dream finally come to rest here among the mountains of Friuli. It wasn't real, it was only a stage setting, an illusion. The effect on both Urvan and Gavrila was disturbing and they couldn't sit still and wait quietly. They kept getting up and walking back and forth from one room to another, observing everything with a faint uneasiness.

Krasnov didn't come back until late at night. He had been carrying out an inspection somewhere. He traveled in a black limousine, moving at a slow speed, both preceded and followed by a mounted escort of twenty-four Cossacks each. The officers of his guard wore dark blue dress uniforms adorned with gold braid on their jackets and fur hats. It was apparent Krasnov was above all a prince and had not wished to renounce an iota of the ceremonial splendor due his rank. His wife, the Princess Lina Fyodorovna, rode beside him. She was dressed with extreme elegance as if on her way to a ball at court. Gavrila and Urvan's first impressions were identical: "My God how he has changed!" They had not seen Krasnov since the campaign in Crimea. He was now about eighty years old and his hair was perfectly white, but his uniform was as impeccable as his wife's dress. When he spoke, however, his voice was nasal from the effects of a head cold.

"My prince, these officers have been waiting for hours to see you," someone whispered. Krasnov looked at them, his eyes somehow curiously veiled.

"They are assuredly two valiant soldiers. Let's hear what they have to say," he said.

Gavrila started to talk but his voice broke and he hesitated as if unsure how to begin. Urvan quickly took over.

"General, we are the commanding officers of the Terek garrison."

"I can see that from your uniforms. How are things going?"

"Not well, your Excellence."

"Because of the partisans?"

"I wouldn't say that, General. We've had very few encounters with them. It seems they're doing all they can to avoid open combat. They are exercising maximum caution, limiting their actions to sabotage."

"Well then what's wrong?"

Urvan felt a choking rush of anxious words in his throat, but suddenly he couldn't utter them before this old man who was now merely the decorative symbol of a failed enterprise.

"It's the morale of the troops. They don't see a way out. They've lost hope...."

"Our plans provide for an eventual confrontation with the Reds and their allies. Our present duty is to defeat the partisans, who are of course all Communists. Bolshevism must be combatted, wherever it surfaces."

"Certainly, General."

"Thus you see, things are quite clear."

"But, Excellency, victory seems no closer.... On the contrary it seems even farther away than before. The war is going badly for our side...."

"Who says so? That's mere enemy propaganda. The fact is the Red Army is being held in check on all fronts."

He went on to point out that the raw material of victory consisted in believing in the goodness of one's cause and one's leaders, as well as in courage and self-denial. They must fight on until final victory was won.

Gavrila and Urvan realized that either Krasnov had no understanding of the actual situation, or else he was denying it even to himself. Nothing he said reflected the reality of their predicament. Instead he seemed to be talking about a fictitious state of affairs. Thus, they thought, poor old Krasnov was only a visionary. He too had turned into a myth, one more myth they had believed in for years. There was no way he could provide the help and advice they had been seeking.

They set off to return to the garrison profoundly discouraged, convinced their mission had been perfectly useless. With anguish and chagrin, they had to admit the lowest-ranking Cossack soldier understood the situation better than any ataman and it was now up to the army to save itself if it could. In fact the orders received from Domanov, Shkuro, Naumenko, and Polunin reflected the same content and point of view as Krasnov's. They appealed to the honor and the extraordinary fortitude of the Cossack people. Urvan's and Gavrila's disgust with the war had become intolerable, and was now augmented by a heavy burden of guilt for their part in leading their nation to ruin. They felt trapped in the face of imminent disaster. So this was what their leaders proposed: keep fighting to the end, in other words until you are all massacred. The only solution they proposed was death.

Thus in Urvan's mind the images of the atamans looked up to for so many years now lay like broken idols fallen to the ground. He set about distancing himself from them mentally and decided he was no longer obligated to obey their orders. He refused to consider slaughter as a solution because he loved life and he loved his people. There had to be some way out. The first step was to continue as long as possible to avoid any direct confrontation with the partisans. This should be relatively easy if the only commander in question were Vento, who was well aware time was on his side and would naturally favor the same strategy. But Saetta wanted a fight at all costs. It was now a contest between the two of them. The eternal rumors in the village discounted Bora and Sonia, insisting they had left because of disagreements with the other partisans. Some said they had fled beyond the Isonzo to join the ninth corps of the Yugoslav partisans, others maintained they were in hiding for fear of reprisals directed by Saetta, whose position in the guerrilla force was growing stronger, and still others reported they had simply gone off to fight in another area.

On their way back to the village Gavrila and Urvan had to cross a German-controlled zone. As they approached a grove of beeches they came to an abrupt stop at the sight of partially decomposed bodies of partisans hanging from branches of several trees. Crows, foxes and other scavengers had already been at them. The German command had forbidden removal of the bodies as a warning to local people. It was a scene from an ancient barbaric era, when people were governed by terror and cruelty. Gavrila felt they had fallen into a new dark age — wolves, bears and other wild animals had returned to dwell with men, even inside their cities....

Neither spoke, realizing that outside their territory even more terrible things were happening, and they spurred their horses on to hasten their return. After giving the password to the sentinels they dismounted and proceeded on foot. At a certain point they thought they heard a woman crying. Since they were not far from Alda's house Urvan paused to listen in concern. He had heard Alda's mother was no longer in her right mind and prone to fits of weeping at all hours.

As they passed by the barns they heard an occasional soft nicker from a sleeping horse. They could make out the dark outlines of the mountains in the distance, their summits still white with snow. A light breeze from that direction touched their faces and now and then they detected the rustle of some small nocturnal animal moving about. It was one of those nights when there seemed to be no war.

Around that time the garrison wanted to organize a seasonal festival like those in the *stanitsy* on the steppe when they used to celebrate the melting of the snow and the coming of spring. In the course of the evening all individual differences among the Cossacks disappeared, no matter who they were or what they had done. Whatever was past was forgotten, or seemed to be. Even Urvan danced and sang and the Cossack women performed the dance of the birches, taking such tiny steps under their long skirts one might think they were being pushed along on invisible casters. Most of the night was given over to song and dance at the villa as well as in other houses.

Then they all went to bed and fell into peaceful sleep since the festival of springtime had chased away all thoughts of war, or *partizany*, or Reds, or of the homeland they'd left with no hope of returning. But their awakening was cruel indeed. The sound of a barrage of gunfire awoke those in or near customs headquarters, then reached the whole village. The Cossacks bounded from their straw pallets as if startled by a nightmare. Each man pulled on his *valenki* as best he could, buckled his belt, donned his *chekmen* or overcoat, slung his rifle or pistol diagonally over his shoulder, crisscrossed his cartridge belt on his chest, set his fur hat or *kubanka* on his head and they all rushed in disorder toward the barracks, where the last shots were just dying down.

By the time they got there the noise of rifles and Stens had ceased entirely and those who had fired them were already gone. The men who had been guarding the partisan prisoners lay motionless on the floor of the barracks hallways or on the ground in the courtyard. All the prisoners had been freed. The surprise attack had knocked down the Cossack guards like ripe pears shaken from a tree. They hadn't expected a raid that evening, or rather, in a certain sense, they had thought about it even while everyone else was celebrating the rites of spring and had kept their eyes open with just such a thing in mind. But then they too were overcome by the general revelry going on close by, so they brought out jugs of wine, and drank and danced like the rest. After all they were Cossacks and they couldn't be expected to behave differently. The temptation was simply too strong and they had given in. Thus they had fallen into the trap set by Saetta. The guards lay where they had fallen, in distorted and awkward positions, in the midst of pools of dark blood beginning to congeal. A few were not yet dead and they moaned or moved a leg or an arm. Blood was everywhere, on their hats, their cartridge belts, their *chekmeny*, their boots, on the silver medallions that hung from their belts.

Akmek, who had rushed in with the others, thought they looked like hens slaughtered by a fox who, despite all measures to shut him out, manages to get into the chicken coop and wreak havoc. He was overcome with resentment and hatred as well as remorse for having forgotten the possibility of an ambush that night. Some partisans had also fallen, prisoners as well as attackers come to liberate them. The Cossacks were enraged. Their anger at letting themselves fall prey to an attack was increased by grief for their dead and dying comrades in arms. Bodies lay sprawled here and there outside in the courtyard as well, as if scattered by death itself, the essence of war, which continued to sow disaster and reap more victims.

Those prisoners who had given the Cossacks such a boost in morale, whom they had paraded in wagons from one garrison to another so all the *kazak* people could exult in their success, the living trophies which had made up for so many failures — the *partizany* had either taken them back or left them dead on the ground. Anyhow they were gone and their captors were left as empty-handed as if they had tried to hold on to a gust of wind. Meanwhile the *kazak* went on dying and there was no sign the carnage would let up. Everything conspired to continue it. Perhaps another massacre was going on right now. At a certain point during the night of the festival they had heard a volley of gunfire from small arms as well as machine guns, far away in the distance.

Urvan and Gavrila arrived on horseback and observed the scene with somber faces and few words. Their first thought was to make sure the doctor was taking care of the wounded, and he was. Then they had the men line up the dead from both sides in preparation for burial. Taking an oil lamp to see more clearly in the still dim light, Urvan peered at the faces of the dead partisans. They were very young, mere boys Girei's age or younger, and their expressions reflected astonishment at their fate.

But one was not young, but rather a man of thirty or perhaps even older, bearded and wearing tattered clothes under a worn-out coat. Urvan wondered if he were a soldier who had come to the end of a long odyssey. His expert eye noted the marks of war, scars where minor wounds had healed, a frostbitten foot. Maybe he was a veteran of the Russian campaign.

Urvan returned the next day to take another look at the partisan dead laid out on the red tile floor in the barracks hall. He gazed at their abandoned bodies, the bloodless pallor of their faces, the wounds that someone had wiped clean as best he could, and was touched by the strange dignity of death. For a long time he stared at the motionless limbs, the blond or chestnut hair of his now helpless adversaries. The Cossacks poked at the bodies lightly with their leather *valenki*, feeling an atavistic thrill of pride at the contact with their fallen enemy.

Each one was acutely aware there is no sight as defenseless as a corpse. Anyone could do with it what he chose. Vento's and Saetta's men lay lifeless, without thought or memory, with open wounds and bloody clothes, long beards, partially open mouths and eyes that hadn't been properly closed. Urvan gave notice that the families could now claim their dead. Everyone already knew who they were because an obscure wireless communication system had already spread the news. Thus people from distant villages arrived with horses and carts to take away the remains of their relatives. Some victims were actually local and Urvan's opinion that all the young men — there were almost none left in the village — had gone to the mountains to fight was thus confirmed. So was his conviction that the entire local population supported the partisans.

This was not news. Even old women who lived in the village were partisans without guns or Stens, quite prepared to fight in their own way. Urvan decided it had been madness to assume these two populations could live together, and couldn't forgive himself for being ingenuous enough to believe in such a silly illusion, even during brief moments of extreme weariness.

Each side buried its dead and now a river of distance flowed between the two communities. Yet during that time an unofficial, undeclared truce prevailed. Day after day passed with no raids or ambushes, no incidents of sabotage, only church services, benedictions read over coffins, and long lines of mourners, both local and Cossack, wending their way to the cemetery.

"Do they have to bury their dead next to ours?" said one old man, whose grandson had died in the attack.

"Where else can they put them? In the woods? They're not animals," replied a woman.

"They've got their own military cemetery on the other side of the lake."

"Yes, but they died here. Along with ours."

"Still doesn't seem right."

"Why not? The dead aren't fighting each other. The war's over for them."

Stepan the priest blessed the bodies and celebrated the official funeral in the barracks. Then the deceased were interred in the village cemetery with crosses at their feet, while the women quietly wept. Urvan's expression was somber and reflective. More than ever he felt he was part of a lost generation, crushed by the evil fatality of history. Destiny had carried the *kazak* people to this cursed place, just as adverse currents in the Caspian or the Aral seas drove swimmers and fishing boats off course and took them where they never meant to go. His whole generation had been condemned by the war. In fact he and Gavrila had been pursued by an evil fate for years, from the time of the civil war, and it pursued them still. God only knew how things would end for them....

Every now and then they received scraps of news about the war. It was reported the Red Army was now less than a hundred kilometers from Vienna, but the reports were vague and unverified since Carnia was in a state of siege. Encircled as it was, neither weapons, nor food, nor news could reach them, nor could they themselves communicate with the outside world.

Urvan kept brooding over his idea that the Cossacks' situation was different from the position of every other people on earth because they had no place left to go. All the others would soon be able to celebrate the end of the war at home in their own country. Even the Germans, who had deported women and children and sent them to their deaths in concentration camps, even they had a place to return to. But the *kazak*, no, he had no place on earth to call his own.

He went on Sundays to listen to the Orthodox priest in the great hall of the barracks, which they used for a church. But Stepan's sermon sounded empty and meaningless because he couldn't point to a single sign of hope for his people, wandering aimlessly and abandoned to their own devices. Like the ancient Hebrews after the destruction of the Temple in Jerusalem, the *kazak* was left with nowhere to go. This provoked a deep sense of guilt in Urvan's mind, as if he had violated a law, an ancient sacred principle, and now he must pay the penalty. One of the Cossack songs lamented, "Oh brother mine, how hard it is to live in a foreign land!" But it was far more difficult to live in a foreign land when one's own home country was lost forever. Urvan could see a hundred different signs of the coming collapse of the German forces and their allies. He sensed the faster, almost precipitous, pace of events that would finally tumble over them all and bring this war to an end....

Individual soldiers began to defect. Almost every morning when the Cossacks assembled or went to get their rations they noted the absence of a friend or comrade, perhaps the one who slept on the next pallet. No doubt he had slipped away to join the partisans or gone to surrender to the Allies now advancing from the plain. The Cossack army was a sinking ship and the rats were starting to leave. This was the beginning of the end, the time when nobody listens to orders but simply acts on his own.

In their hearts Urvan and Gavrila couldn't condemn those who had fled under cover of night to the *partizany* because it might be a way for one man to solve his problem when no general solution existed. Each day life became more difficult. Now the specter of hunger began to loom larger. Every evening as soon as it got dark the Cossacks set out in search of the food the local population tried to keep hidden with all the ingenuity they could muster. Villagers avoided going out at night because a hungry Cossack engaged in a hunt was very dangerous and it was obviously best to avoid him.

Hay supplies were almost exhausted and it would be an interminably long wait until the first new crop was ready to cut. The starving horses wandered about looking for stray tufts of rotted grass or gnawed at the tender bark at the base of young trees, leaving them peeled and strangely white so that on moonlit nights they showed up like bones. One could almost see the poor animals grow thinner from one day to the next and despite their shaggy winter coats every rib was clearly visible.

Some of the Cossacks traded their horses to mountain people from distant villages in obscurely bartered contracts. Others regarded these transactions as the ultimate renunciation, a sign of extreme despair, almost an abdication of human dignity in exchange for the inferior status of a gypsy or vagabond. However, maintaining their horses had become a nearly impossible burden. They turned their mounts loose to forage for themselves, but some of the animals seemed to be lapsing into a sort of madness brought on by stress and hunger. They wandered like ghosts through farmyards, along roads and mountain trails, whinnying in desperation.

As the Cossacks watched them in distress they saw the frenzy of the horses as a sign of their own fate. A current of decadence, exasperation, of predatory and murderous cruelty swept through the garrisons. Officers of all units feared they could no longer control their men. Whatever happened from now on would be decided by unleashed passions, random chance and fear.

One day near the beginning of April a group of Cossacks rode up toward the *Salvadi's* clearing to look for food. The general spring thaw was just beginning up there and the melting snow dripping off the trees sounded almost like rain. The woods and the path were still wet but the sky was a bright clear blue, without a trace of a cloud in sight. Burlak was leading the group and he rode along with little thought of caution, because hunger drove him and his men onward with an evil urgency. But when the houses and wooden haysheds and huts came into view the Cossacks were met by a sudden lethal barrage of gunfire from automatic rifles and Stens.

Burlak felt an urge to bitter laughter. He had always suspected the *Salvadi* was a secret ally of the partisans, despite Urvan's and Gavrila's opinion to the contrary. Now the truth had come to light but it was too late. All their cards had been played and the war was nearing a bloody conclusion. "My friends, we've waited a long time for an open fight with the *partizany.* Well, the moment has come. Fire at will," he said. The partisans were shooting not only from some of the huts, but from the woods as well, having taken every precaution to avoid encirclement. They too had come to the *Salvadi* to replenish their supplies of livestock, but they had kept their eyes open and those surprised inside were already fleeing frantically into the woods.

The gunfire was intense and many men from both sides fell stricken on the wet grass or into the underbrush with wrenching cries or suffocated gasps. But then the partisan fire suddenly diminished and the Cossacks realized they were firing into a void. The guerrillas, always poised for flight, had given up and simply evaporated. Burlak and the others were quick to discern that this time as well as before, someone had warned the partisans and put them on guard. They smelled an informer — spies were an obsession with them.

They set about picking up their dead, glancing now and then at the fallen partisans, but with less curiosity than before. All at once an apparently dead partisan lying contorted on the ground leaped to his feet and dashed away. Akmek saw him and shouted to the others.

"Take him alive!" ordered Burlak.

Thus began a pursuit both desperate and terrifying for the fugitive, the Cossacks bellowing like madmen. Without knowing or understanding why, they reverted to an atavistic habit of frightening the enemy with savage yells. The youth kept running and actually succeeded in putting some distance between himself and his pursuers, when he stumbled on the root of a tree and sprawled on the ground, his face twisted in pain. He tried to get up and go on but he limped badly. In a matter of seconds they grabbed him. Burlak, Akmek and most of the others couldn't contain their joy at having at last got their hands on a spy. For them he wasn't just any spy, he was the Spy par excellence, the Absolute Spy, the embodiment of all the spies they had forever imagined and sought. If they had always somehow gotten the worst of so many encounters with the partisans, it was because of the Spy, who had informed the enemy of their movements and foiled their plans.

The prisoner was Ugo. The Cossacks had always suspected him, but not really seriously, because he was the only young man in the village who dared mingle with them openly. But now they had caught him redhanded, and this time he couldn't deny it. They tied him up and began to taunt him with sarcastic comments.

"So, little pigeon, you can't fly away anymore, can you now?"

"Where are your folks? Did they go off and leave you all alone in the woods?"

"You must have run pretty fast to get here in time to warn your friends...."

"Only this time, my boy, you've stepped in a trap...."

They moved closer, with raucous laughter, touching his chest with their rifles. One of them kept poking him with either the handle or the whip end of his riding crop. Later, as they rode quietly and cautiously back to the village, with the captured animals already slaughtered, cleaned and partly skinned, they left a trail of blood from both slaughtered animals and wounded men. Akmek, who had slit the throats of the sheep and goats, was covered with blood. Visibly satisfied at having been the one whose sharp eyes had spotted the spy, he was in a cheerful mood. Once again he'd put one over on the *partizany.*

But the other survivors were silent as they brought back the dead slung over the horses' backs. Even Burlak, who rode at the head of the column was enveloped in a cloud of gloom about his people and himself. He was positive now he wouldn't be able to return to the villages on the Terek, and never, no never again, would he see the Circassian Mountains, the land of his ancestors beyond the Caucasus.

Akmek's thoughts were not much different. True, he was outwardly pleased at having finally captured the spy, but underneath he too was bowed down by a leaden weight of sadness. Several pairs of boots in good condition hung from his saddle, as well as overcoats and fur caps with their identifying stripes, all taken from the *partizany* who had died in the battle. It was decidedly a sad thing to despoil the dead, even for somebody like him, but the *kazak* was just a poor vagabond with no resources of any kind and he needed clothes because nobody would give him any. He had to take things where he found them, without quibbling over details. The *kazak* was indeed in a desperate plight, suffering from cold, hunger and fear.

But he tried not to think about it and to console himself with the fact that they had fended off the ambush and the partisans had suffered losses as great as their own. The thought of the spy actually made him laugh. He had always had enemies and the mentality of the ambush was instinctive with him. Fighting the partisans, having to shoot them, was perfectly natural to him. Why shouldn't he? It was them or him. The partisans were the present enemy and they had to be resisted. Perpetual warfare was man's destiny. As for him, his attitude toward the whole question of enemies was simply part of his nature — wasn't he descended from those mountain tribes of the Caucasus who periodically raided the Terek Valley settlements and carried off livestock and horses? To put it another way, in his veins coursed the blood of the Abreks, the wild horsemen who were always ready to face gunfire, kill the enemy, and flee back into the mountains. Akmek was used to a poor nomadic life, accustomed to living on plunder and being hated by stable populations. There was nothing new in his present life, just the continuation of the life he and his forbears had always led. He didn't really know why he had joined the Cossacks or why they had allied themselves with the Germans and he had no clear idea of who the Reds were and why they were supposed to be an enemy. All he knew was he had somehow ended up in this place and there were people here who shot at him so he had to shoot back. Nothing, or practically nothing, had really been different for his Abrek ancestors. He didn't know much about this world but one thing he was sure about — destiny didn't change, never grew kinder. It kept watch on you like a falcon, just waiting for the right moment to sweep down and seize you in its outstretched talons.

That was why he always kept his gun handy — an old flintlock that had once made Girei laugh. He never let it out of his sight as if it were part of his body, the extension of an arm or a leg. His horse was an equally essential and irreplaceable part of his world. He couldn't imagine life without a horse. It would be like having one arm or being crippled. Thus he loved his horse, stroked him, curried and brushed him, urged him on affectionately with a, "Trr, trr." Without a horse life was no good at all. When people had played that ghastly trick on him, stolen his mount and slaughtered him for food, he had quickly acquired a new one from another valley, making a two day excursion to go and get him.

On their return from the raid Akmek cooked for the survivors of the expedition. Since it wasn't cold — in fact from the Russian point of view it was mid-spring weather, he made his preparations outdoors. After all, stones or bricks were tiresome for the *kazak*. He preferred to live in the open air. In somebody's cellar Akmek found an old spit with a handle to turn it, then cut some sturdy forked hazelnut branches to hold the spit, whittled them down to size and drove the unforked ends securely into the ground. When he had transformed an entire sheep carcass into a savory roast of mutton, the veterans of the day's action gathered around, sweaty, dirty, stained with blood and mud, sat down on stones or wooden stools and devoured Akmek's offering. Because they had eaten well and drunk their fill that day and they saw the world as beautiful and problem-free.

Akmek had already forgotten about the spy. But Burlak couldn't wait to begin the interrogation. Akmek had drunk too much, which gave him a somewhat guilty conscience, perhaps because he was an ex-Muslim, converted only superficially to Orthodox Christianity, perhaps because the wine reminded him of Alda's death, Girei's grief and the whole unfortunate incident. Burlak had drunk no wine, but he had not abstained out of respect for the Prophet, who didn't matter to him. As the most sober among them, it was he who ordered the Cossacks into the prisoner's quarters as soon as they finished gnawing the last bits of meat off the bones in their greasy hands.

"On your feet, *partizan*. Your time has come," said Burlak.

"Time for what?" said Ugo in a steady voice.

"Time to tell us where the other *partizany* went."

"I don't know anything about them. They're like the wind. Here one minute, gone the next."

"No, my young friend. You've always told them everything. With them you are a damned chatterbox. Now you're going to spout off a few things to us for a change."

"I'm not a spy. I just happened to be up there. The partisans surprised me just like they did you. I only went up to see the *Salvadi*. I'm a shepherd too."

"Maybe you are, maybe you're a shepherd and a friend of the *Salvadi*. But you're also a spy."

"That's not true. The partisans have robbed me too, lots of times. They've stolen at least a dozen head of my sheep."

"My boy, don't make me lose patience. I have very little patience to lose."

"I don't know what to tell you. I'm not a spy and I don't know anything about the partisans."

Furious, Burlak picked up a riding crop and snapped it in the air. A primitive rage welled up in him like a wave and he could already feel the battle cry rising in his throat. Playing with his razor sharp dagger and scimitar he could barely resist the terrible desire to use them. He was remembering not only all the times the partisans had baffled and defeated him, but the fact that Marta too had thwarted his desires. Everyone knew Marta was an easy woman. Before Urvan she'd had other lovers. This infuriated Burlak because he could no longer deny being strongly attracted to her. Just the thought of her created a vague restless torment in his mind. But he knew with absolute certainty she'd never be his and the only effect he'd ever had on her was fear. He clearly remembered her terrified face that day when he'd gone into the farmyard of the villa and stared at her as she stood by the window watching him chase the goose around. The looks on both their faces had said all there was to say. Burlak liked to boast to his comrades about scorning women. But Marta fascinated him, bewitched him like a sorceress, a weaver of spells. But she would forever say no to him. She was a woman capable of going to bed with a poor nobody who found himself in the worst kind of troubles. But not with him, never. She'd continue to say no to him until time ran out.

Why? Was he ugly or contemptible? Not at all. He was a fine looking man, handsome even. His eyes were Asian but his mustache was trimmed in European style and the scar on his cheek, made by the blade of a scimitar, that was no disfigurement — it was a sign of honor for a man, a testimony to his valour. He was tall and strong with well-proportioned limbs — any woman would find him good looking and attractive. But not Marta. The minute she laid eyes on him she shuddered, he could read the shadow of terror on her face. She sensed in him the mysterious legendary violence of ancient Asian warriors and could not help but think of the blood he had caused to be shed and the enemies he had killed.

Burlak had never asked anything of Marta and for the most part had avoided even speaking to her because it would be contrary to his Circassian pride. He was bold with everyone else, men as well as women, and it was only with her he became hesitant, his mouth too dry to utter a word. Now he avoided her entirely, not to spare her feelings but because he couldn't endure the blow to his pride when he read that ultimate refusal in her face.

Such were Burlak's thoughts as he struck Ugo with the riding crop. The boy screamed with pain, but still refused to answer. Burlak kept hitting him, again and again, determined to loosen his tongue and get every last secret out of him. Burlak himself had twice been punished this way on Urvan's and Gavrila's orders, but now he was the one wielding the whip and calling the dance.

"Where's Vento now? Where's Saetta?"

"I don't know, I don't know...."

"A few more blows and you'll remember everything. What's become of Bora? Where are their headquarters? Malga Pitis? Malga Zoia? In Rodau's alpine huts? Or the *Salvadi's*?"

The blows continued without respite. Ugo had fallen to the floor, his face, hands, and back bloodied. He tried desperately to protect himself but the only move he could make was to turn his head away.

"All right are you ready to talk now? Where are the leaders? Are they going to get together soon?"

He kept badgering the boy with questions, never letting up with the whip, certain this was the only way to bring him out of his mutism. Ugo was covered with bruises and blood, and his open wounds burned as at the touch of a red-hot iron. He knew Burlak would not stop, he had a will of iron, and he also knew his only chance to save his skin was to betray his friends. Then he felt a rush of overwhelming pride — never, never was he going to tell Burlak anything. He was still conscious enough to understand he himself was finished — he was dying in the cause of freedom, as so many of his comrades had done. The very fear of what was happening to him strengthened his resolve and he decided to let his savage tormentors see just how defiant he was.

"You'll never take them, never. They're always moving, like the clouds in the sky, and every day there are more of them...."

Infuriated, other Cossacks raised their whips and the blows rained down like hail.

"Now are you ready to talk?"

"Never. But you — you'll all be wiped out. Not one of you will get out of this valley alive. You'll die, die, die, every last one of you...."

A final terrible rage possessed the Cossacks and they beat Ugo until he struggled no more. Akmek bent to look at him. Ugo's neck was horribly bloody and swollen, his back striped purple and red, the skin in ribbons.

"This one won't ever talk again," said the Tartar.

"Why not?" asked one of the others.

"He's dead, the whip severed his jugular vein."

"Oh well, who cares. One less *partizan*."

Burlak had to stifle his disappointment. At last he had had the chance to get hold of the secrets of the organization, and now he was right back where he had started from, almost completely in the dark. He'd have to go on feeling his way carefully, relying on guesswork wherever the *partizany* were concerned — it was like trying to find your way through a dark cellar at night. Akmek stretched his cold stiff limbs and looked out the window at the high peaks still dusted with snow. He shuddered uneasily, and those unknown mountains up there suddenly appeared to be traps set to close off all exits from the valley, should the Cossacks try to escape. All the men felt subdued and melancholy. Ugo, like Alda, had died at their hands, and thus once again a mocking destiny had thwarted their plans. It was a terrible blow to Burlak's pride. He felt as if something had come apart and disappeared into the night and all his projects were now subverted and undone. But this time his characteristic burst of rage was somehow stifled.

"What are we supposed to do with him now?"

"Hide him. Bury him the way we did the two Germans."

"Sooner or later they'll find him."

"Why worry about that? By the time they find him we'll be long gone," said Burlak.

He gave the order to clean the room and make sure not a single trace of blood remained. Meanwhile he did nothing, just stood and stared at Ugo's body, as if suddenly conscious of a powerful attraction to death. There was something inviolable in the lifeless corpse of his enemy. Now that Ugo was on the other side of the mysterious boundary he was surrounded by a sacred aura. He had passed through the gate and he knew what lay beyond it. Was it another life full of gardens and watered by fountains, like the one described in the book of the Prophet, or was it merely silence and nothingness, as Akmek believed? Burlak didn't know, couldn't make up his mind which one was right. He had them lay Ugo on a table, untie him, and extend his arms and legs so he appeared to be at rest. Then he lightly touched some of the purplish bruises with one finger. It irritated him to have disfigured the boy so brutally. A finely placed puncture between the eyes or a bullet in the heart would have made a much cleaner job of it. Now that he'd achieved his revenge it meant nothing. He told the men to wash the boy's wounds and thus began a strange transformation. As the swellings began to go down and the skin grew pale, Ugo took on a singular beauty. He was a tall muscular youth with the physique of an athlete or a woodcutter. Burlak had observed that Christians laid out their dead with their hands joined on their chests, bound together with a rosary. He wanted his comrades to do the same with Ugo, even though there would be no coffin and no funeral.

While Burlak watched them carry out his orders he kept thinking sooner or later it would be his turn, death was moving closer and closer. Ugo had been an implacable enemy, had performed his duty to the end and Burlak had to respect and admire him. Now that Ugo was on the other side all Burlak's former rage had evaporated. Ugo had been a worthy adversary, had conducted himself with honor. He was a real man, as courageous in every way as a Circassian warrior. But death had taken him away because war was the triumph of death. Death was the most important and inevitable reality and he accepted it with respect, without the horror and refusal experienced by women like Marta or Dunaika. For this reason Burlak never even considered fleeing from death, simply waited, standing firm, for it to come after him whenever and wherever fate decreed.

They wrapped Ugo in a blanket and buried him at night in the sandy gravel near the river. The news of his disappearance spread quickly. Rumor had it that he no longer felt safe in the village because his connection with the partisans had been discovered, so he had fled to the mountains to stay with them until the war was over. But his mother was not convinced. If he had done that, Ugo would have found some way to let her know. Besides, she had a premonition. She began looking for him everywhere, without telling anyone. Her melancholy figure dressed in black became a familiar sight. Only once in a while, when she was all alone and no one could hear her, she would wail softly. Then, oddly enough, she and Alda's mother, drawn to each other by their mutual grief, began to wander about together, their subdued weeping only occasionally interrupted by a sudden sob.

The Cossacks couldn't bear the sight of the mourning mothers, or the sound of their lamentations. Convinced they would bring bad luck, they made every effort to avoid encountering the two women and actually hoped some accident of war would eliminate these grim reminders forever.

Then came a minor spring flood caused by a sudden snow melt after several days of sirocco and the swirling waters cut into the river bank nearly uncovering Ugo's body. It was Arturo's dog Baldo who discovered him. His barking summoned Luca. When the boy saw a hand and the corner of a blanket sticking out of the sand he began to shout. People came rushing and began to dig out the body. The signs of the whipping were obvious and a shudder of horror ran through the entire village. People shut themselves in their houses and scarcely dared set foot outside. They peered through the barred windows or the doors of their houses, shocked and terrorized by the realization that any Cossack could change without warning into a raging madman and commit every imaginable excess.

This attitude only further exasperated the Cossacks. Urvan could see how the divergence between the two communities he had tried so desperately to prevent had now become a gulf of disastrous proportions. He could hardly find the courage to look into Marta's eyes and his conversations with her were forced and awkward. He didn't know what to say, how to explain that historically speaking the Cossacks had emerged from barbarism only moments ago, not centuries, and the slightest shock could set them back.

Marta too was terribly tired from too much anguish and too much responsibility. For years now she had carried the burden of worry for Caleb, Signor Aaron, Signora Esther, Haha, Urvan, and now Anita, who was soon to give birth. She looked forward to that event with dismay as one more thing to further complicate a situation already hopelessly confused. It seemed to her despite all possible good will no place could be found where that baby would be safe. The future loomed ever more threatening and cruel....

She would have liked to send Anita like a package through the mail to some remote island in a peaceful ocean where no one had ever heard of this war. Was there such a place? Or was even that a mere dream? She was so weary and demoralized she found herself overwhelmed by an impulse to flee, or even more than that, by the most compelling desire she'd ever felt to fall into a deep sleep and not awaken until the war and all its dreadful scars were completely wiped away by time — to sleep the sleep of Rip Van Winkle, whom Caleb had told her about so many years before.

But these moments of exhaustion and loss of hope were always brief. The usual Marta would reemerge, full of energy and purpose. Once again she was the woman nothing could defeat for long and her resistance to the surge of compassion for those around her was less than ever. She felt for all of them, more and more intensely, unable to defend herself against overpowering pity. Pity for her neighbors and the members of her household, pity for people in general caught in the terrors of war like baby chicks who glimpse the dark shadow of a buzzard circling in the sky. She empathized with their collective desire to run away and hide in a cave in the mountain, in the vain hope of finding a moment's peace. They were all possessed by a terrible nameless fear of unknown forces about to crush and annihilate them. Perhaps it was more than fear of the war — it was fear of life itself and the play of cosmic forces. Her fellow human beings reminded her of terrified kittens, looking about for a protection that doesn't exist.

Everyone tried to find some sort of defense, a belief in Providence, in a God who would protect them like a bell jar. Marta thought of paintings she had seen depicting the Madonna stretching her mantle over poor frightened sinners. That's what everyone wished for. If there was no mother hen to keep them safe, why not a heavenly mother who watches over her children? And what other hope was there, when faced with the grim reality of the death camps where Signora Esther and Haha's family had been exterminated.

Thus she too sometimes wished she could hope for the Madonna's protection, although she suspected such beliefs were only the result of the human yearning for salvation and defense. She thought the Heshels' villa had seemed to provide a refuge for those who had so willingly come to live there and perhaps she herself was part of that protective atmosphere in the midst of war's pandemonium.

Of course everyone wanted to live. The instinct to survive was inexhaustible and ubiquitous, even in the animals: Baldo; the Cossacks' horses, now thin as skeletons; the camels, who had brought an enigmatic hint of the Orient to the valleys of Carnia. Sometimes Marta went back to her secret place by the mossy spring in the woods or to the cave with the indecipherable prehistoric graffiti on its walls. Breathing the strange atmosphere of the place, imbued as it was with life from an ancient past, gave her energy, renewed her strength and restored her hope. The spring, the wood, the cave, the inscrutable graffiti were for her a manifestation of the arcane fascination of life itself. After passing through those places, which she thought only she knew about, she felt refreshed and ready to begin again.

Despite all that was going on around her she fervently desired a life of her own as soon as possible. She wanted children by Urvan, who was now her man. She wasn't going to give him up and she was as worried about him as Dunaika was about Girei. Thus she set about trying to devise a plan to save him for herself. The two of them might retire to the cave with blankets and a supply of food and wait until the front with all its lethal consequences had passed through the area. Or they might surrender to the partisans. For instance to Vento, who could not be unaware of the way Urvan had carefully avoided confronting them. But would Gavrila be able to save himself? And Dunaika? And little Luca? And what about the whole Terek garrison? How would they ever escape the trap that was closing all around them?

Maybe she would be able to save two or three Cossacks, but not all of them. That was impossible, even more impossible now that the local people had risen in a storm of fury against them. She didn't know what to do, where to look for a way out. She constantly made and unmade plans. Maybe the best move would be to convince them to lay down their arms, to surrender and let the victors know the Cossacks were finished with war for good.

But she really had no definite ideas and certainly no experience to guide her. All she knew was that the war was coming to an end. The Allies had retaken France and crossed the Rhine, the Russians were about to invade Germany from the east and their armored divisions were already devouring the immense Balkan plains. It was the last act of the tragedy.

Now that the end was finally at hand, now that it made no sense to continue the struggle because the outcome was already determined, precisely now the partisans and the Cossacks were fighting each other ferociously and without restraint. The patriot raids increased and there was frequent news of clashes and massacres in other valleys. Many young men on both sides were dying, but the Cossack losses were far heavier. As the momentum increased they became more stunned and disoriented, unable to ward off the enemy assaults, like helpless tuna caught in nets, then clubbed to death in a relentless hail of blows. The partisans, smelling victory, grew bolder every day. They had come to hate the Cossacks as much as the villagers did and dreamed only of finishing them off. For the partisans the enemy was a destructive wild beast, now mortally wounded. The Cossacks knew the end was almost upon them and they seemed to hear the approach of death from all sides like the obsessive beat of an African drum. Dazed and unable to act, Urvan let himself be carried along by the force of events. He could see perfectly well that the old generals and traditionally revered atamans had no strategy, no contingency plan, no hope. They just went on blindly, talking about resistance and outraged Cossack honor in a kind of delirium reminiscent of Hitler's ravings from his bunker in Berlin. But all this was madness....

Gavrila had even stopped dreaming of returning to France to the secluded estate in Berry. He could almost hear the horses of the Apocalypse bearing down from all directions on him and his people. Angry and desperate, he wondered again how he could have believed so blindly in Krasnov, that old man who still lived in a czarist past imprisoned in a lunatic dream. How could he have thought the worn-out Cossack Army, whose oldest soldiers still carried nineteenth-century flintlocks used to fight the Abreks, might defeat the Bolshevik giant that now dominated Holy Russia, more powerful than ever? How could that battered remnant of the past ever liberate the biggest country on earth?

For him and his comrades there was no return and no future. Their Ithaca had disappeared in the clouds, or rather, they had never even glimpsed it from afar, nor felt the island wind nor heard the song of the birds. For Gavrila Ithaca no longer existed, neither in Friuli, nor in Russia, nor in France. The only reality was this never-ending war. He had developed a theory and went about repeating it to his friends in a low monotone, almost a whisper: not only the ***kazak*** but modern man in general had no home, because his life and thought had been overwhelmed by chaos. There were no more certainties, no more guarantees, no straight paths that led to definite places. Modern man didn't know where to go because he no longer believed in anything. He had become incapable of simple essential thought, and he was lost like a sailor who navigates with no port in mind, among sirens and monsters without end.

Girei, Urvan and Marta listened with furrowed brows, not quite understanding his disquisition, but the colonel's bewilderment chilled them like a cold wind and left them ill at ease. Urvan either didn't comprehend at all or interpreted things his own way. He translated Gavrila's words into his own idiom and applied them to the *kazak's* present predicament. Nonetheless, almost from a kind of physiological necessity he persisted in hoping.

The defections continued. One day they discovered the priest Stepan had vanished, along with his meager collection of communion vessels. He left a letter in which he invited the whole Terek garrison to follow his example: "There is no more hope for us. All we can do is try to survive. The only thing to do is to surrender our weapons to the patriots of this country, who have every right to defend it." Such was the substance of the letter. Urvan had trouble deciding whether to read it to the men or simply to tell them Stepan had disappeared. He opted for the second course. Maybe the priest was right and desertion was the only viable solution. But he himself couldn't do it, nor could he bring himself to encourage others to. Now with Stepan gone Urvan felt his people were left without even the thin thread of hope based on religion.

Urvan and Gavrila communicated less and less, almost avoided each other. Gavrila preferred to spend time with Girei, trying to explain his doctrine to the youth, who listened and understood as best he could. The colonel spoke of the irrevocable loss of the concept of the happy island, which meant that modern man had to get used to living without that kind of hope. Humanity, he said, had reached a point where more and more often entire populations would be left homeless, chased out of their land and condemned to nomadic life, crucified by cruel circumstances, driven into blind alleys by enemy armies and perpetual war. But most important of all, the very idea of a *patria* had vanished, the order of thinking that created and perpetuated a familiar mental place where men felt secure and validated.

There were no more orders to give to the soldiers of the garrison, nothing left to do but wait for the beginning of the end. Thus Gavrila whiled away the time talking to the boy, who regarded him wide-eyed as the older man expounded his depressing conclusions, hardly relevant to the present situation, and resembling momentary flashes of prophetic utterance which made no more sense than random snippets of a lost text. Girei thought Gavrila was right, that he spoke the Sibylline truth, but it wasn't so much the words that convinced him as the fact that Alda was dead and it was Girei's own comrades who had killed her.

For Girei, Alda's death permeated an infinity of other things, darkened so many aspects of life. Even his former acceptance of Cossack traditions and customs was now eroded and fragmented. When he heard that Ugo had been beaten to death, his own treasured riding crop of braided leather suddenly became hateful to him and he tossed it into a corner and never touched it again.

Sometimes he felt as if from the day Alda died he'd been living in a nightmare in which everything was falling apart. He couldn't get her image out of his mind, that day of Epiphany when she'd come out on the balcony wearing the peasant costume and the necklace of coins on purpose to dazzle him and ignite his ardor. He could still see the glitter of the gold coins, still hear Alda's laugh, as her words rejected his advances while her gestures told him clearly she was his. Sometimes he almost forgot she wasn't still alive — she was too young, too full of life to have anything in common with the idea of death. It seemed quite possible he could again ride his horse into the entryway of her house because she had let him see her in the splendor of her girlish beauty....

He had thought of her as his woman, his in Cossack terms, the way his people defined such things. Many times he'd called her "witch" and "she devil" to himself because she tempted him and provoked him with her looks, her gestures, her words and her refusals. Again and again his mind returned to that day he had ridden into her house, just as if he were going to carry her off on his horse. How he would have loved to take her with him to a hay shed, up there where the *partizany* camped, those same *partizany* he had probably encountered without knowing who they were, and they hadn't touched a hair of his head.

Then, coming to himself, and almost frightened by the intensity of his imagination, he cancelled those dreams as too bold and fabricated another, twice as impossible. He and Alda stood before the priest Stepan on their wedding day. Of course he still perceived women as witches and she devils, as Akmek called them, but he also recognized a virginal integrity in Alda, a quality she expressed in her laughter and showed in her display of the gold necklace. Such purity demanded gentleness, respect and homage, not the usual Cossack brutality. He decided Alda had a double nature and he might have been able to know and experience both sides of her, if only she hadn't been killed.

He didn't understand much about how the war was going in general. Sometimes lately he couldn't even imagine how he, his mother, and his little cousin had ended up so far away from home. He didn't really know why they were fighting on the side of the Germans, whom he detested, and against the partisans, who simply wanted to rid their land of invaders. And he was completely baffled by what he heard about the Georgian battalion, stationed in another valley. Apparently they talked with pride about the great Russian Army, about Moscow and Red Square and Stalin, who was a Georgian like them. But if that was so why were they fighting on the

German side? Then there was Stepan, the priest, an "Old Believer" who had always been antagonistic to the Reds and the Communist state — now he had fled for protection to the partisans who were friends of the Communists. Why would he do that? And what was going on with the Cossack generals? Vlasov, for example. Had he acted out of principle or was he just an astute opportunist? If he detested the Reds why had he become a hero of their army in the defense of Moscow? And then, once he was taken prisoner, did he join the Nazis simply to avoid the concentration camp or did he really believe they would defeat the Bolsheviks? It was all like a huge kettle of boiling confusion, a babel of nonsense so mixed up and contradictory there was no hope of finding a hint of order anywhere. The whole situation was as puzzling and obscure as the colonel's theories.

Gavrila had become a solitary wanderer. He roamed about the village and even beyond it at night, at the risk of becoming the target of a volley of shots from a Sten. Girei took it upon himself to go with him, thereby making sure he came back to the villa at a decent hour because the boy had to go to bed. One night they passed a house with a lighted window.

"They're crazy. There's the blackout," said Girei.

"Even blackouts are useless now."

"Do you mean the war is lost, Colonel?"

Gavrila said nothing, still looking at the lighted window, where a tall female figure wearing a black shawl stood still as a statue. Suddenly she noticed the two Cossacks outside, flung open the window and began to shower them with curses. The colonel recognized Ugo's mother. She wandered about at all hours, and it was well known that every time she encountered a Cossack, or saw one of their military fur hats or a pair of *valenki* she'd begin to hiss a series of invectives, which erupted from the depths of her spirit with volcanic energy. Sometimes her imprecations mingled with the inarticulate moaning of Alda's mother, who often accompanied her and who had completely lost her wits, didn't know what she was doing and stumbled about blindly, with her clothes on backwards and the wild-eyed look of a skittish horse. Every now and then the whining and howling of the two women would echo from one end of the village to the other. They might come up behind an unsuspecting pedestrian at any time with no warning and their notoriety had spread throughout the whole valley. In fact the Cossacks had renamed the village, "Mad Woman Town."

Still the Cossacks retained a degree of respect tinged with fear for the two unfortunates, especially Alda's mother, who seemed hopelessly and permanently deranged. Since they traditionally regarded insanity as a sacred malady, they crossed themselves in superstitious panic if they happened to come face to face with one or both of these "souls marked by God." But at the same time they felt sorry for them because they were like the Cossack mothers and babushkas who had also lost their children in the cruelest possible ways. Nonetheless they couldn't bear their lamentations and curses and fervently wished they'd be struck dumb or that an order would be given to put a bullet between their eyes to end their suffering and let them finally rest in peace.

# The Birth

When Gavrila encountered the two women he too was distressed and his desolation intensified. He still preserved his gentility, his courtesy toward women, his antiquated formality in human relationships, despite the fact that such things had no place in a world turned completely upside down. But he was more and more conscious of himself as a man who had lost all significance. He thought it was now too late for all but one component of life, an aspect that for him had always been inseparable from home and country. Wherever he lived he had always had a woman, and thus even here in Friuli he had found a companion. She was neither Cossack nor Friulan, but a refugee of uncertain nationality and mixed ethnic origin, who spoke Italian with a strong foreign accent. When Marta found out about her she felt reassured on the colonel's account, even though Gavrila seemed to act like someone who has lost everything and doesn't care any more. Once in a while, however, he seemed to evince an attitude dangerously similar to the mentality of the generals and the atamans. He would indicate that perhaps the only solution was resistance to the end in order to save the Cossacks' honor.

"Colonel, I beg you. I don't even want to hear such talk."

"You don't want to hear about honor?"

"Not that way. It would make more sense to talk about duty. And everybody's first duty is to save their own life."

"I don't see how."

"There's always a way, if a person really wants to survive...."

The worse things got, the more Marta needed the intimacy of a family. Sometimes she wished she were pregnant so Urvan would regard the two of them as an authentic family and his first loyalty would be to her. She continued to rack her brains trying to think of an idea for saving her whole tribe. Within the circle of her larger scheme, she worked to trace a smaller private circle around herself and Urvan, a plan based upon the idea of going to America. She had no clear idea how to go about such a project but in the back of her mind, almost unconsciously, she had always felt that "going to America" meant saving oneself, blotting out the past entirely and beginning life all over again.

Hence her principal formula was this: go to America. Would it be possible? She would have to plan very carefully because she knew she tended to have a somewhat mythical approach to reality, but then she was also practical-minded and so she set about looking for methods to reach her goal. The first stage was to make sure Urvan remained in hiding until the war was over and the front had passed through their area. He would have to agree that the *kazak* should be left to his own devices and he himself should be concerned only with the two of them, because they were indeed a family. Salvation would be more likely if they all looked out for themselves. Marta kept repeating her arguments to him, but he neither agreed nor disagreed. He listened attentively, with a gentle frown, then kissed her silently and remained lost in his own gloomy reflections.

"Once the storm is past, we'll sit down and figure out the best way to get to America," said Marta.

"To America?"

"Yes. After all that's happened we can't stay. They'd hate you here in this village. That's why we have to leave and go to America. You can find a job as a typographer over there. It's the only possible solution. At least that's what I think. What do you say?"

He said nothing, but as he listened to the honeyed sweetness of her words he too began to conceive a faint hope.

After the Americans withdrew from their wartime alliances, might they not be able to find a piece of steppe, or something similar, for the surviving ***kazaki***? The word "America" sounded positive, it radiated hope.

By now the partisans were bold enough to come out of their hideouts en masse and descend into the valleys. The instigator of this move was not Vento but the younger, more impatient and arrogant Saetta. He had gotten rid of Bora and Sonia, though no one was sure how or where.... In fact even Vento, who had kept the situation in hand for so many months, had been rudely sidelined. Apparently he was now deprived of all authority and had to submit to Saetta's orders. It was rumored Saetta wanted to liberate all of Carnia before the Allies arrived, that he was politically ambitious and was already planning his post-war career.

Vento, Saetta, Sonia, Bora — people seemed to have nothing else to talk about. Marta was interested in Vento because she had developed a theory about him. In what she heard about his overall strategy and the details of his actions she thought she recognized a style she knew very well. One of the partisans Girei had encountered up in the alpine huts of Madroias had sent his regards to Marta — that partisan might very well have been Vento. During his entire guerrilla adventure Vento had consistently tried to avoid confrontation and bloodshed, just exactly as Urvan and Gavrila had. And she was well acquainted with a certain man who was sick to death of war because he had fought on too many fronts and seen too many dead. He was one of the "poor soldiers" whom she had adopted as her own. Ivos. Hadn't he told her about the terrible fate of the Italian soldiers in Russia? Were Ivos and Vento one and the same? She really thought so and it was a consoling thought because if Ivos were in command there was hope the last stages of the war would not be played out as useless slaughter, and perhaps the storm would pass with minimum damage.

Around this time the partisans captured old Akmek one day when he was out looking for hay for his horse. They held a summary trial and condemned him to death for the murder of Alda and Ugo — the partisans were always completely informed about what happened in the village. When Akmek heard them discussing a grim bloodthirsty individual he didn't recognize himself in the portrait they were depicting and thought they were talking about somebody else. Of course he had been present when Alda and Ugo had died, and had acted the way the others did, but he really didn't quite understand why those two ended up dead. Neither he nor any of his comrades had meant to kill them, at least that's the way it seemed to him. They had died mostly because of mere chance, or evil destiny or possibly because the Cossacks had so much pent up rage from all their various misfortunes.

However, from the moment he was taken prisoner and the trial began, Akmek knew it was all over — death already held him in its grip. He looked at his arms, his legs, thought of his feet in his leather *valenki*, even imagined his face, all as belonging to a corpse. He almost saw his body riddled with bullets then buried in the stony mountain earth. The arc of his life was descending. Man came from the earth and to the earth he would return. His moment had come, he thought with melancholy resignation. He heard the low hoarse chant of destiny, like the song of a drunken *kazak* and all his orthodox pretenses vanished, leaving only the old hopeless Muslim fatalism. "Old Akmek, you're already a corpse," he addressed himself as if he were talking to another person. He prepared to die as one who has lived in the proximity of death for a long time, but at the same time he felt he was being wronged, there was something forced and contrary to nature in the way they were treating him. He wanted to go on living, making love to women, riding horses, hunting partridges and wood grouse, singing the *dumy* and playing the balalaika.

At the appointed time he stared intently at the eyes of the young men who made up the firing squad, but they tried not to look at him. He realized they too felt they were being forced to do something meaningless and against nature. He could sense their shame at having to point their rifles at an old man, and in a flash of intuition he believed all men shared something universal that tended toward peace and the preservation of life. But he didn't know where that universal impulse came from and now he would never be able to find out. It was an eternity too late. As they led him to the wall of the dairy shed he wanted to ask them: "Boys, why kill old Akmek? Why not let him live? Squirrels and moles and badgers are allowed to live? Why not Akmek?" But the young partisans kept their eyes on the ground, determined not to meet his gaze. They knew they were being propelled by something much stronger than they were, a force they couldn't resist despite the fact the war was nearly over, the Allies were approaching and in a few days everything would be decided.

The news that a partisan tribunal had tried and executed Akmek for his crimes was a shocking offense to the Cossacks, especially to Burlak and the others who were particular friends of the old man. Many of their number had been killed in ambush or in combat, which was normal and acceptable. Enemies were expected to kill one another. But the idea that a partisan tribunal should apply its own laws to a Cossack — this was a profound outrage. The law of the partisans was not their law and they denied its jurisdiction. Their faces flushed with rage, they spit on such a law and trampled it under their boots as a shameful and cowardly thing.

Hence the whole garrison was in an uproar and the desire for revenge was intense. They had found Akmek's body on a trail near the village on the day after the execution and the

Cossack women prepared him for burial. They carried him to a meadow near the barracks, laid him out on a canvas tarpaulin on the newly sprouted grass of spring, placed two coins over his eyes and lighted candles at the four corners of the canvas. Men and women filed past him, crossing themselves and whispering that other Cossacks, with or without their horses, had gone off to join those very partisans who had condemned Akmekkhan to death. Things were becoming more senseless and chaotic every day, nothing that happened was either justified or reasonable. Maybe the Good Lord himself didn't understand this bloody mess and had turned his eyes away in disgust, refusing to have anything to do with it.

They wrapped Akmek in a sheet and placed him in a coffin of freshly planed spruce planks that still smelled of resin. Then they filled the coffin with spring flowers taken from the woods or back-yard gardens. Dunaika embroidered the name "Akmek" on a handkerchief and laid it over the old man's face. Then from afar they heard the screams and guttural lamentations of the mothers of Ugo and Alda. Some of the men quickly took measures to prevent the two from coming close enough for anyone to make out what they were saying.

The funeral took place on a clear April day, with the Cossack military band playing the funeral march and someone carrying the icons and relics at the head of the procession. They had all the necessary equipment for a funeral except the priest. But was a funeral without a priest really a funeral? The women wondered aloud and didn't know what to say. Akmek's friends carried the coffin through the village to the cemetery. They were followed by a soldier leading the old man's horse by his rope bridle and although he'd only belonged to Akmek for a few months the animal seemed to understand his master was inside that wooden box because he kept sniffing at it and shaking his head. Akmek's friends, especially the older ones, cursed the partisans, convinced they were Godless Communists just like the Red Army, which had now reached the outskirts of Vienna. They placed a cross inside the coffin at Akmek's feet and fired three volleys as a farewell salute. Then his comrades spoke of his remarkable skill as a hunter, his cleverness, his zest for life, his talent for singing and playing the guitar. Dunaika passed among them with a plate of boiled dried peas — it was too early for fresh ones — offering each person a spoonful. Akmek's old friends kissed him, then closed the coffin and finally lowered it into the grave. Everyone threw a handful of earth over it, then a few of the soldiers filled in the grave and planted a wooden orthodox cross on which they had carved Akmek's name.

Thus, instead of entering a tired stage in which no one was much interested in continuing, the war between partisans and Cossacks flared up more intensely than ever before. Every action on one side provoked a counteraction on the other and one vendetta followed another, often accompanied by shouted insults from soldiers drunk on grappa. The Cossacks couldn't utter the word "*partizany*" without verbal violence: "Damned cursed bastards! A plague on all of them! The devil take them! Death to them all, every last one!"

The war was degenerating into pure savagery. In a nearby valley a young partisan was trampled to death by a Cossack squadron's horses. They rode over his body repeatedly until nothing remained but a bloody mass of mud and pulpy flesh. As for the Terek garrison, they too were out of control. No one paid any attention to either Urvan or Gavrila. They might as well have been voices crying in the wilderness or birds of ill omen that no one heeds. The men were possessed by the demons of revenge, tormented and obsessed to the exclusion of everything else. They gave no more thought to the future, seemed oblivious of the fact that the Russians were now in the suburbs of Berlin and every military action they themselves might take was totally useless.

One evening near the end of April Anita felt her first labor pains. Her baby didn't know this was the worst possible moment to be born — in fact to the baby the situation simply didn't matter. All the residents of the villa were in a state of agitation. Even old Haha, who was deeply fond of Anita and Marta, couldn't stop pacing back and forth from one room to another as if he'd been bitten by a scorpion. Baldo realized something unusual and exciting was in the air and kept getting under everybody's feet as he bounded about not wanting to miss the big event. At one point he startled Dunaika, who had taken charge, and made her drop a basin of hot water, but dog and woman both miraculously escaped being scalded.

"I can't put up with any more of this. Someone's got to get hold of that animal and shut him in!" she shouted.

"All right, all right. I'll do it," said Luca reluctantly.

But he couldn't catch Baldo by himself and had to ask for Girei's help. When they had safely imprisoned the dog in a tiny room he whined and scratched at the door, desperate at missing all the excitement outside as well as inside the villa. They could hear the distant sound of gunfire from rifles, machine guns and all kinds of weapons. What exactly was happening, they wondered. Had the Germans begun their retreat? What was transpiring in the other valleys? Had all the partisans come down and attacked the *kazaki* right in the heart of their villages? More likely the English and Americans were coming....

Girei realized that for all his vaunted pride as an indomitable Cossack male, full of disdain for the weaknesses of women, he couldn't bear to hear Anita's cries of pain. He wished he could run away to the woods or the river, far enough so he wouldn't hear the faintest echo of those screams. He was amazed at this discovery about himself, astonished to find out he was different from what he had thought himself to be.

"You want to come with me?" asked Urvan, noticing how distressed he was.

"Where are you going?"

"To bring back the midwife. It's almost time."

Girei was happy to get away. It was now completely dark and as they walked through the deserted village they could see distant flashes of artillery fire, and would have given anything to know what was going on in the whole territory of Carnia where the destiny of the *kazak* was finally playing itself out. Urvan thought of his Cossack brothers scattered throughout those mountain valleys, certain each one of them was touched by the same quiver of intuition he himself felt, the knowledge they were on the threshold of fatal and final events. The terrified midwife didn't want to leave her house and it took some time for Urvan and Girei to reassure her and persuade her that at least for now their village was safe and nothing drastic was going to happen. She screwed up her courage, swallowed a shot of grappa, and followed them to the villa. The whole house resounded with Anita's wild screams — the poor girl was protesting with all her strength. But Marta and the babushka were unconcerned, and Urvan was equally calm. He still remembered his wife's cries during her labor twenty years before. Women were destined to give birth in pain — it was a law of nature sanctioned by the sacred texts.

True, he felt sorry for Anita, but he accepted this cruel law and wasn't unduly upset. Gavrila was nowhere in evidence. Urvan thought he might have gone to the command barracks to oversee the garrison, but he wasn't really sure because the colonel had lately been so remote, so strangely detached from all that was happening. Perhaps he had gone to visit his inscrutable refugee woman, whom some said was a war widow, hoping she'd help him forget the frenzy of these horrible days. But he couldn't find out now because things here were happening too fast and he had other obligations. Dunaika and the midwife were in a jolly mood, chattering to each other in satisfaction because the birth was progressing exactly as it should, with no sign of complications. But Urvan was uneasy, feeling he had not done all he could and decided on impulse to go and get the Cossack doctor. The doctor was really a veterinarian, but he was extremely knowledgeable, took care of people as well as animals and had helped usher a number of little *kazaki* into this world. With such a plan in mind Urvan went out once more into that night of distant battles, perhaps thinking he'd learn its secrets. He could still hear rifle, machine gun and mortar fire, now joined by the menacing drone of fighter planes. His heart contracted with a suffocating pang of fear. Fear of the unknown. Then from a distance he noticed a Cossack from the garrison bargaining with a local peasant, trying to sell his horse. No doubt he was ready to take less than the animal was worth just to be free to go off and surrender to the partisans.

Urvan neither approached nor said anything. He had no more will to give orders or advice. The shipwreck was already happening and it only seemed fair that every man should follow his own instinct, find his own way, whether it led to salvation or disaster. If the comparison with a ship was valid they were at the point when it was "every man for himself" and the shrewdest had already bailed out. But if the ship was already sinking into the dark sea the whole Cossack nation was going down with it and the wreck had begun months or even years ago. Urvan was seized with a fit of trembling as he considered the disaster facing the Cossack army, the hopeless uncertainty of their future. It was time to tell them to go, but go where? What could he say?

As he entered the villa on his return with the veterinarian he heard the newborn baby's cries. He smiled. When he asked

Dunaika's permission to go into Anita's room and wish her well, he got a scolding from the babushka. She shook her finger at him and made him take off his muddy *valenki*. She was actually scolding him simply because he was a man and it was men who made women pregnant and brought this pain upon them. "Men!" she thought resentfully, recalling her own husband and the labor pains she herself had endured so many years before.

At any rate the doctor and Urvan were ultimately allowed into Anita's room. They found her in bed, propped up against a mountain of pillows, smiling in radiant satisfaction because she was more than ever the center of attention. Sooner or later everyone came by to see the baby, a boy with a ruddy complexion, who mostly slept, not caring a bit about what was happening in the world around him, but woke up predictably five times a day to nurse vigorously. Anita didn't have much in the way of intelligence or initiative, and people easily took advantage of her, but at least she was blessed with robust health. Two days after giving birth her face showed no sign of the pain endured and her breasts literally overflowed with milk, so the baby could eat his fill.

Determined the new mother should have what she needed, Marta intensified her search for food from the peasants. The results were good, as some crops were beginning to mature and since the war was definitely winding down, the peasants, as astute as ever, were beginning to breathe a sigh of relief and open up their ultimate reserves.

Despite all their troubles the atmosphere in the household was cheerful, contagiously cheerful. Even Baldo bounded about the rooms, wagging his tail and inviting people to play. He acted as if the recent happy event authorized him to show off and act the clown to his heart's content.

Urvan spent as much time as possible at the villa, and when he had to go out he did so with regret. The mood outside was different and there was no telling what might happen. He hated to go to the barracks or into the village, because he inevitably heard bad news. The ***kazak*** had now lost all feeling for law and had reverted to the violence and cruelty of his nomadic ancestors who wandered the steppes of central Asia. For example, when one young partisan had been unable to resist coming down to the village to visit his girl friend, a number of Cossacks had surprised him and when he told them the purpose of his visit, they seized him and cut off his testicles amid shouts of ribald laughter.

Within himself Urvan rebelled against all this, tormented by a sullen angry urge to abandon the Cossacks to their own destiny. Burlak had replaced him in their affections, let Burlak take the responsibility. His own mission was finished. They hadn't let him carry it to its logical conclusion anyhow. So perhaps Marta was right after all? Didn't he have a right to withdraw, to go into hiding until the last spasms of war were stilled? Yes, Marta's idea was a good one — go seek out Vento in the mountains and surrender to him. Once you gave yourself up and laid down your arms, the nightmare was almost over. Maybe that's what Gavrila had done, since he seemed to have disappeared. But then, perhaps he had gone into hiding with his woman, thrown his uniform of a Cossack colonel into the weeds, repudiated his past and set about preparing once again to flee to France....

Urvan decided to look for him, to talk to him, try to discuss the subject at least indirectly. He wasn't sure where the woman lived so he asked Girei to accompany him. When he knocked on the door no one answered. It was locked. "So that's how it is, Gavrila. You've gone off without a word," thought Urvan, as he tried unsuccessfully to find a way to open the door. They discovered an unshuttered window at the back of the house and Urvan called Gavrila's name several times. The only answer he got was the barking of dogs, invisible now because night was coming on. He was on the point of giving up when a sudden doubt seized him.

They went back to the rear of the house, broke the window glass, and at the risk of being mistaken for thieves and exposed to a volley of bullets whizzing past their ears, they went inside, Urvan first, then Girei. Urvan wanted at least to make sure the house was unoccupied. All the windows except the one by which they had entered were shuttered and it was completely dark, but a strange inhibition prevented Urvan from turning on the electric light. They groped their way blindly from room to room with the help of an occasional glimmer of moonlight, which came in as Urvan opened some of the shutters. He knocked on each door he came to, then entered and found every room in perfect order. Nothing was missing and there was no sign of a hasty departure.

When he reached the bedroom he knocked again, waited for a response, then very slowly opened the door. There on the bed lay Gavrila and the unknown woman, carefully dressed and composed. Gavrila wore his colonel's uniform, minus cap and *valenki*, the woman was clad in a black dress, looking as elegant as usual and lacking only shoes. They might have been sleeping: their eyes were closed, their faces serene, they betrayed no sign of any suffering. Besides there wasn't the slightest trace of blood anywhere, no froth around their mouths nor any other evidence of poison. The enigmatic woman of uncertain origin must have known the secret of a substance that killed without pain, inducing a peaceful permanent sleep. There was no doubt — there in her dresser drawers or among the jars and boxes of makeup and powder she had kept the lethal powder handy.

Urvan took the full measure of his solitude and the heavy responsibility that weighed upon his shoulders. He knew exactly what he had to do, even though he wasn't sure how to go about it. He bid a silent goodbye to Gavrila and his woman, who had chosen to take their leave without noise and commotion, discreetly avoiding the final convulsions of the war.

"What should we do?" whispered Girei.

"Leave them here."

"Leave them here? Not bury them?"

"No, our people mustn't know they're dead. The villagers will find them and bury them, once all this is over."

Girei didn't agree. He firmly believed the dead must be buried because otherwise their souls would never rest in peace, would wander about through the darkness in extreme distress, frightening the living. But he didn't argue since Urvan was the garrison commander and he should know and decide what to do in every situation. Girei felt he himself had inexplicably matured since Alda's death — every day that had passed from that moment on had the value of a year for him. Suddenly, looking up through the window toward the mountains, he saw a fire.

"It's the huts of Madroias," he said.

"So it is," said Urvan. "Shall we go see what's happening?"

"All right."

"It may be very dangerous...."

Girei shrugged. Along the trail, where the grass was beginning to grow, they met refugees on their way down from the alpine village, pushing handcarts piled with hastily salvaged household effects, and leading a cow or pig. Urvan and Girei watched without a word and the shepherds and peasants of the *Salvadi's* little settlement looked back at them in unmitigated desolation, continuing on their way without the slightest pause.

The two Cossacks knew these were the eternal results of war and invasion. They had already seen such things in Poland, in the Balkans, and in other places they remembered only vaguely, as in a dream. Moreover the refugees from that remote village reminded them of their own arrival here, after wandering across much of Europe in an endless pilgrimage. They reflected that what they were seeing was as nothing compared to things happening elsewhere, for instance in the Torre valley where many towns had been burned, where the Germans had actually set fire to some houses with the people still inside. Despite all their troubles the Terek Cossacks' valley was an oasis of peace compared to the rest of the region.

Urvan saw his people as both victims and invaders. They suffered the consequences of the war, but they also increased its destruction. They had come from far away with their horses and wagons and now they had helped provoke the exodus of more refugees who didn't know where to go. Destiny had thrown invaders and invaded together in the same predicament.

Urvan and Girei didn't arrive in Madroias until about eight o'clock in the evening, but there was moonlight so they could survey the scene. The houses were truncated, roofs burned and caved in, walls black with soot. Here and there dying flames flickered where the remains of a beam, a plank, or a door still burned. On the garden path behind his house they found the *Salvadi* lying face down on the grass, wearing his military overcoat and his heavy boots. In the muddy weeds nearby lay the *kubanka* of white lambskin, identical to those worn by the atamans and Cossack princes. Urvan was certain now that the *Salvadi* and Vento had been defeated by Saetta and Burlak, who were triumphantly squeezing out the last dregs of the bitter essence of war — those two had the relentless demons of war in their very blood. All around Urvan and Girei heaps of coals still glowed, fanned by the wind blowing through the blackened openings that had once been windows and doors.

However, not all the inhabitants of Madroias had fled. Several stood quietly by, looking at the desolation. There were even a few searching for boards they could use for a makeshift roof to keep out the rain and cold, and here and there someone began pounding nails with a hammer. There were also several children. Two were picking up planks from a pile at the back of a farmyard, and carrying one at a time to their father, who was standing on a roof. Another little boy, much younger, wasn't working, but happily swinging back and forth on a rope still dangling intact from a beam over a threshing floor. As the rope went back and forth the boy rhythmically moved in and out of the glow of the fire. Nearby stood two tiny girls looking on with an air of sleepy astonishment.

Urvan and Girei sat down on a low wall, crumbling and blackened. The youth found himself suddenly thinking of the song about the Cossack boy who had returned to his village and found his house burned and his father and mother killed by the Russians, the boy who had sat down under a tree and concluded the song with the sad refrain, *"Ahi, dai, dalalai!"* It was Akmekkhan who had taught him that ballad. But this time the village was Friulan and those who had destroyed it were Cossacks, but Girei decided that didn't matter because the ballad applied to all wars, all recurring disasters, which happened in every climate everywhere on earth. People had fled their ruined villages thousands of times in the past and the same thing would happen thousands of times in the future. Nothing had changed since that old song was written, and the same events would repeat themselves over and over because war was eternal and would go on creating refugees and nomads pushing carts full of household goods along dusty roads somewhere or other forever. In fact they themselves would soon have to load up their wagons and set off for who knows where. Now that Gavrila was dead his words came back to Girei, his theory that modern man would never have a homeland to return to, that destiny was destroying one homeland after another, that all men were now condemned to eternal nomadism, dragging the broken-down wagon of their hopes after them. Those ideas had sounded bizarre and unfounded before but now he was beginning to understand the depth of the colonel's meaning.

Returning to their own village they came upon the Cossacks who had burned Madroias. They were sullen, silent and ill at ease. Among them was Burlak, who had led the expedition. For a long time he had brooded over the *Salvadi's* complicity with the partisans and had cherished a desire to get even. Now that the whole question was irrelevant and the war was already lost, now he'd had his revenge. The old man was lying up there on the path, his body full of lead and his white *kubanka* hadn't saved him this time.

Girei and Urvan went back to the barracks. Total confusion prevailed and no one knew what to do next. The telephones weren't working but it was known that the generals and the atamans, after having called repeatedly for resistance to the last man in the name of the Cossacks' honor, now had changed their minds and were leaving it up to each separate garrison to decide their own fate. There were rumors that elsewhere the Cossacks were surrendering en masse to the partisans. Urvan and those close to him judged these rumors false on the grounds that after what had happened they would know they'd all be executed like Akmek. Mass surrender was no longer a plausible option.

Every soldier was now suddenly aware of himself as an invader and destroyer. The men were generally disoriented, and floundered about burdened by a sense of imminent disaster, like birds whose wings have somehow been covered with sticky mud. Only now were they beginning to recognize and assess a situation they'd always kept hidden from themselves behind some strange sort of curtain. Wine, song, festivities, military actions, their own physical vitality, or self-delusion — all these things had reinforced their refusal to consider their plight realistically and in depth. Perhaps it was a sign of the mysterious vitality of a people who didn't want to die and had to cry out to the world their will to go on living. But it wouldn't work anymore. The chips were down. It was obvious they didn't know which way to turn from the alternatives they spoke of: some proposed surrendering to the Allies, who were now very close, and others were preparing to set off for Austria, or rather, toward annihilation because they wouldn't be able to remain in Austria and they couldn't go back to Russia. But since Austria was closer to their steppes and the land of the Black Earth it seemed charged with an enigmatic attraction, an invisible power to save. So they decided to retreat toward Austria.

Now Marta, her face drawn by worry, kept pleading even harder for Urvan to leave the others to their own fate and make up his mind to stay with her. The idea of separation was so wrenchingly painful to both they couldn't bear even to think of it.

"Urvan, you've got to decide. You're no longer obligated to them. They can join the Cossacks from other garrisons. You can't help them anyway."

"Alas, you're right about that...."

"Then, you accept my idea? I know so many hiding places. And it will only be a matter of a few days. Until the storm passes, that's all. Everyone knows you've done the impossible to keep worse things from happening. Nobody would dare touch a hair of your head."

"Well, maybe."

"You see what I mean? And besides where would you want to take your men? To face the Russians? Better to stay here and wait for the Allies."

"You're probably right."

"Stay here Urvan. It's the only thing left to do. You can never go back to the Terek steppe!"

"About that you are terribly, sadly, right...."

"Stay. You'll work things out. We'll stay in hiding for a while. Then things will get back to normal...."

Urvan kissed her, smiled tenderly, answered in uncertain evasive phrases. The force of Marta's attraction was immense, the waves of sympathy from her sweet body were nearly impossible to resist. Perhaps her surroundings joined with her to urge him to stay — the villa, the little town, the other valleys, the whole region. Here at least he had found a place to distract and mitigate his *kazak* desperation. Yes, based on what little he knew of the village, Marta and this place were one entity and he almost couldn't tell where the attractions of the woman ended and those of the land began. With its rivers and its green mountains, its people, and especially its women, in some ways so like Cossack girls and babushkas, Friuli itself combined with the essence of Marta's persuasive appeal.

What if he really were to stay? What if he and she had children of their own, established a new family together? Started life over in a new world after the endless misfortunes of the war? Would this be possible? Could he detach his own future from the fate of the *kazak*?

Marta couldn't stand the thought of losing Urvan. She had lost Caleb, Arturo, and Ivos, but her feelings for Urvan were different, more tenacious and intense. Their lives had been more tightly interwoven because they had been together longer and time had turned him into a husband figure on whom she felt she could rely for the rest of her life.

But even as she pleaded with him, or expressed her passionate love with looks or gestures, Marta knew these cruel times made it impossible to plan a private or personal future. Again she thought about America. But then her mind returned to Anita, the baby, Haha and Signora Esther, who might return, though it seemed she'd vanished into another world. No,

America wouldn't do. She couldn't go that far away. The only solution was to keep Urvan here, to hide him for a while until people's resentment died down and then to find some sort of work for him there in the village. She kept repeating her proposals to Urvan and although he didn't say yes, he didn't say no either and he seemed to agree. Never before had they made love so passionately. Despite their own innumerable problems and the chaos all around them, they threw themselves into each other's arms like two lovers reunited after years of forced separation.

One night Urvan quietly got up and she, barely awake, asked him where he was going.

"Just to the kitchen to get a drink. I'm thirsty."

"Try not to make any noise so as not to wake up the others," said Marta, turning over and settling down in bed. When her regular breathing assured Urvan she was indeed asleep, he thought, "No, I won't wake anyone, not even you." He quietly picked up his clothes and went out in the hall to get dressed. Girei, Dunaika and little Luca were already waiting in the courtyard, according to instructions. They had followed Urvan's orders in every detail and their escape was so far working like a meticulously thought-out strategic plan. Unfortunately Luca had a slight bronchitis and a touch of fever, but they had to leave without delay. They had made secret arrangements with all the other Cossack garrisons throughout the valleys of Carnia. Urvan could almost feel on his lips the final yearning kiss not given to Marta for fear of awakening her and arousing her suspicions. Out in the courtyard he, Girei and Luca, in turn, hugged the dog and Baldo wagged his tail and whimpered softly as if he too understood he mustn't make noise and wake anyone.

Only one person in the villa noticed the Cossacks' departure into the darkness — Haha, of course, who slept as lightly as a hare. He got up and went to a window, opened the shutters with no more noise than a woodworm or a moth would make, and silent as a shadow stood watching the little group set off in the cool night air. Luca turned to look back, saw him and waved. Haha waved back.

They went to the peasants' barn, a good distance from the villa, hitched the horses to the wagons and started off in the penetrating dampness, taking the narrow road to the village. Here there was major animation. In the piazza and the main street a procession was forming, made up of wagons, horses, and the remaining Cossacks from the garrison. The vehicles had been readied the night before in careful secrecy. The Cossacks had loaded them with everything they could get that might assure the survival of men and horses for at least a few days. Soon the soldiers holding the bridles gave the signal to the horses, the usual, "Trr, trr!"

The long column began to move, as quietly as possible, but the villagers had heard and were watching from their windows. So it was really true, the Cossacks were leaving — certainly the Germans would do the same and the war was over.... Someone expressed a wish that the partisans would come down and wait for the Cossacks in some narrow valley and massacre them all. A mysterious intuition had awakened Alda's mother from her delirium, as well as Ugo's mother, and the two of them began to shower the fugitives with curses and threats interwoven with their general moaning and lamentations.

The long column wound its way down the valley road. The only sounds were the horses' hooves, the squeaking of the wagon wheels, the rhythmic step of the men on foot — there wasn't room for them all in the wagons. Someone had taken a live goat or sheep, others led cows, all in the hope of having food along the way. Where were they going? They were heading for the Gorto valley and then after a long march through other valleys they would reach the Monte Croce pass and from there take the route that would finally cross the frontier into Austria. After that? After that, nobody knew. Urvan's information didn't go any further. It was remarkable that he'd been able to find out as much as he had.

This was then the retreat. Retreating was perfectly natural. All defeated armies retreated before advancing enemy forces. Their plan was clearly outlined up to the moment they arrived in Austria. But at that point they would face the unknown. Among the dozens of peoples who had fought in the war, or had declared war at the last minute against an already collapsing German regime, only the Cossacks had no place to return to. In the damp cold April night they felt inexpressibly weary of war and desperately discouraged at having to take up a nomadic life once more.

Now that the retreat had begun and the interminable column of wagons had begun to move, sorrow accompanied every Cossack like an invisible companion who walked beside him along with the surviving horses. The men marched with heads down, holding their rifles balanced against their chests as if to rest their tired arms. The women and children rode in the wagons. Urvan and the wiser more prudent men kept glancing toward the mountains or the sky, whence the gravest threats might come. At every unusual noise they started, then shouldered their rifles, ready to resist even in these desperate conditions. There was still a bit of snow on the summits and on one side of the road the river roared like a flood. That roar was to become the persistent background sound of the retreat.

A strong breeze was blowing through the valley and the weather soon turned bad. The temperature suddenly plunged and the wind began to sting the Cossacks' faces with tiny frozen drops. Winter seemed to have returned unexpectedly to the mountains and it too had taken on the guise of a treacherous enemy. Fear, as usual, lent force to the rumors already circulating. In the valleys to the north, it was said, partisans in search of a vendetta had already come down to cut off the retreat and engage the Cossacks in combat.

Urvan thought about the archaic system of reducing noise to a minimum so no one would hear the passing of the horde, for instance binding the horses' hooves with rags. But they'd have to do something about the wagon wheels as well and at this point such complicated measures were almost impossible.

It was bitter cold and seemed to be getting even colder. Urvan was immersed in gloomy thoughts. At least he found some comfort in the image of the sleeping Marta, who might not yet be aware of his absence. He remembered the bodies of Gavrila and the widow, left to the mercy of the villagers, but one dominating anxiety overruled all other worries — where were they going and what would become of them? There must be some room for hope somewhere. It simply wasn't logical that an entire people should disappear, and they had to end up with some place to live. But he couldn't shake off a dark clinging pessimism. Even so he wondered if sooner or later a few of them might return to the shores of the Terek, maybe the innocent children. Luca, however, as if things weren't bad enough, had taken a chill and his bronchitis was worse. Dunaika had wrapped him in a blanket but she could tell his fever was rising.

At the confluence with the Gorto Valley the Terek Cossacks met and joined another retreating column. The entire Cossack people, no longer daring to call themselves an army, were anxiously gathering together in an instinctive effort to survive. Every one of them had felt a stirring like a flutter of wings, an arcane urge to count the survivors, to cling to one another and try to banish the returning cold, the fear, the desperation. It was the same instinct that binds together a herd of bison on the North American plains, or elephants in the African forests, a need for the group to unite in the face of whatever dangers might lie ahead. It was the survivors' instinct.

Various nightmare possibilities haunted them. The first and most terrifying was that Saetta had sworn to exterminate the Cossacks before they got one foot across the border, not to let one Cossack escape alive from this territory they had claimed to conquer. Nobody spoke of Vento anymore. He must have left the partisan brigades and now he too was probably a fugitive, a refugee, like Bora and Sonia before him, and maybe he was wandering those mountains like them, looking for a way to save himself. But these were only rumors, there were always rumors. Certainty had become an extremely rare and almost unknown phenomenon.

The second nightmare, less immediate but even more frightening, was the possibility of accidentally running into the Red Army, which had now occupied Prague and Vienna. But what was the exact plan for this retreat? Where were they going? No one had any precise information. Someone whispered about a certain German general, Kaltenbrünner, who had a plan to withdraw into the Alps and resist. The Alps would become another Gothic line, and there among the snows, the rocks and the glaciers they would fight to the last man. The plan was to be named "Alpine Fortress." No one who heard this talk made any comment. People simply shook their heads in silence. But they all knew, from acquaintance with centuries of warfare, that such a plan was pure madness.

There was one other rumor, a report that Vlasov and Krasnov had met in a Friulan village and given the order for the retreat to Austria. What then? Nothing, apparently. There was no need to think about what should happen next. They should stop there and reinforce their hopes, because never in history had an entire people been eliminated.

Anyhow all the rumors agreed on at least one point: they should unite and proceed together toward Austria. After that they'd have to wait and see. In fact all the valleys throughout Carnia: Gorto, Incaroio, Valcaldo, San Canzano, Timau — all were filled with long lines of Cossacks converging in the direction of the Monte Croce pass, like streams in flood flowing toward an outlet to a major river.

The rain kept falling and the horses and wagons moved forward with constant effort on roads deep in mud. Now and then a few perfunctory volleys of gunfire came from the woods and the men fired back with similar listlessness. Then someone reported that Colonel Zulukize's battalion of Georgians had fallen into partisan hands. It turned out not to be true. Instead the Georgians, who had never missed a chance to boast about the Russian army, Red Square and the great Stalin, and who apparently had allied themselves with the Cossacks only as an absurd joke, had simply gone over in a block to the partisan side.

As the rumors continued to circulate the *kazak* continued his trek toward the pass. The only certainty for now was the long march ahead through cold and rain and mud. Sometimes violent storms broke out and the frigid rain showed signs of turning to sleet. The ominous roar of the swollen rivers paralleling the road was never far away. Luca's fever showed no sign of diminishing and Dunaika, Girei and Urvan grew more and more worried, but they didn't know what else to do except keep the child wrapped up in blankets inside the wagon. But the concern for Luca did not reach beyond his relatives and friends because everybody else had problems too and the entire horizon for these people consisted of nothing but troubles and anguish.

At a certain point along the road they were joined by the Circassians, who were coming from the Torre Valley. An almost palpable cloud of bloody iniquity seemed to hang over them. People whispered that when the partisans had come down to negotiate their surrender the Circassians had fallen upon them, cut their throats and collected the blood in buckets. Then they had blown up the barracks where the atrocities were committed in the hope no one would ever find out. But the news spread immediately and now everyone regarded the Circassians as if they were ogres and cannibals. Urvan found himself looking at them with Marta's eyes, an indication, he thought, that though she had remained at the villa sleeping peacefully, she was following him like a shadow.

All the Cossacks, whether guilty or innocent, murderers or not — all were tired, anxious, wet to the skin as well as cold and hungry. They stopped at intervals, made camp, lighted fires with great difficulty and cooked their miserable provisions. They ate with guns handy, always afraid of hearing the sudden rattle of automatic weapons in unseen partisan hands.

The column was growing larger all the time. By the time they had reached the Gorto Valley it was estimated they were at least thirty thousand, but now they were no longer organized according to where they came from, but simply all mixed up together. There were men from the valleys of the Terek, the Don, the Donets, the Kuban, the Ussuri, the Amur and the Ural rivers, from the Caucasus mountains and from as far away as Circassia and Turkestan. An entire people was on the march, or rather representatives of numerous different peoples, all of whom, however, belonged to a single nation with a common origin.

The latest war news reached them. This war that had seemed so endless, with no hope of any solution, this interminable nightmare from which they thought they'd never awaken — this conflict, like all others before it, was not, after all, going to last forever, and had indeed reached the last stages before the collapse. One after another the German garrisons were surrendering to the partisans or the avant garde of the Allied forces. They had lost all their arrogance and they too were wrapped in a cloud of bewilderment, now that the iron discipline to which they had so long been accustomed had simply dissolved. No more shiny boots, impeccably shaved cheeks, short perfectly cropped military haircuts. Now, like the Cossacks, they were stumbling along in disorder, deprived of all certainty, involved in the same tragedy. Urvan's men watched them with bitter satisfaction. At last the Germans were discovering how it felt to be frightened and disoriented, desiring only to be free of the trappings of war and to go home to their bombed cities and ruined countryside.

The wind and rain kept increasing. Heavy gusts rattled the leather covers over the wagons. Nevertheless a powerful momentum was propelling the Cossacks toward Austria. Perhaps it was based on the tattered remnants of an old attraction once perceived as destiny. "*Österreich, Österreich!*" Yes it sounded good, while the word "Friuli" now belonged to the past, the worn out past devoid of hope. The woods and fields of *Österreich* awaited them, but for what purpose they didn't know. Maybe, in their situation, all they could expect was to leave one place for another, like any other nomadic people.

The horses and wagons transporting the funds of the *Feldbank* passed by Urvan. He had heard that the strongboxes were to be buried with their contents beyond the frontier. Not in Italy but in *Österreich* because the frontier beckoned with some sort of magic. When the rain ceased the column stopped and made camp once more. They ate roast mutton, sang in a subdued tone some of the ballads from the Volga and the Terek valleys, as well as the *dumy* about death and defeat. Then they lay down on the straw inside the wagons and tried to sleep for a while, all of them completely exhausted. Luca's fever continued to rise and to sap his strength like an evil spell.

At dawn they set off again toward the end of the valley, following after the thousands of Cossacks who had already exited to cross the Valcalda Valley and reach Timau. Here the dreaded partisans appeared with an offer to negotiate the surrender of the fugitives. A Cossack major spent a long time discussing terms for giving up their arms, but then when the partisans came forward he gave the order to open fire. The patriots cried out and fled. It pained Urvan to see this kind of treachery continue. Giving one's word had lost all meaning — the possibility of any kind of trust now belonged to the past. He recalled that the whole adventure of the Cossack Army had begun with a betrayal, Domanov's complicity in the murder of his commander, and now it was ending with the treacherous act of this obscure garrison commander. The day of Cossack honor was certainly over.

The partisans decided to attack the next day. Perhaps their offer to accept a surrender had also been a trick, and Saetta might have cherished a plan to drench the valley in Cossack blood. During the night, plagued by insomnia, the Cossacks talked among themselves and tended to exaggerate the number and strength of the partisan troops. Nonetheless it was evident they would not be able to cross into *Österreich* without a fight.

The person least concerned about all this was Dunaika, who was desperately worried about Luca. The mere touch of a finger on his cheek was enough to reveal he was burning up with fever. He no longer spoke coherently or opened his eyes, only rambled in delirium, his breathing ever more labored. The veterinarian said the infection now involved the lungs as well as the bronchial tubes. He was dangerously ill and they had no means to treat him. Dunaika blamed herself. Why hadn't she stayed at the villa with Luca? Why hadn't she kept him there with her, even though it would have meant permanent separation from her people?

The next day began with a hellish blast of gunfire from the partisans on the heights, a veritable barrage followed by an attack by Saetta's men. A bitter house to house battle ensued like Stalingrad on a small scale, another of the thousands of mini-Stalingrads that had marked the course of the war. There were heavy casualties on both sides and it was immediately obvious that Saetta's decision to block the Cossack retreat was going to cost many human lives. The Cossacks fired from the windows of houses and the partisans replied with hand grenades, hoping to stun their enemies, then blow them to bits inside the buildings.

Burlak, along with a group of his most faithful followers, had decided to resist to the end. He was no peasant from the Terek valley — he was a Circassian born to fight. The Circassians had always been warriors and "surrender" was the most ignominious word in their language. He was sure he had arrived at the end of his earthly adventure and his thoughts now turned entirely on images of final destruction. He and his comrades began softly chanting traditional ballads about war and death. He knew his wild pleasures had ended forever and death was near for himself and his friends. Even before the war, in fact from the time he was old enough to fight, the image of his own death had kept him company in a confused subliminal way. He had always known he would die in battle. Now the moment had come, and nothing could save him from the *partizany* he had hated from the first day he set foot in this territory. He had hated them because they were the enemy and you had to hate and kill your enemies or be killed by them. He knew he would die of multiple wounds, because that morning he had smelled the corpse within himself. It was to be a day when death reaped a bountiful harvest in the ranks of the opposing armies. He heard the gunfire, the explosion of grenades, the noises of this final decisive battle both partisans and Cossacks had postponed a dozen times, but always known would ultimately take place. Burlak knew nothing of what was happening elsewhere. As the quintessential Circassian, he would fight his personal battle, the battle he had always glimpsed as a waiting shadow ahead, knowing he'd had no choice but to die fighting. He couldn't turn back. All this was perfectly clear.

But he would sell his life at a high price and leave this obscure village with a lasting image of who the Circassians were and what they could do. He would get his revenge for the deaths of so many of his friends. Thus he fought ferociously with the courage and determination of one who knew this battle would be his last.

Burlak had a vague notion that the world was dominated by violence, plunder and war and you had to deal with these things. He fired his rifle without respite and each time he saw an enemy fall he felt a surge of joy. The battle, like all battles, was bloody and chaotic and it was impossible to tell which side was winning. But the triumphant partisans were as thick as flies around Burlak's little pocket of resistance.

"Surrender! You don't have a chance!" they shouted.

"A plague on all of you!" came the reply.

For Burlak his little band was like those elite platoons of Janissaries once pledged to defend the Turkish sultan to the death. If he managed to hold out until the end perhaps the other Cossacks might get through the partisan lines and reach *Österreich.* With this in mind he decided to try to attract as many partisans as possible in the hope that his comrades might seize the opportunity to escape. He had been wounded several times but not yet in any vital organ, and even though he was bleeding profusely he was so excited he scarcely felt the pain and went on fighting. He had plenty of ammunition because he had built up his supplies over a period of months in anticipation of just this sort of confrontation. But now he seemed to be driven only by fate. He had always believed a man would know when his hour had come. He and his faithful followers, these same men who had burned Madroias before they left the garrison, were facing their ultimate destiny.

# The Gorges of Plöckenpass

The battle was dying down. Most of the Cossacks had gotten through and by evening were moving on, but they had left many dead behind. The houses in the town were riddled with bullets, their timbers splintered, their rooms filled with dead. Wounded men, crying out in several languages, tried to drag themselves out in the open on terrain made slippery with blood.

Burlak sensed that the living were gone and only the dead and dying remained. A clear line of demarcation now separated life from death and he was here on this side of that line surrounded by corpses sprawled in all sorts of distorted or indecent postures. The gunfire was gradually becoming fainter and less frequent, the mortars and artillery had fallen silent, and there were no more explosions of hand grenades. Burlak was cold and he realized it was not only from the temperature but because he had lost so much blood from multiple wounds. He heard the partisans' shouts of victory and oddly enough he didn't hate them any more. They had won, but what difference did it make? It was only fate and this time fate had been on their side. Fate ruled the world and everything happened only because it was written in the great book of Necessity, a much richer text than even the book of the Prophet.

He was growing weaker and he realized there were no more living men around him. All the wounded were now dead. Without realizing it he was inwardly chanting the *dumy* dedicated to the dying. The Cossacks had a song for every moment in life. He thought of Alda's death, the brutal beating that had killed Ugo, the partisan who had bled to death after being castrated. Those memories vaguely bothered him now because some part of him, now grown terribly weak, regretted such acts. He was leaning against the remains of a wall knocked down by artillery fire. He was ready to set off on his last voyage, his last migration, entirely alone, as he had always been. He was going far far away but without moving an inch. He didn't know where he was going, because no man knew what lay on the other side, and all the stories about it were only fairy tales....

After Burlak's death the partisans also felt surfeited with massacres and death, even though they had been provoked and tricked. Despite Saetta's plans and his orders, they were intensely weary of fighting, wounding and killing. It looked as if Vento's strategy was coming back into favor, although Vento was no longer present among them. They no longer cared about stopping the Cossacks' retreat. Let them go, let them follow their own destiny.

The long march of the *kazak* continued, as did the wind and rain, mercilessly beating against the leather wagon covers. Now and then they heard a single shot behind them but the noise of battle was stilled.

When they entered the Timau Valley Urvan, Girei and Dunaika saw scattered bodies of Cossack soldiers as well as dead horses. Local people had already begun to eviscerate the animals because their hunger had turned them into scavengers, like hyenas. Getting their hands on a big chunk of horsemeat meant surviving for a few more days and maybe until the last crazy blast of the war had passed. There was no time for the Cossacks to bury the dead, at most only a few minutes to take their coats, their *valenki*, their *kubanki*, whatever might be useful for the living. Dunaika moved about holding Luca constantly in her arms, wrapped in a blanket, as if it were dangerous to leave him in the wagon where death might steal him away more easily. But her efforts were in vain. At a certain point the babushka realized Luca was no longer hot.

"The fever has gone down," she said to Urvan and Girei.

The two of them touched and examined the little boy at length.

"The fever has gone down because he is dead," said Urvan.

"What are you saying, Captain? You're mad!"

"He's right, Mother. Luca is cold because he is dead," said Girei.

"No! He's not dead! I don't believe it! It's just his fever has left him!"

"Give him to me, Dunaika. I'll take him to someone and ask them to bury him in a cemetery."

"No, he's not dead! He can't be dead. It's not true...."

The babushka wouldn't let go of the boy and kept talking to him in a low voice to awaken him. But Luca neither moved nor opened his eyes and finally she was convinced. She began to sob weakly, but still didn't want to relinquish her hold on his body, wouldn't even put him in the wagon because she wanted to spare him the jolts of the road.

At the entrance to the Monte Croce pass the immense caravan stopped once more to rest both men and horses. Again they lighted campfires to dry their clothes somewhat and warm themselves. Girei took Luca, still wrapped in the blanket, and gave him to a local woman to bury. He carved Luca's name into a fir plank so his grave would not be nameless. Urvan took some silver coins out of his pocket and offered them to the woman.

"Even a funeral costs something," he said.

"All right, I'll take the money," said the woman, looking down so as not to meet his eyes.

They soon set off again, up the winding road through the pass. Along the way they passed places where houses and border posts had been blown up.

It was early May but still very cold and before long a snowstorm came up. The wounded in the wagons moaned in pain or rambled in feverish delirium. On either side of the road patrols on horseback kept watch for partisan ambushes, but the partisans were no longer interested in attacking that caravan of desperate survivors. As they climbed higher the road was flanked on both sides by vast forests of spruce and fir. During the night a mounted column in white alpine uniforms passed them — General von Pannwitz's Slavic troops. Civilian hostages the German divisions had decided not to shoot came rapidly down the road in the opposite direction. A universal weariness prevailed all along that road, a yearning to let everything go, to shake off all the murderous rules of war. The darkness was filled with the sound of the squeaking wagon wheels, of heavy uniforms and overcoats brushing against each other. Because the snow melted as soon as it touched the ground, the road was deep in mud and horses slipped and wagons tended to get stuck.

They arrived at the border in the middle of the night and a sudden shout went up: "*Österreich! Österreich!*" They seemed to be within reach of a mystical salvation, now that they had crossed the frontier. They stopped for several hours, then set off again at dawn. They could see the gray snow-covered Noric Alps of southern Austria. Yes it certainly was *Österreich* but this did not yet mean peace, rest and safety, and it was nothing even faintly resembling their homeland, which was still hopelessly far away. In fact Urvan's anxiety was only increased by the knowledge they were actually moving toward the Red Army. All day long they continued their march uninterrupted. Toward evening it began to snow again and they found themselves facing another night fit only for wolves and smugglers. The wind whistled from every direction, creating blinding snow squalls.

Under the snow the road was covered with ice, just at the point where the Plöckenpass was flanked by steep ravines.

The horses picked their way along with extreme caution but the odds were against them. Suddenly one of the smaller wagons skidded toward the edge of the ravine and despite the horse's desperate efforts, bracing his hooves and stiffening his legs, he couldn't hold his ground. It was Dunaika's wagon. The Cossacks closest to her shouted the alarm and Urvan and Girei rushed to help but they were too late. The runaway wagon and the helpless horse went faster and faster down the slope until they were precipitated into a free fall and after the woman's anguished scream from the bottom of the gorge there was silence.

Urvan and Girei were struck dumb. Now the two of them were the only ones left of the little group with shared memories of their temporary Friulan home, watched over by the benevolent figure of Marta. They looked at each other in silence while Dunaika's friends wept and wailed. Eventually the mourners calmed down, consoled by the realization that Dunaika at least would no longer have to suffer the pain of the retreat and the uncertainty of the future. They moved on through the night, carefully and slowly, because they were still in the zone of steep ravines. "Christ have mercy on us!" whispered the women, beating their breasts. They felt they were following their own path to Calvary, having only passed the beginning stages despite the length of the journey behind them.

The men were able to march at a good pace because they had grown up on the steppe and the taiga — they were used to hardship and their endurance was considerable. But their desire for a respite, their longing to stop and set up felt yurts and sleep on a pile of straw, was becoming obsessive.

The woods around them were dark and cold and the drip of rain and melting snow increased the discomfort. From the rear guard came the news that Krasnov had given the order to surrender to the Allies. A wave of relief spread through the caravan, as the wagons continued to slip and slide on the frozen road. Then suddenly they heard a distant roar of fighter planes. "On no! Not here! Not in the midst of these gorges!" thought Urvan. He gave the command to set the wagon brakes and he himself leaped to grab the brake handle of a wagon belonging to a Cossack Muslim widow with three children. She had lost her husband in the battle back in the Gorto valley. The planes were upon them in an instant, strafing and dropping fragmentation bombs. The terrified horses broke into a mad gallop, dragging the braked wagons behind them and capsized wagons, horses and people plunged into the cursed ravines of the Plöckenpass. Instinctively Girei looked toward Urvan, just in time to see him go down among the screams of the other victims, still holding on to the widow's wagon brake. The planes made several passes over the column and when their cruel carousel was ended Girei realized he was one of very few survivors of the entire Terek garrison. The road and the ravines were full of dead. He sat down on a boulder at a turn in the road and held his head in his hands like a man in a trance.

A short distance beyond the ravines the Cossack Army did surrender to the English. They were obliged to make camp at Peggetz, along the Drava River, which was swollen from the spring thaw and recent rains. There the Cossacks set up felt yurts and constructed makeshift buildings. The few surviving horses went down to the river to drink. A cheerful mood settled over the survivors because all the remaining members of the Cossack Army were here together. It was a vast reunion of their people. Around campfires the men exchanged stories of wartime adventures as they roasted venison from roe deer they had taken in the Austrian woods.

The weather was mild, the Drava high, the mountains still topped with snow. The storytelling flourished, especially as a way to remember and honor the innumerable dead left behind by the now decimated and exhausted *kazak* people.

Girei also had much to say about his own losses, his mother and Urvan who had perished in the ravines of Plöckenpass, Luca, who had died of bronchial pneumonia and whose death Dunaika had refused to accept, Gavrila, the aristocrat who had lived in France for so many years and had chosen to die with his companion of unknown nationality. The old men talked about the disappointing war between Whites and Reds, the war they had dreamed of beginning again, with disastrous results.

The encampment was huge, holding tens of thousands. An atavistic spirit permeated the yurts and shacks, as if the *kazak* people had been rejuvenated by hundreds of years. Despite all they had been through and despite their greatly reduced numbers, they were buoyed up by a certain optimism because the English had taken no measures to disarm them. Everyone puzzled over the question of where they might be sent after that quarantine subject to unknown conditions. There would certainly be some place for them in the vast British Empire. They would be perfectly happy at the end of the earth as long as there was a river, a steppe, a savannah, so they could pretend they had returned home.

But then some sinister signs began to appear. The Cossack General Staff, in other words all the generals and atamans, whom the people had followed blindly for years and almost transformed into mythic figures: Krasnov, Shkuro, Polunin, Naumenko — or those tainted with ambiguity like Vlasov or Domanov — all of them were taken away to a hotel in Lienz called "Zum goldenen Fisch." The English said they had done this to honor these distinguished figures and spare them the humiliation of living in uncomfortable camp conditions they weren't used to. But an old Tartar whispered to Girei that the English had cleverly deprived them of all their leaders and without their atamans the Cossack people were like a huge body without a head and wouldn't know how to make the most minimal decision.

Then the English requisitioned all the surviving horses and the men felt this deprivation as a deep wound that tore their manly honor to pieces. But that wasn't all. Next the armored strongboxes of the *Feldbank* were confiscated and at that a subtle fear began to take possession of the people in the camp. They surreptitiously studied their captors' faces trying to discover some signs of their intentions. What were the English planning? Why were they little by little depriving their prisoners of everything they valued?

One day the British commander-in-chief, General Alexander, had his chauffeur drive him around the periphery of camp in his jeep. The Cossacks watched with intense curiosity loaded with unspoken questions but the general maintained a cold glassy stare, as if he didn't even see them. And yet throughout the camp the *kazak* persisted in repeating the fable invented to overcome his fear: "They're going to send us to Australia. There's plenty of land down there. What they need is strong arms...."

Australia was extremely far away, but what did that matter? The *kazak* was a nomad by his very nature. Distance didn't scare him — he'd be content just to have someplace where he could survive. Then at the end of May, Alexander demanded they hand over all their weapons on the official pretext that disputes might break out in the camp and lead to bloodshed. After one more unmistakably ominous indication, the Cossacks had no residual doubts about their fate. The English general ordered all the remaining officers in camp onto trucks and drove them off with the excuse they were invited to participate in a conference on questions dealing with the *kazak* people.

The officers looked at one another, overcome by unequivocal suspicion. As they rode away in the trucks through the brilliantly green valley of the Drava they saw long lines of British armored vehicles in the meadows on either side of the road. Before they reached their destination some of the officers smelled the sharp odor of betrayal and threw themselves off the moving trucks. Some, unhurt, fled into the woods, while others sustained injuries or even fractured their skulls on the asphalt. Those who were left were driven to Spittal — there was of course no conference. Instead there were prisons, where the officers were confined to await being handed over to the Russians. The English had known of this plan all along because it had been drawn up at Yalta by the three Great Powers in response to Stalin's precise demand that all Cossacks should be turned over to the Soviets. The English and Americans had not hesitated to agree.

Thus the betrayal intuited in so many sinister signs was obvious to all and desperation took possession of those left in the camp. A madness comparable to the behavior of Alda's and Ugo's mothers was in the air, as if the two deranged women had followed them invisibly and hung over them with all their curses and maledictions.

The officers were taken to Judenburg to be turned over to the Soviets. Many tried to run away and were mowed down by British machine gun fire. The ***kazak*** was now mortally afraid. He knew his fate as well as he knew the palm of his hand. Summary trials awaited him, after which he would stand with his arms bound behind his back and face a firing squad. Or perhaps those judged less guilty would be sent off to forced labor camps in the remote corners of Siberia, where they would live like convicts, these men who had been born free as the wind to gallop over the limitless spaces of the steppe. Although they lived each day in fear and desperation, they continued to grasp at the flimsiest of hopes. They elected Kruma Polunin as a new camp ataman to replace those so treacherously taken away. Then they sent letters pleading for help to the king of England, but those letters ran aground in the offices of the British General Staff and never reached the sovereign.

On the first of June, after the priest had celebrated mass in the camp, the announcement was made. Everyone had known it was coming and everyone had stubbornly refused to believe it — all the Cossacks were to be forcibly repatriated. The news provoked instant panic as it spread throughout the camp like a sudden terror that turns a herd of bristly wild pigs into a maddened stampede. There were crazed attempts to flee en masse, quickly halted by the rain of British machine-gun fire. Then hundreds of *kazaki* turned to a different mode of escape, the only one left. Howling like wounded beasts they threw themselves into the frigid waters of the flooding Drava. It was an act of collective suicide almost without historical precedent. Only in ancient times could possibly comparable events be found, for instance after the conquests of Carthage, Numanzia or Jerusalem.

The piercing screams were followed by a tragic silence. Days later, much farther downstream, the river began to give up the bodies of the drowned victims. The impassive English used long poles to pull the cadavers toward shore, then piled them up like wet logs on the banks. The Drava was full of floating gray bodies, swollen like wineskins. But that was not the only kind of death the *kazak* invented for himself. When the English had demanded they surrender their weapons many a soldier who had managed to conceal a pistol under a clump of sod or a pile of leaves now used it to shoot himself in the head. Every morning the first light of dawn revealed dozens or, as time wore on, even hundreds of suicides in the makeshift wooden barracks of the camp. People hung themselves by belts, by twine braided together to make it stronger, by sacks torn into strips or any other material they could adapt to their purpose.

A few, even up to the night before they were to be turned over to the Russians, managed to flee into the underbrush of the nearby woods. Girei was among them. A surge of vitality, an imperious urge to survive had ignited his spirit, and he refused either to die or surrender to the Soviets. His desperate will to live drove him to flight. He hid for an entire day in a thicket of hazelnuts and alders, only a few hundred metres from the camp, shivering from the cold and the fear of being recaptured, hungry and alone. Then that night he set off toward the mountains like a hunted wolf.

It was not long, however, before he began to relax. He knew the English were unswerving in their purpose, but unlike the Germans they did not pursue fugitives with relentless determination, nor did they make use of trained Alsatian dogs to track them. They had formally respected the terms the Yalta agreement and if a few Cossacks escaped, as far as they were concerned, let them go and good luck to them. The important thing for Girei was not to show himself and above all to stay clear of patrols. During his first days in hiding he lived on berries, wild mushrooms, unripe fruits and milk he sucked directly from the udders of goats sought out in the barns of the most isolated farms. He adapted rapidly to this kind of life in harmony with nature, exploiting whatever resources might keep him alive. He quickly learned what plants and fruits were edible, deciding to live this way as long as possible until the dangers threatening him disappeared entirely.

He began to come out of his temporary shelters, alpine huts and haysheds, only when he was sure the surrender of the last remaining Cossacks was already a fading memory in the minds of the victors. Then he soon learned that he had understanding allies among the Austrians, whether peasants, artisans, or woodcutters. They had heard about the suicides in the camp and knew something of the long odyssey of the *kazak* people. Thus an aura of sympathy surrounded the small number of fugitives scattered among the mountains. The Austrians invited them into their houses, fed them, provided them with civilian clothes, kept them for long periods of time on their farms, giving them work and food as they would their own compatriots. The war was definitely over here too and people were trying to forget the wounds it had left and to let them heal with time. These were simple people with an instinctive horror of anything that suggested persecution: concentration camps, manhunts, pursuit of fugitives. It was the opposite kind of behavior that appealed to them.

Thus Girei stayed in turn with peasants and woodcutters, finding warm refuges that reminded him of Marta's villa. He worked alongside the people who lived in these mountains and the hill country, always keeping the question of his future in mind. He was cautious and reflective as he tried to figure out what might be the best course to follow. At first, remembering Marta's conversations with Urvan, he began to think about America. He dreamed of going as far away as possible from the place where his *kazak* people had met such a tragic fate. Now he knew he'd always be a man without a country and he wanted to take advantage of that situation in the most economically advantageous way, leaving this continent behind and cutting off all ties with the past. But it would take patience. He'd have to wait until the bitterness left by the war had dissipated and things went back to normal, with ordinary people living ordinary lives.

America, America.... That was where desperate people went to start a new life — Jews who had survived the death camps, displaced persons, people who had lost everything, maybe even their own identity, and needed some kind of myth to believe in. The most important thing was to avoid the occupation forces, especially the English. After that he'd have to figure out how to get to America.

Girei had changed a great deal. The knowledge that he could depend only upon himself, that he was one of the few free survivors of an act of genocide, had galvanized his intellect and rendered him extraordinarily prudent. He had learned to control himself, to be patient, to plan carefully and specifically, to adapt himself to a multitude of different possibilities.

Then, as the months passed, his American project gradually faded and was replaced by nostalgia for Marta's house. Gradually he came to understand it was there he wanted to return, for now the villa was the closest thing he had to a home. The people he had known there were like a family, and might indeed take the place of a family. Thus once he decided he could make the trip with minimal risk, he crossed the border and following little traveled paths, made his way to Marta's house. He was welcomed with surprise and joy and great curiosity. When he told them what had happened to the Cossacks no one seemed to know much about it. All they had heard were vague and sometimes conflicting rumors. As he described the tragic fate of the *kazak* they could almost hear the implicit refrain: *"Ahi, dai, dalalai!"* This was now his sorrowful chant, full of misfortune and grief. All his sad story needed was a popular poet to put it into verse and song and dedicate it to his people so they would never forget their past.

Everyone in the villa had imagined something of the sort had befallen the Cossacks, yet they were strongly affected by Girei's story. In turn Girei was struck by the fact that Marta had cut her magnificent rust-colored hair. It was now only a few inches long, but it was already beginning to curl as it always had. It made her look younger and even more attractive.

Marta mulled over the thoughts she had lived with for such a long time. When Urvan had gone away in the middle of the night, managing not to wake her, for days and days she had gone about with an image fixed in her mind — an image of Urvan leading the survivors of his garrison toward a homeland that didn't exist. She had lingered with desolation on the idea of a people marching onward toward annihilation, toward death and deportation, victims of a cruel destiny that forbade them to return home. She thought about Urvan and the vastness of his Slavic soul, haunted by nostalgia and melancholy. Now that the fear and violence were behind her, her memories came crowding back. The tragedies of the war, both near and far away, seemed to hover like heavy wind-borne clouds over herself and the people around her.

She was more than happy about Girei's return. As the only living Cossack in the whole valley, perhaps in all of Carnia, he brought a certain richness to her caravansary of survivors, whose human warmth and melancholy happiness interwoven with the demands of daily living had finally freed the villa from the nightmare of war. Marta felt as if her soul had been frozen into another dimension and now at least three-fourths of it had thawed out and started to live again. Life had begun anew and regained its savor, and a homey air of quiet domesticity pervaded the villa.

Here at the villa Girei occasionally encountered someone he had met once before up in the alpine hamlet of Madroias, the man who had asked him to carry a message to Marta. It was Ivos, or rather Vento, because they were one and the same. Thus this famous partisan commander had returned to the village where Marta lived. He refused categorically to be addressed as Vento and preferred not even to talk about the war and the partisan campaign. He was mortally tired of such things and desperately in need of peace, even in thought and speech. Indeed he would have wished his dreams to banish all but peaceful images, but that wasn't possible and it was in his dreams that the war often came back to trouble his nights. At present he was managing the Heshel farm, which by a strange twist of fate now belonged to Marta, who had never owned anything nor even wanted to. When the

Heshels had acquired the farm and the villa they had put them in Marta's name to circumvent the racial laws and avoid other complications. Now that the Heshels were all dead the property was a posthumous gift to Marta. But in a sense it really wasn't a gift at all because from the moment Caleb fell in love with her the whole family had adopted Marta as one of their own and when Caleb died she was the only child they had left.

Little by little, as time passed, the terrible wounds of war, which everyone had thought were incurable, began to heal. Vento kept hoping time would slowly chase away the ghosts that still haunted him. He sought solace in the silence of the woods and fields.

It was late autumn and as the days grew shorter the household was busy preparing for the long mountain winter. There were still many shortages and they had to be sparing with their provisions, although Marta no longer felt obligated to sell any of the Heshels' family legacy of gold and silver. Now, however, no one would have questioned her about such transactions.

Vento and Girei went off to the woods to gather chestnuts and came back with bulging rucksacks. Then they roasted them in a pan full of holes or peeled them and boiled them in a cauldron. The gypsy Haha, not wanting to be in the way, walked along the river to collect the wood washed up earlier when the water was high, then brought it back home to saw, split and stack neatly for the winter.

Anita's little son, whom she had named Arturo, now kept her occupied all day long. She bathed the baby, patted and powdered him, changed his clothes three times in a row, trying to decide which outfit he liked best. She liked to imagine he was some sort of prince in disguise, whose true identity was known only to her. Although she didn't say the words aloud, she seemed to be telling him: "Ah, my pretty young one, only I know who you really are!" Actually, however, even Anita didn't know who he was. Only one thing was certain, according to Marta — he was the son of a soldier of the disbanded Italian army. After the armistice many young men had fled to the mountains in order to escape either fighting alongside the Germans or being sent to a concentration camp. Surely Arturo's father had no idea he had a child, and where that soldier was and what had happened to him were anybody's guess.

As she reflected on Anita, observing her closely, Marta found herself remembering her former perception of the Heshels' villa as a shelter or refuge for people who had lost their homes. It was still true. Actually the villa had sustained almost no damage as the front passed. Some of the many machine gun volleys had chipped and scratched an external wall here and there, but that was hardly serious. And Ivos had already repaired them. Ivos, whom people persisted in calling Vento, was one of those men who knew all sorts of trades. Thus he could manage masonry perfectly well even though he was a professional surveyor. Busy as he was with the farm, he still found time to direct repair work on houses damaged by gunfire, or to draw up plans for new construction to replace those that had burned.

He was outdoors working all day, but almost every evening he came up to the villa, in fact he simply couldn't stay away very long. Girei wondered why Marta had cut her hair. It was rapidly growing back but for the moment she looked as if she were wearing a curly goat fleece on her head.

"I like it this way," she replied to his question.

"I don't believe you," he said.

"Well, you're right. So don't believe me. But I'm not going to tell you."

"I'll find out anyway."

Marta smiled and shrugged her shoulders, but Girei didn't give up his investigation. When he asked Anita she started to cry, mumbled something, then wouldn't talk anymore. It was Ivos who finally told him the whole story.

As soon as the war was over, after the partisans had come down from the mountains and the English and Americans had installed their occupation forces, Marta was accused of collaboration with the enemy. There was no lack of evidence, she had been the lover of a Cossack officer, a member of an invading army allied with the Germans. Marta had the impulse to tell the whole story, including her own particular secrets, but she feared no one would understand. It was too complicated, too subtle and too personal and the investigating authorities were not given to making refined distinctions or picking up nuances. If she looked at the facts realistically and objectively, she had to admit they had a strong case. As a result, she and other women who had gone to bed with the invaders were taken to the assembly hall of the barracks once used by the Cossacks. And there they were tried.

All were sentenced to having their heads shaved. A barber who had been a partisan did the job in a few minutes. The young girls wept, protested, and tried to insist they'd been slandered, inventing all sorts of false alibis, but there was no way they could avoid their punishment. Two robust female partisans, used to carrying guns up in the mountains, held them still, one by one, in the "execution" chair and the barber busied himself with cheerful diligence. As soon as they were released from the iron grip of their captors the girls rushed to look in a mirror, which the judges had cruelly made available. There before their horrified gaze the mirror gave back an image of ridiculous bald heads like those of wigless mannequins in clothing-store windows.

Marta did not rebel, told no lies, invented no false alibis, in fact said nothing. She awaited her turn with patience, inwardly smiling at the strange ironies life sometimes produces. At the very moment her turn came up, Ivos rushed into the room, despite the efforts of those in charge to keep him out.

"I'm Vento, Vento! You all know who I am!"

"But you have no authority here."

"What do I care. I'm here to talk to whoever organized this spectacle."

"You aren't allowed to interfere in this matter...."

Vento exploded in anger. He grabbed one of the partisans in attendance at this supposed court of justice, and shoved him several meters aside.

"Are you ready to listen to me?" he asked.

"All right. All right. What have you got to say. Now that we're a democracy."

Vento explained Marta's complicated story, how she had tried to save Aaron and Esther, how she had been Caleb's woman, then Arturo's — and he had gone missing in Russia — then his own. Yes, she had also been the lover of Urvan, the captain who had desperately tried to avoid a confrontation between Cossacks and partisans, and worked as hard as he could to keep his people within the law and prevent them from resorting to violence, as long as anyone would listen to him.

"All that may well be true. But she's still a collaborator," replied the partisans.

"She helped anti-Fascist activists, deserters, exhausted soldiers sent to die at the front."

"It's possible to make mistakes even in that context."

"You don't understand anything about this woman. You don't know her. But I do, I know all about her...."

Her self-appointed judges shrugged. Marta had gone to bed with a Cossack, an enemy and an invader. For them that was enough. In the meantime the atmosphere in the room was beginning to change. The other girls and young women, who had been willing lovers of Fascists and Germans, hoping their side would win, were realizing that Marta's case was distinctly different from their own, although they wouldn't have been able to explain exactly why.... On further consideration of the fact that Marta had taken in an old gypsy wanted by the Germans, had cared for a wounded partisan, had tried to hide and save Jews, the judges found themselves suddenly less opinionated. The possibility they might be about to commit a judicial error, so to speak, made them un-comfortable. At this point the barber took matters into his own hands.

"While you're thinking about it, I'll go ahead with the others."

"Fine, very good. You take care of the others and we'll re-examine this case," said the judges.

Vento withdrew to a corner of the hall with the other partisans and set about explaining Marta's actions at length and in detail. Every once in a while the so-called judges would glance in her direction, as if they hoped to discover the answer to the mystery this woman represented to them. They were actually making their way clumsily toward a decision to reconsider the case, moved by the sympathy Marta always elicited, when, turning once more to look at her they were astonished. She had seated herself in one of the chairs in front of the mirror and begun to cut her own splendid long hair with a pair of scissors picked up from the barber's table. Vento ran over to stop her.

"Marta, what are you doing?" he asked.

"You can see perfectly well what I'm doing."

"Marta, you're crazy. Can't you see they're getting ready to reverse their decision?"

"I don't care what they decide. I once read about a place somewhere in the world where widows cut their hair as a sign of mourning. I've been widowed three times. Urvan is dead. Arturo is dead. Caleb is dead..."

"But Marta...."

He didn't know how to finish the sentence. Everyone in the room was watching Marta — the judges, the barber, the other young women, those still unshorn, as well as those already shorn and wearing a kerchief on their heads. In fact the girls had almost stopped crying. All were staring hypnotized at Marta. Nobody quite understood what was happening before their eyes, but they knew it was something anomalous and it touched and disturbed them. Nobody said a word, while Marta continued her task, as serenely absorbed as if she were arranging her hair to please a waiting young man. She gave herself a complete trim, leaving only an inch, more or less. When she finished Vento was the first to notice she still looked pretty. Actually her gesture of self-mutilation had made her even more attractive. "Marta, Marta," he thought to himself.

Then he said, " Come with me. You've nothing more to do here...."

"Yes, I'll come with you now...."

They returned to the house without speaking. Vento was thinking Marta had cut her hair because Urvan had chosen to go off and die with his own people, and she would never see him again, and her dream of going to America would forever remain just a dream. Her sacrifice of her hair was a sort of religious ritual. After all, when nuns took the habit they cut their hair, didn't they?

Girei, once he learned the truth about Marta's hair, was strangely moved. He decided this evening was a time for story telling and confidences and added his own contribution by describing the final stages of the Cossack Army's adventures. His mind still dwelt on his people — decimated, deported, dispersed — on the many who had chosen death in the frigid waters of the Drava or had hung themselves from the beams of the barracks. He pondered the fate of those consigned to the Russians, wondering what had become of them.

He felt much older than his years because of the burden of all those experiences. He was one of the tiniest minority of surviving *kazaki*, the small number who had fled and were now probably dispersed on more than one continent. He and those others were the only ones who would remember the Cossack tragedy and the grandiose project that had begun it, the dream that had ended dashed to the ground and trampled underfoot. He was acutely conscious of his identity as a survivor, a lonely individual marooned in infinite solitude....

Now that he had come back to stay, he might have been able to think realistically about becoming Alda's fiancé, if only she were still alive. His mind returned to Gavrila's mysterious theories expounded to him in those last days, and he felt as if he were at last beginning to grasp the subtle elusive truth they contained, even though he couldn't actually define it. At least he now knew what the colonel had meant when he kept repeating that modern man had no *patria*, no homeland. It was certainly true for the Cossacks. And for the gypsies. It had been true for the Jews for two or three thousand years. A glance at old Haha's face, at his habitual lost and bewildered expression, was enough to convince anyone he had no home anymore. Perhaps the home he once had was nothing but the gravelly bank of a stream, or the dreary outskirts of various cities where his people camped in their caravans. But now even that was gone and his tribe and their caravans had been dispersed and destroyed. Even this most minimal home had been taken away.

In a world turned upside down by war how many other populations might there be who had been driven out of their homes, whose numbers had been decimated, whose return was now blocked by newly erected boundaries and barriers, or political systems and conditions so changed as to be hopelessly confusing? Those people were also doomed to wander in unknown foreign lands where they knew no one and no one knew them. In Girei's still boyish and somewhat primitive mind these reflections were new and unusual, not really like what he had always felt and thought about before.

Vento found Girei an interim job as a manual laborer, but meanwhile took the time to teach him the skills of masonry and bricklaying. Girei, completely unfamiliar with this kind of work, was quick to discover new potentials in himself. He not only learned the trade, he developed a taste for work. Since he still felt the need for a guide or mentor, Vento became his role model and he worked along with him.

Nonetheless Girei continued to dwell on the implications of the things Gavrila had told him, to reflect ever more deeply, more subtly on those ideas. Ultimately he found himself pondering questions even more difficult and obscure. It seemed to him that perhaps as a result of the war as well as other more perplexing causes, something intangible had insinuated itself into the mind of contemporary men. This unknown factor prevented people from retrieving their identity, from finding themselves as they once had been, rediscovering their former authentic thoughts and feelings. Maybe an entire world, a world once known and loved, had been dissolved by the war. Maybe all people were now exiles, refugees, citizens without a country, even setting aside the vicissitudes of the war. It was their very soul that had no home, no familiar place, no certainties, no consoling dimensions, and thus they didn't know where to go or what to hold on to.

But after a few months, having entered into the routine of work, he wasn't even sure he would want to go back to his *stanitsa* on the banks of the Terek. This didn't mean Friuli had now become his home so much as it meant he had accepted the loss of the lands on the Terek. He would have to be content with his substitute home here at the villa, in the village, the valley, the woods and the mountains, because this was all he was going to get. There wasn't anything else. Perhaps what he had yearned for was a dream, an expression of the profound nostalgia so typical of Russians and Cossacks. Now and then he still played his guitar and sang the *dumy* for his friends and for himself. But he realized his homeland wasn't there in the *dumy*, just the dream and the desire. There was no more *patria*.

He felt like an exile and a foreigner, but he decided so was everybody else, for one reason or another. Nobody could find the way back to the beloved old home. The character in the fairy tale who had scattered crumbs on the path found the birds had eaten them all, and whoever scattered colored pebbles with the same intent would find they had been washed away by the rain. Girei was becoming a young man whose thoughts wandered off in strange directions. Vento, Marta, Anita and little Arturo were his friends. He liked to talk to them, and enjoyed their company at mealtimes when he shared their bread or polenta. But sometimes he needed to be alone and let his mind wander through his memories, like a fox exploring the woods at night.

His speech was becoming more Italianized. He was happy to talk to local people, providing they didn't insist on bringing up his past. But he greatly preferred to converse with Vento and Marta. He felt the two of them possessed something he desperately needed — wisdom. Vento did not seek out the company of other ex-partisans because he realized they had begun to invent shining imaginary countries adorned with all sorts of wonders he no longer believed in. They were dreaming of a new golden age, wanted to change everything, sweep away all the old injustices, as if it were up to them to change the world and build a new society as easily as you'd build a new house.

Vento had no patience for this sort of talk and quietly opted out. Like Girei he felt he was no longer the same man he had been before the war. War ages people, especially reflective people. Only Marta seemed still young, despite her thirty-four years, but then she was different, always had been. She seemed to have an inexhaustible hidden reserve of youth. It was as if time had not touched her. But Vento felt much older. His beard and hair were tinged with gray and he thought of his partisan adventure as something that might as well have happened twenty years before. If by some aberrant destiny he should be called back to such duties, he wouldn't have been able to find the strength to carry them out. It would be as if Robin Hood had to return to Sherwood Forest after an absence of twenty years. Sometimes he felt as if his responsibilities as a partisan commander, the decisions he had made, and the deaths of so many friends still hung over him. He had developed a habit of speaking slowly and his conversation was always imbued with a quiet melancholy.

When he thought about it he was astonished that during those months in the mountains he had shown a talent for guerrilla warfare he never knew he possessed. Throughout all the villages and valleys of Carnia, and even further away, his name was legendary. People still talked about his incredibly clever and daring tactics, his extraordinary subterfuges and tricks that caught the enemy off guard. He had invented a partisan campaign out of nothing, no experience, no previous knowledge, and yet he had succeeded far better than Bora or Saetta. He didn't know why. Maybe it had something to do with being a person who tended to think things through, who was not likely to act out of passion, who wasn't motivated by burning hatred.

But he remembered the dead willingly, for instance Bora and Sonia, whose bones had been discovered in a dry stream bed up in the mountains at the end of summer when all the snow had melted. People had wondered for a long time what had happened to them, making up all kinds of hypotheses. The truth was the two of them had been liquidated by their own comrades for dissension about how the war should be fought.

Once in a while Vento went back to his own village down in the foothills but he really couldn't live without Marta. When he wasn't working he would sit with a half-spent cigar in his mouth, quiet and sober in everything he did, conversation, eating a meal, even the way he moved. He needed nothing, never asked for anything from anyone. But now and then he would look over at Marta and she would quickly turn away because she knew the meaning of that look. Vento couldn't help but think of himself as a sort of stray, a solitary reject, because he could see further than others did and couldn't participate in their hopes for the future.

He was absolutely certain that sooner or later there would be another war, other guerrillas or partisans would take refuge in woods or mountains somewhere in the world, and other villages would be destroyed by flamethrowers or doused and burned with cans of gasoline. There would be other firing squads and other vendettas, and dogs would bark in the night on the trail of a fugitive from an invading army. He knew in his heart that all the things he had known and suffered would recur, here or in some other place, because men carried war in their bellies like an endemic sickness that periodically rekindled a fever to kill and burn and destroy. His task and Marta's, in fact the task of anyone who didn't want a new war was a labor of Sisyphus — always doomed to begin again as soon as it seemed to be finished.

Still it was possible he, Marta, Haha and Girei might form a little island of common sense and wisdom in a world full of confusion and useless uproar. Marta, however, continued to be haunted by the melancholy shadows of the past.

"But I'm here. Now. I'm alive," he said to her. "What we had between us we can have again...."

"Yes. Yes, I think so...."

"Well then, let's get together. What are we waiting for. We've already wasted so much time...."

"Yes, you're right. We're aren't that young anymore."

She started talking about marriage, but with a certain enigmatic indecision, as if she still had too many unfinished matters pending. She often mentioned going back to her village in the upper valley of the Natisone River. It had been many years since she'd been there, but for one reason or another she kept putting it off.

One day she heard on the radio that according to terms of the peace negotiations her village was now on the other side of the border, had in fact been ceded. It was nothing but a tiny hamlet, a few little houses built of river gravel, but nonetheless she was saddened to lose it, to know she couldn't just go back there when she wanted to. Now it seemed fearfully far away in time and space. Maybe she'd never return again to visit the graves of her relatives.

As she continued to think things over she was gradually coming closer to accepting Vento's proposal when something happened, which was so bizarre it resembled a wartime legend. According to village rumors, a strange vagabond had been sighted in the old abandoned mill beside the river, the very place where Marta had come upon Ivos, lost and wounded in the leg. For all that anyone knew he might as well have come from the moon. Grass and straw clung to his long straggly beard and tangled gray hair — he certainly didn't concern himself with his appearance, and was obviously unacquainted with barbers and combs. Instead his only interest seemed to be rendering his refuge habitable and organizing his life in that place.

Everyone assumed he'd stay a few days and then move on, as so many other victims of the war had done. But it wasn't likely he was a veteran because if so he had returned very very late, outside any reasonable time frame, when all the legacies of the war had been signed and sealed, so to speak. Some men had returned, some had died in combat, others in the *Lager*, but by now everyone's fate was known. There was no room for surprises or unfinished business.

Thus the adults more or less ignored the bearded vagabond, but the children were curious and often went to see him, sometimes with an excuse, like asking him to sharpen their pocket knives because he had a grindstone. Then they'd stay and watch him, look around his habitation and ask him questions. He would answer in monosyllables, most often a yes or no, as if he'd forgotten how to say anything else, talk being useless as far as his way of life was concerned. Boys and girls would go inside his house and poke around, examining everything they found. He saw no harm in their curiosity and they didn't bother him so he let them do as they pleased. After a while, however, the older villagers began to pay more attention to him, because he seemed somehow familiar — there was something about his face and his manner that made them feel as if they should know him. Maybe he was a native of their valley who had lost his memory in the war, and survived as a confused relic of his former self, an awkward stuttering scarecrow who didn't even know who he was. He aroused compassion as well as curiosity and his neighbors began quietly to come to his aid.

The members of Marta's household also took an interest. Who could he be? Someone began to go through the list of the missing from nearby villages, those who nobody thought would ever return now. Maybe the war had indeed robbed him of his memory and his capacity for rational thought, but had left him with some vestige of consciousness or instinct to guide him back here, like a migratory bird that always returns to the same place and no one knows quite how. Marta began to watch him from a distance, following his movements, his gestures. He didn't know anyone was watching and thus his behavior was perfectly natural, and as she watched, Marta sensed a kind of flutter of excitement and her interest increased. Where had he come from and what paths had he followed in his wanderings? What had he been doing since the end of the war?... He never smiled, never looked at anyone or talked to anyone, apart from his monosyllabic responses to the children. If anyone stopped him and asked him questions he avoided their eyes, and moved away, possessed with an obvious desire to flee.

One day Anita came home in a state of extreme agitation, hardly able to put two words together. She was holding her baby tightly against her breast, as if she'd had a terrible fright and was trying to draw comfort and courage from the little boy.

"I...I met that...man," she said to Marta.

"He scared you? He said something bad to you?"

"No, no...he ran away...."

"Then why are you all upset?"

"I recognized him. He's Arturo...my brother...."

"What are you saying Anita? You're imagining things. What...."

"No, I think it's really him, even though he's terribly changed...he looks like a...like a beggar."

Marta couldn't believe it and yet at the same time she herself was shaken and disturbed. Good God, was it possible? She'd have to have a closer look at him, seek him out, question him, but try not to scare him or arouse his suspicion. Somehow they'd have to get him to cut all that hair and trim or shave his beard so he'd look a little more like he used to.... Marta tried to go about her housework but she couldn't keep her attention on anything until the mystery was solved. She went out, accompanied by Haha, Girei and Anita and they headed for the old mill. She knocked on the door, but there was no answer. Her heart was beating so hard she had to stop and catch her breath for a moment. Then she knocked again, softly. She waited, then tried the door. It was open, but inside, although the interior of the mill had been skillfully converted to a living space, no one was there. Only a jumble of miscellaneous objects apparently picked up from rubbish heaps, construction sites, people's back yards, or other neglected places — tin cans, pots and pans, old umbrellas, worn out shoes whose leather was cracked and split, pieces of wood, rusty nails, a whole bazaar of shabby castoffs. In the drawers of tables were piles of newspaper clippings with pictures of the war, as well as rags and woolen socks,. All these things might be useful to a homeless tramp but Marta could make no sense out of them, nor see any point to keeping them.

"Let's wait. He'll be back," said Girei.

"Yes, of course," said Marta.

But she wasn't really sure. She began to examine the accumulated relics, hoping to come across something that might reveal the man's identity. She searched for a long time, in every corner, anxious and worried, almost forgetting where she was or whom she was waiting for. Certain things: a few photographs, a piece of shrapnel, or a dilapidated doll caught her interest and she remained for a moment in pained suspense, studying the objects in her hands, drawn against her will into painful reflection tinged with pity. Scraps of memories of her brief relationship with Arturo came back to her — before he had gone off to Greece, then to Russia, and she felt she was slipping backward into a time she had believed lost forever. Arturo, Arturo.... But was it really possible that Arturo had been living here in the midst of this hodge-podge, this dreary muddle of meaningless rubbish? What could have happened to him to bring about such an unheard-of metamorphosis, a breakdown of all memory and identity? Where could he have come from...a hospital, an asylum? Or a Russian concentration camp, way off at the edge of civilization, the very place where the last remnants of the Cossack Army might have ended up? One aspect of all this she did understand, however: whatever it was that had befallen Arturo, it was her business to find out and do something about it.

She tried to remember everything she could about this stranger, every time she'd seen him and what she had noticed, every trace of emotion he had aroused in her. She tried to analyze the vague feeling she'd had that he was somehow familiar. And how had she been able to let him live there like that on the outskirts of the village, like lepers in medieval times, who had to go about with bells fastened to their feet?

It was getting to be a long wait. Girei looked anxiously at Marta, wondering what she would decide to do. It was getting dark, and the colors of the sunset shone through the windows, reflecting red on the mountain ridges, and creating an air of suspense and expectation throughout the valley.

"What should we do?" asked Haha.

"I don't know. I really don't know," said Marta. "It's getting colder. He should be coming home. We could light a fire for him while we wait."

Anita's baby was tired and hungry. At intervals he'd begin to cry and rub his eyes despite her efforts to distract him with various objects she picked up and put in his hands. But Marta took pity on the little boy and decided they couldn't wait any longer. She added more wood to the fire, cheered by the thought that when the stranger returned he'd find warmth and comfort. Then she gave in to necessity and went back to the villa.

All night she was troubled by weird dreams in which the image of the tramp kept appearing in various guises. Her first thought when she awoke was: "Has he come back?" It would be odd if he hadn't. There was no reason in the world why he shouldn't return to the refuge he'd so carefully prepared for himself. As soon as she finished her indispensable chores she went back to the mill.

He wasn't there. The wood in the cast-iron stove was now a small pile of ashes and nothing had been touched since the night before. There were no keys to the doors and she wondered if any place could have been more vulnerable to intruders than this old mill, where she had found one man and lost another. She was profoundly certain the vagabond would never come back. For some inscrutable reason he had simply gone away. Perhaps when Anita encountered him she said something inept that frightened him off and he was now looking for another refuge. A poor lost bird, she thought...but was he really Arturo? If he wasn't why had he ended up here of all places? And where had he come from?

Whoever he was, thought Marta, giving way to a strange melancholy, he was more forlorn and displaced than anyone she'd ever known, and she'd known so many hopeless stateless people. Not only had he lost his home, he didn't even remember it. And it might well be that our truest home, the only one that really belongs to us is indeed our memory, because it remains when everything else is gone. This man, whom she'd hardly noticed at first, was deprived of even that consolation. She must try to find him, he couldn't be far away.... Vento arranged to borrow a small truck from a cooperative of ex-partisans who had started a transport business. He and Marta drove all over, through nearby villages, and even into the other valleys that had witnessed the tragic exodus of the Cossacks. They stopped dozens of times to describe the man they were looking for to anyone who would listen — a ragged wanderer with a veritable thicket of hair and a long unkempt beard, an unforgettable sight. But all the people they met listened with puzzled expressions, then shook their heads. It was as if the man had dissolved into nothing. He must have taken the lonely paths frequented by smugglers and fugitives.

After a while Marta felt as if she were chasing after a phantom, almost as if the wanderer himself had never really come to her village. The only material evidence of his presence was the collection of miscellaneous junk they had found in the mill. He must have amassed it like a patient beaver, tormented by an obsession to survive. Marta was overcome by a desolate stinging sorrow, a sadness that penetrated to her very bones and for which there seemed to be no remedy. She, the Marta who had given shelter to so many people, so many victims of war — how was it possible she hadn't even noticed or recognized the most deprived of all? How could she have failed to recognize Arturo? Could the war have so changed a man as to make him unrecognizable to those who loved him? These ideas kept buzzing about in her head like a swarm of wasps whose nest has been burned. Her mind simply couldn't rest.

One evening, after the second day of fruitless searching, she looked up and saw Vento watching her with a perplexed and troubled air. He'd done everything he could to help her, even procured the truck to go out and find the man who would perhaps permanently displace him in her affections. He had gone along with her plan without the slightest objection, making no mention of his own desires. Now, in her search for a ghost, she was beginning to forget him.

"You knew we'd never find him, didn't you?"

"I was trying to help you...."

"You were going along with my crazy idea, without saying a word...."

"Oh well now, no need to overstate."

"You are a sensible man and I'm a mad woman. I don't know what I want anymore. I feel like crying...."

Dazed and confused, she asked him to stay for supper. It turned into an evening that might have been cut out and sewn together, or perhaps dreamed up, by the most bizarre of minds. Girei recalled his Cossack friends, but in disconnected sentences, because Marta kept interrupting to ask some question about them but she was really thinking about the missing vagabond. Then Anita and the baby went to bed, as did Haha, amazed at himself for staying up so late. He usually went to bed with the chickens. Then Girei said he was tired out from his day's work and he needed to get some sleep too.

"We're the only ones left," said Ivos to Marta.

She didn't reply. He didn't want to distress her anymore than she already was and got up to get his things together and return to his lonely room. But Marta had a different idea. She felt firmly convinced now that something that had been slowly growing over time had reached maturation. For an instant she might have been back in the old mill on the night when she found the wounded Ivos. But that was a long time ago, so many things had happened, and all those images and all those memories were still there behind her merged into a shadow that couldn't quite be shaken off.

"Tonight you aren't going. Tonight you're staying here," she said.

"And tomorrow?"

"Tomorrow too. And every day after that."

Vento's habitually pensive face was touched momentarily with something like a smile. He picked a fragment of moss out of her hair, a minuscule souvenir of their prolonged search for the man without a memory. Then, slowly, as if now there was no hurry, he took her in his arms and held her close in the silence of the night. Everyone in the house was asleep, and everyone in the village, and everyone throughout the whole valley because they all had to get up and go to work the next day. There was still so much to do to hasten the return to normal life. Then Vento looked down at her and saw her eyes glistening with tears. He said nothing but couldn't help thinking that between him and Marta there would always be shadows and ghosts — the mysterious vagabond who had appeared for only a few days, and Caleb who had fallen into the ravine and Signora Esther engulfed in the *Lager* and Urvan, who had slipped away from the villa one night without waking Marta and had marched for days only to end up broken and lifeless at the bottom of one of the gorges of Plöckenpass, and the endless column of the Cossack people who had kept on trudging ever onward toward annihilation.

Things would never be the same for him either. Yet he knew now he had truly come home. His old feeling of rootlessness, of being a man with no place that was really his own, had almost vanished. The woman he held in his arms embodied such a place — she was his home, his world, his Ithaca finally and forever recuperated.

*This Book Was Completed on October 15, 1998 at*
*Italica Press, New York, New York and*
*Was Set in Galliard. It Was Printed*
*On 60-lb Natural Paper by*
*LightningSource*
*U. S. A./*
*E. U.*
* *
*

www.ingramcontent.com/pod-product-compliance
Lightning Source LLC
Chambersburg PA
CBHW030352020726
47493CB00003B/780

* 9 7 8 0 9 3 4 9 7 7 6 2 3 *